RING OF CONSPIRACY

By J. Robert Kinney

Visit and follow me online!
www.jrobertkinney.com
www.twitter.com/jrobertkinney
www.facebook.com/jrobertkinney
jrobertkinney@gmail.com

"Our new Constitution is now established, everything seems to promise it will be durable; but, in this world, nothing is certain except death and taxes."
– Benjamin Franklin, in a letter to Jean-Baptiste Le Roy, November 1789

"—far above all rule and authority and power and dominion, and above every name that is named, not only in this age, but also in the one to come."
Ephesians 1:21 (ESV)

CAST OF RETURNING CHARACTERS
From *SPLINTERED STATE*

The Team
Franklin Holt – Former low-level Russian mob, now unofficial consultant with the Special Intelligence & Security Agency (SISA)
Jacob Sloan – one of the Directors at SISA, former elite spy now on desk duty
Shannon Faye – SISA Agent, works for Jacob Sloan
Evelyn "Eve" Chase – Freelance tech guru/hacker

Terrorists
Phoenix – Mysterious leader of Nasha Volya (NV)
Nathan Hook – former FBI, outed as NV & imprisoned
Graham O'Brian – former FBI, outed as NV & imprisoned
Maria Perovskaya – Member of NV, original descendant

Franklin's Family
Irving Holt – Franklin's father
Jeremiah & Tara Holt – Franklin's brother & sister-in-law
KJ Holt – Franklin's nephew, son of Jeremiah and Tara

Chapter 1

The first shovel load of topsoil missed the mark and landed on a brand new pair of alligator skin dress shoes. A cascade of pebbles and grime showered over their scaly leather, causing a thick layer of dust and dirt to settle on the hide.

"Sorry boss," Abram Danko mumbled as he avoided the irritated gaze of the man wearing those shoes. He knew what the glare looked like anyway, a stern frown, wrinkled forehead, and eyes that shot daggers. Such was the normal look of their boss and Danko had been on the receiving end enough times to visualize it vividly with his eyes closed. Intensity was the only emotion the man was capable of expressing.

"Just keep digging," the boss ordered, his abrasive voice tinged with a quiet anger. The large, burly man slowly and intentionally shook each foot rid of its unwanted coat of earth.

Danko and his partner Ruslan Volk soon fell into a rhythm, one scraping a heavy shovel into hard-packed dirt while the other slung his payload from their slowly deepening hole. Neither spoke a word for several minutes as the pile of dirt at the side of the pit slowly rose. It felt creepy enough out here in the church graveyard without having to add the patter of awkward small talk to the mix. Eerie tendrils of moonlight glowed and sliced through the canopy of trees overhead, casting long shadows across the grass and making it difficult to see beyond an arm's length.

Danko supposed that was for the best; it made it easier to imagine he was somewhere else—anywhere else— without the extra visual of a multitude of worn headstones reminding him they were surrounded by dead and decaying corpses. The steeple of the local parish looming overhead did no favors either; its towering presence created a deep sense of foreboding.

Dead bodies had always given Danko the creeps. He supposed it went back to a fear of his uncle. Uncle Louis had been...eccentric and irreverent. He was known for being a little too cavalier with the coroner job entrusted to him. When Danko's mom and dad went on one of their drug-induced hallucinatory vacations, Louis would bring young Abram to the lab and perform autopsies in front of the child. The whole procedure had been scarring. Uncle Louis eventually cracked and was arrested for using one recent homicide victim as a ride-along passenger in the front seat of his '72 Chevy so he could use the carpool lane. Now, Louis was never mentioned at family gatherings—rare though they were—except for occasional whispers of how Crazy Lou was managing at Sunnydale Psychiatric downtown.

The two had been digging for fifteen minutes or so— Danko guessed—when a dull clang rang out through the crisp night air, right as Volk slammed his shovel into the dirt. The sound brought the attention of the man above them and he cautiously made his way into the pit to examine their discovery for himself.

"Yes, yes...this is it..." he murmured in a gravelly voice. "Keep digging. We need to get this open." Showing disregard for the same shoes he'd so carefully dusted off, he climbed out again and gestured his two "employees" back to work. The pair nervously shrugged and started digging again, but an abrupt shout startled the men and they looked up to spy a lone figure jogging towards them, dodging headstones across the grassy expanse.

"Hey there!" a man's voice rang out through the crisp air. "What are you doing here? The cemetery is closed." The groundskeeper, a hefty man in his late 50s, was making his rounds. They'd timed their activity to avoid this scenario, but he'd arrived on the scene earlier than expected.

"Merely paying respects to a friend." Their boss spoke calmly, with a hint of arrogance and a sneer on his lips. He knew the groundskeeper wasn't going to drop the questions based on that flimsy excuse, especially when he spotted the growing hole they were making in his cemetery.

"We closed at sundown, young man." The large man continued to waddle furiously towards their location. Danko and Volk watched as their boss casually repositioned his hand inside his leather jacket. He said nothing as they watched the groundskeeper advance. "What do you think you're doing?? You can't do that! I'm going to call the police!" He'd noticed the disruptive nature of their activity. He unsnapped his cell phone from a belt clip on his waist.

"You don't want to do that." The boss took a final drag on his cigarette and tossed it to the ground with a flick of his wrist, snuffing it out with the sole of his alligator shoes.

"Digging up a grave is a felony offense." The obese groundskeeper fumbled with his phone, flipping it open with a loud click. "The police will sort this out when they

5

get here." He never managed to finish dialing. A sudden pop sounded—echoing across the cemetery—and the large man stumbled backwards, his mouth slackened and agape. Two more pops in rapid succession and he slumped to the ground with a loud thud. He twitched once and then all movement ceased.

A pink mist hung in the air where he once stood. Danko turned to see his boss with a fiery look in his eyes and a silenced MSS Vul—standard issue for KGB spies in the 1980s—gripped in the hand of his outstretched arm.

No one uttered a sound for several long seconds as they watched him holster the fired weapon and slowly rebutton his jacket. He turned to face them, their eyes wide and their bodies frozen. He flashed a wry smile— they hadn't been told about the possibility of someone being murdered. He hadn't even elected to mention he was carrying a gun, though they probably should've guessed. But now that they understood what lengths he was willing to go to, there would be no double-crossing tonight.

"What are you waiting for? You want someone else to come investigate the rumble from that whale hitting the ground?" The words were biting and sharp, but had the desired effect. Danko and Volk redoubled their efforts and sank their shovels into the unforgiving ground.

It wasn't another five minutes before they uncovered their find. A long wooden box lay before them. Unremarkable, really, it was light brown and plain, with no distinguishing features. Not even the customary cross with which so many coffins in this quaint town were etched before burial.

Much like its topside appearance—only an unadorned concrete headstone to mark its location—the box showed no signs to indicate the identity of the individual contained within. But as Danko knew, that only made it more mysterious. He'd been hired for this job without being enlightened on any details, but he was no idiot. Ever since arriving at the cemetery, he'd been piecing it together. Combining the unusual appearance of the grave at this specific church in this tiny town with the physical nature of the box, being remarkably still intact and not yet deteriorated, he felt reasonably certain whose postmortem residence they were currently disturbing.

"Open it!" their boss commanded.

"You want *us* to open it?" Volk finally spoke up, a twitch evident in his shaking voice. "That wasn't part of the deal. You just told us we had to do the digging..."

His voice trailed off as the boss tugged back his jacket a few inches, revealing his shoulder holster. The man's right hand rested on the grip of the weapon he'd utilized minutes earlier. "I still have three rounds. How many do I need?" His meaning was clear. Volk and Danko nervously glanced at each other before turning back to the coffin.

Both leaned over and gripped the edge of the wooden box, bracing themselves for what they knew lay inside. Counting to three, the men wrenched upward, pulling the lid with them. The stench of the stale air caused them to recoil.

A cloud of dust and dirt—and God only knows what else—exploded in a poof from the previously sealed chamber, coating the two men.

"Is it there?" Their boss, for the first time, sounded genuinely jubilant about the prospect of finding his treasure inside. Indeed, it was there, a small drawstring bag clutched beneath the crossed arms of the decedent. What exactly he wanted with such a frivolous item

7

belonging to a dead man eluded Danko, but he wasn't being paid to speculate on motive. Volk gingerly reached into the tomb and pulled it out, holding it delicately between forefinger and thumb. He passed it upward out of the grave to his superior, who looked giddy as he grabbed the dusty, odorous item. He pointed at a metal briefcase laid next to the hole.

"Payment is in there, in full," the man remarked. Then, he spun on his heels and, without glancing behind him, he disappeared into the night. Right as he did, the clock in the church steeple rang out.

It was midnight.

Chapter 2

The quiet purr of her black motorcycle died as Shannon Faye pulled into a shadowy spot at a side entrance to the park—tucked along one side of the gravel lot, near the trees—and killed the engine. But she didn't dismount. Not yet. Instead, she took a minute to survey her surroundings.

It was nearly 2:30 in the morning and the night was dark, almost an inky blackness, which made it hard to see very far. The one streetlight, marking the entrance to the parking lot, had burned out. Some ambient light from downtown peeked over the treetops, but very little settled down the steep grade to the lot.

The lot sat empty, save for a solitary dark Mustang parked on the far side of the lot, but she knew the park wasn't. Cars were conspicuous and the people she was here to observe wouldn't risk being spotted because a passerby got curious about their expensive vehicle. No doubt they'd found other transportation here before trekking deeper into the park to avoid being seen or heard.

She listened for a minute for any sounds of human activity, but hearing none, Shannon dismounted from her bike and pulled off her helmet, flicking her hair over her shoulder. The recently-dyed long locks, a rich dark nougat, were pulled back in a severe ponytail.

With her engine killed and helmet removed, she cocked her head to one side and listened again. A single bird screeched from a nearby tree. Some species of owl, she supposed. Almost instinctively, she ran a hand through her hair. There'd been occasional stories of Barred Owls attacking runners in this area, with one theory being that they mistook women's ponytails for an animal of prey, probably squirrels. But after a few seconds and no appearance of a dive-bombing bird, talons outstretched in attack-mode, she smirked and figured she was safe.

No other noise penetrated the blackness, giving the night an eerie feeling. It was as quiet as she'd ever heard the park. Most nights, you'd hear a hint of music and clamor emanating outward from Dupont Circle, a popular nightlife scene with college students, or from one of the few universities in the area, but tonight there was nothing. A soft drizzle hanging in the air probably kept everyone indoors, she mused, and university students weren't due to return to campus from summer vacation for another week.

She softly laid her helmet on the seat of her bike, patted her pocket to ensure her camera was safely secured, and began to hike into a wooded area just off the parking lot, in the direction of the Taft Bridge with its famous lion guardians at either end. You couldn't catch a glimpse of the giant leonine statues from so far below where she hiked, but they were one of her favorite parts of the District.

She'd always found something familiar and majestic about lions in the muted way they carried their power. They didn't flout their power, prancing around, but presented themselves regally; no one would dare to mess with a full-grown lion. No wonder they were called 'Kings of the Jungle.'

Shannon moved slowly and deliberately, tracking the main path about twenty feet to her right, until she passed beneath the towering arches of the bridge's concrete supports.

It had been roughly six months since she'd helped stop a terrorist attack at the Lincoln Memorial. A century-old Russian anarchist group—long-believed extinct—had re-emerged with a new name, Nasha Volya, a new globalized brand of ideology, and seriously strengthened connections in influential places. Attacks had taken place, simultaneously, in cities around the globe, including several in the United States. And not all had been foiled, like the one in Washington had.

A lot had changed since then. A couple high-profile targets had been captured. An FBI Director, Graham O'Brian rotted in a federal prison cell, though his agent, Nathan Hook, had escaped during a prisoner transfer a few months ago. Even one Senator had been outed as a sympathizer and deposed. Three others were being investigated. And countless other government officials were under suspicion.

But it was costly. One of the FBI's best, Agent Joanna Talbott, had lost her life at the Lincoln Memorial that day, gunned down by Hook, her traitorous partner. Several others died at the Rayburn Congressional Building attack. One of the local masterminds, a mysterious woman known only as Phoenix, had vanished into the wind without so much as a trace. And a heavy cloud of doubt and cynicism hung over the whole industry.

Life in the intelligence business was challenging now as well, more so than normal; virtually no one could be trusted.

Not your boss.

Not your employee.

Not your coworker.

After the events of that weekend, Director Sloan—his life-saving actions had prevented dozens of casualties—had personally vetted the others in their new inner circle. The only ones she felt comfortable trusting anymore.

Director Sloan was a legend, both in and out of the intelligence community. His undercover work decades before for the top-secret Midnighters was oft-rumored about, but he'd privately confided to her that his exploits abroad were even wilder than the stories. Now a bit older, and quite a bit rounder, he'd worked his way up the ladder and still cut an imposing figure as a desk-bound Director at the Special Intelligence and Security Agency, SISA. He'd seen—and done—more than anyone and he'd rather die than allow some new group to unravel his life's work. But his job running a federal agency meant he needed to be careful. He still ran in powerful circles, both domestically and abroad. Even now, he was meeting with other intel heads in Budapest to discuss a potential cooperative counter-terrorism initiative. He wasn't due back for a few days.

Other than the two of them, there were three more on the team.

First was Franklin Holt. Unlike her, he wasn't an agent; he'd even spent time as a member of a local Russian mafia before cleaning up his act and writing a fictionalized memoir. The now-deceased Agent Talbott had been his ex-wife—estranged, but they'd been in the process of mending fences—so he had a personal stake in fighting. He was a bit of a wild card due to his shaky past and troubles with alcohol, but his motivation was revenge, so lack of trust wasn't an issue. He had a family to worry about though, an ex-military father who fought in Vietnam, a brother and sister-in-law, and their young son. The brother, a local D.C. professor named Jeremiah, had proven useful with research, but Franklin refused to involve his family any further than that and Shannon didn't blame him. Not after what he'd been through already.

Next was Evelina Chase. Eve was a technology guru, a computer hacker if you will. Young and naive outside her digital world, but her technological abilities were second to none right now. She'd first made her name working freelance, but when the government eventually took professional notice of her skills, she'd taken on some intelligence community projects as well. Officially, she operated as a non-government employee, which gave her certain leverage and access to off-the-book channels Shannon and Sloan didn't have. But it did mean she had to be extra careful poking around federal servers; the feds weren't fond of outside individuals accessing their networks. But she was more than up to the task.

Finally was Dominic Randal, her partner at SISA. An agency legacy with a famous, now retired, father, Dominic carried a chip on his shoulder, but he was intelligent and resourceful. Dominic was true blue—red, white, and blue, that is—with loyalty ingrained in his bones. He'd been by Shannon's side when they took down a major arms dealer a year ago and, while he'd taken a leave of absence when his father had a stroke, he'd proven to be a dependable partner and friend. Even if he wasn't active with the team at the moment, Dominic was reliable and she knew he'd be there in the end.

That was it. Five of them. Others obviously existed, but with no way of knowing who they were or whether they were trustworthy, they were stuck with each other and only each other. Which was why Shannon had been tasked with tonight's mission alone. The other four were scattered and stretched thin right now, leaving Shannon as the only one in position to crash this meeting. 24 hours earlier, they'd intercepted chatter indicating a meet-and-greet of a handful of high-rolling sympathizers to the Nasha Volya movement. No word on why they'd chosen to convene and no names had been given, but Sloan had cracked the location. A small, sheltered structure in Rock Creek Park.

So here Shannon found herself, creeping through shrubs and trees in the dark while wearing long-sleeved clothes in mid-August humidity. She had to get close enough to hear their conversation. Or at least identify a face or two.

She heard them before she saw them. A group of individuals standing in a circle, about ten in all.

The glowing red light on the nightstand read 2:52am, but Franklin Holt's mind couldn't sleep, couldn't relax, and he stared at the ceiling of his hotel room, counting the spiderweb of cracks that stretched from wall to wall. He'd always struggled with insomnia, but the last six months had been especially brutal. Ever since losing Joanna. It used to be a problem of regret, his mind racing with thoughts of inadequacy, anxiety and depression, but lately, he'd been more afraid of sleep.

How much longer could he go on like this?

It was the dreams he dreaded. Nightmares, he supposed. And he didn't want to invite them in. But they weren't your typical, garden-variety nightmares— fantastical scenarios of being chased by a monster, conjured by his brain to terrify him; they were memories his mind kept reliving. Real memories. Over and over. Like a broken record that kept getting stuck on the same few lyrics of a bad song.

The worst part was, he wasn't able to move on. He couldn't. Normally losing someone can be mitigated by getting back to normal life, by distracting yourself with the mundane inanities of everyday living. But that was impossible for Franklin.

His life had been officially upended the day Joanna died in his arms, but the truth was, he'd been dragged into this mess before that. Kicking and screaming, but he was trapped now, strangled in an iron grip. The moment Silas Sherman showed back up in his life—first on the street almost as a mirage, then later appearing uninvited in Franklin's apartment—Franklin hadn't been given a choice. And now, he needed to see this through.

Joanna would've wanted him to. His normal M.O. when things got tough was to cut and run, to get out of town, to drop all ties. But this was different. For the first time in many years, he was fighting for something. Something that would make his family proud.

But he'd learned that having principles, standing for them, being on the side of good, brought its own consequences. It came with a price. For him, that price was sleep. It was sanity. It was sobriety.

Honestly, he missed her too. It felt so strange—almost embarrassing to have such feelings about an ex-wife who'd once kicked him to the curb—but he missed her. No relationship was perfect, but he knew she'd given him her best—worked her hardest—and he couldn't say the same in return. He'd been ready to change that though, to beg for a second chance. *More like a millionth chance,* he groaned inwardly. And he would never get that chance now. Never again.

He listened to the tick-tock of the clock on the wall of his bedroom, steadily plugging along like a musician's metronome. Between every tick, in the momentary silence between seconds, the anxiety tightened its choking grip bit-by-bit.

He'd already downed two of those little travel-sized bottles from the hotel mini-bar, but they hadn't calmed his mind. They stilled his nervous energy, the pacing and the constant need to move. But not his thoughts, not his mind.

The craving for another bottle lingered too. He'd resisted a third so far, but the desire was an itch he couldn't scratch. His chest felt tight, his head throbbed, and he was imminently aware of every digit on his hands and feet. He no longer felt the need to wiggle his fingers and toes, but he couldn't help wondering what he was supposed to do with them.

Where exactly do sleeping people place their fingers? Should toes be straight or curled? Fingers balled up or splayed out?

Questions he never wondered during the day, when he had the time to contemplate such ridiculous notions. They only emerged when he could least afford to let his thoughts run wild.

Finally, he gave up his resistance and caved. He dragged his legs off the side of the uncomfortably stiff mattress and hefted himself upright. He stumbled to the mini-bar and threw open the door, which smacked against the wall with a bang that made Franklin cringe. He grabbed one of those tiny bottles of rum—Bacardi—and, unscrewing the lid, threw it back. The liquid burned as it washed over his tongue and down his throat, producing a slight shudder.

There. That was better.

He stumbled to the bedside and sank onto the mattress with a sigh. He hung his head until it rested in his hands and massaged his temples, trying to rub away the pain. A monster headache was building from the nape of his neck, near the base of his skull, and spreading outward.

If he didn't desperately need the sleep, he'd consider trying to do a little work. There was plenty to be done. With his past, he'd become the 'Russian' expert in their group, so he'd been relegated to hours and hours of research into the original Narodnaya Volya terrorist group, and the rosomakha—or wolverine—coins that were currently being used to identify sympathizers. But most of all, his task was to find out everything he could on the resurgent organization, the Nasha Volya.

There truthfully wasn't much to find. The group had seemingly materialized out of nowhere all at once. Attacks had taken place on nearly every continent simultaneously, thirteen cities in total. Another were thwarted. And within the hour, every intelligence agency in the world was scrambling to learn who they were and how this organization had flown so far under the radar. And few answers had been uncovered.

Franklin had been attempting to leverage old connections from his time in the local Russian Bratva, but it was a challenge. Most of his former friends were dead or had escaped before the group took off. The few who remained were reticent to talk, afraid of what might happen to them or their families if they did.

But he'd pieced together a few tidbits.

Raising his head, he spotted his notebook discarded on the bedside end table. If he couldn't sleep, maybe some light reading would spark an idea.

Chapter 3

The Rock Creek Park meeting was taking place in a valley, surrounded on all sides by trees. A couple members of the circle wore baseball caps pulled low and one had pulled a hoodie over his head, so Shannon couldn't make out their faces, but the rest didn't appear to fear recognition. Or at least, they didn't expect anyone to be watching tonight. And they were half correct; she didn't recognize anyone. But that was why she brought a camera.

Slowly, she extracted the device from her pocket and began silently snapping away. She'd show the photos to the team tomorrow and, if she got the chance, she might be able to run them through facial recognition. If she was fortunate, the software would trip over someone in the system and they'd have a solid lead to pursue.

They'd been floundering lately with the investigation. Their first big break had been getting Graham O'Brian to talk from prison.

Graham O'Brian operated as a double-agent, working for the Bureau, but Agent Talbott eventually outed him as a member of Nasha Volya. He'd tried to kill her, but eventually, he'd been captured, incarcerated in a maximum security prison. Ever since, he'd been reticent to speak out, but somehow, Director Sloan had squeezed some intel out of him. Shannon wasn't sure how he'd managed it and didn't think she truly wanted to know, but she was glad he'd succeeded. That information had been instrumental in unseating Senator Reid, a nutcase politician from New York. No one was sure how he kept winning elections back home, but rumors abounded that his views were so extreme, even his colleagues in Congress were relieved to learn he'd been arrested and deposed from his seat.

But O'Brian's leads dried up shortly after that. Phoenix was still in the wind. So was her compatriot, Maria Perovskaya, a political activist and descendant of one of the original Narodnaya Volya members who hadn't been seen in months. Other nations saw similar levels of success—or non-success; a handful of members had been apprehended, but most remained unaccounted for.

The revelation that this was a global entity had stunned the FBI and the rest of the United States Intelligence Community. Not a week earlier, they didn't even realize the late 1800s terrorist group had been reborn, and now they were dealing with a group large enough and capable enough to execute simultaneous attacks in roughly a dozen different countries around the world. Once the global casualty counts had been tallied and combined, the February attack skyrocketed up the list of deadliest terror attacks. Worldwide, over 1,500 people had been killed. A large percentage of those were government officials, but hundreds of civilians perished as well.

Shannon didn't know most of those casualties. Faceless names, listed in newspapers and on websites, many in foreign languages. But she did know one. Agent Talbott had been one of her trainers in boot camp at Camp Hale and the two had bonded, first as mentor and mentee, then later friends. Months had passed, but Shannon could still see Joanna's body, lying limp and lifeless, in her mind as clearly as if it'd happened yesterday. An empty vessel. Her friend—whatever comprised her essence, her soul—was gone, moved on to somewhere better, she hoped.

Her stray thoughts and mindless shutter clicking were interrupted as words from the meeting drifted up from the glen below and she refocused her attention.

"I won't!" one man's voice broke through the quiet. He stood tall and portly, wearing a dark hoodie and New York Yankees baseball cap, pulled low over his face. "That will cost me everything!"

"Shut up!" Another hissed, still loud enough to be heard. This one was average height and weight, bearded and wearing a green windbreaker over what looked like a full suit. "Someone might hear!"

"Who's gonna hear?" the first man demanded. "It's 3am and we're huddled in a secluded hole of Rock Creek Park. And now it's raining! No one's around except for a few bloody owls…"

"Just shut up!"

The voices dipped below hearing level again, becoming muffled murmurs, so Shannon decided to creep closer. Careful not to step on a branch, a sound that would reverberate loudly on a still night like this, she crept down the hill until she could make out individual words again. Setting up shop behind a tree, she laid on the ground and resumed snapping photos between two branches as she listened.

"Mark, will you have everything ready in time?" Shannon made a mental note to cross-reference 'Mark' against their lists of potential members. He stayed hidden in a shadow, so she couldn't get a decent look at him, but he was definitely tall and slender.

"Just make sure you're in position and stop worrying about me," the man called Mark barked. Tensions were elevated tonight. These weren't men used to middle-of-the-night clandestine affairs in dark parks. It seemed to be creating paranoia.

"Fine," the first man growled in response, "but if anything's out of place..."

"It won't be," Mark interrupted.

"It better not. I heard from Igloo today and..."

"I said it won't be. Next time they call, tell Igloo to mind its own business," he hissed, adding a few choice words that made Shannon blush.

"Good." After a pause, the first man turned to the group and asked, "Any final questions?"

"Yeah, why wasn't this meeting an email?" a third man croaked. Shannon couldn't identify who.

"Because email leaves a paper trail, you idiot," Mark chastised. He seemed to be the one in charge.

"Let's just get out of here," a woman spoke up this time. She appeared to be the only female in attendance. Her hair was ebony-black and hung shoulder-length, the ringlets just touching her brown leather jacket. "The longer we're here, the more likely someone will stumble on us."

"Like who?" Another groused sarcastically. "Who's going to 'stumble on us' at three in the morning?"

"A drug dealer. A nocturnal medical resident from the hospital. An insomniac jogger, for all I know!" the first man speculated. "All I know is that I don't like meeting like this. Too exposed."

"Oh shut up, Andrew," another man growled. "None of us like this, but you're getting paid plenty. We all are."

Another name! Andrew. Shannon made a mental note.

20

The group bickered for a minute, the anger in their voices eventually fading into a sullen resentment.

"Alright, alright, alright. I get it," the first man piped up, conceding defeat. "Meeting dismissed. Now get out of here."

The circle quickly split, with the participants heading in multiple directions as they left the area. She snapped two final photographs before hastily shoving the camera into its pouch just in time. She glanced up to see one individual, one of the men with a cap tugged low over his eyes was headed in her direction.

She hadn't prepared for that. She'd assumed everyone would take traditional exits, along trails or marked paths back to their parked vehicles or a driver waiting for them. But this man was headed off-trail and tramping through the brush right for her.

Shannon thought fast. The man would be on top of her in seconds. She rolled to her stomach and army crawled to the side, hoping to get out of his way, but she wasn't able to move fast enough.

She was out of time.

"Hey!" The man's startled baritone cut through the darkness like a knife. She'd been spotted.

She leapt to her feet and took off at a run, tripping over branches and skidding on damp leaves and loose dirt, but she kept sprinting forward. She had to get to her motorcycle. She couldn't be caught.

"Hey!" he yelled again. The shock in his tone vanished, replaced with the sharp edge of anger. "Someone was spying on us!"

A muddle of other angry voices joined his as the rest of the group was alerted to her presence. She stumbled as quickly as possible, but running through the woods in the dark only allowed her to move so fast. She could hear the man scrambling after her, not far behind.

The stillness of the night had vanished, replaced with the rustling of leaves and snapping of twigs underfoot as she thundered through the brush toward the parking lot.

Shannon was grateful for the inky blackness and the burnt-out bulb at the entrance to the lot. Anything to hide her identity. Reaching her bike, she slammed the helmet down over her head and sparked the ignition. The engine roared to life as she whacked the kickstand with her heel. Her tires spun for a millisecond before grabbing the asphalt. The bike lurched forward and she tore out of the lot.

But she wasn't fast enough. Another loud engine jumpstarted and tires squealed behind her. A quick glance over her shoulder revealed that black Mustang was on her tail. It made the turn out of the lot as well, nearly tipping on two wheels as it worked to keep pace with her.

The road exiting the park was narrow and winding, so she wasn't able to maneuver much on the wet asphalt, which prevented her from pulling away.

She popped out of the park road and onto the main street, but the Mustang stayed directly behind her as if tethered with a towing chain. Shannon put on a burst of speed to screech through a red light, hopped a grassy median, and onto an interstate entrance ramp. Traffic was light given the time of night, so she could weave around cars and in and out of lanes, but it also provided her minimal cover.

Her motorcycle was fast, but the Mustang had clearly been modified to increase horsepower and it was slowly catching up to her. She soon realized she wasn't going to be able to outrun it. But her bike was more agile than a car, even a fancy sportscar.

At the moment, she sped six or seven car lengths ahead, but the Mustang was fighting hard to close the gap. And it was succeeding.

She opened up the accelerator and zigzagged around one of the few other cars on the road. It wasn't going to stop them, but getting out of their direct eye line, even for a few seconds, was something.

The bike hit seventy, eighty, ninety miles per hour, but the Mustang wasn't merely keeping up. It continued to gain, tracking her every move and outpacing her speed. She watched her speedometer surpass one hundred miles per hour.

Another exit was fast approaching and she knew she needed to take it. It was her only option. But she waited until the final minute before swerving over onto the ramp. It wasn't enough, as the Mustang kept up its pursuit. The exit deposited her somewhere in West DC, but the restaurants and street signs blew past too fast for her to process precisely where she was. Spying a side road ahead, she hit her brakes and yanked the handlebar to the right, her tires screeching as the bike wavered, struggling to stay upright.

Her rear tire screeched in protest and fishtailed dangerously, but she somehow kept her balance and soon found herself tearing the wrong way down a one-lane, one-way street.

Stealing a quick glance behind her revealed the Mustang had engineered a successful turn as well, but it'd cost him several car lengths.

They raced through one of the residential sections of the district, hurtling down a narrow street the wrong direction at over sixty miles per hour. It was a recipe for disaster. It felt suicidal.

But Shannon knew better. Residential areas in this part of town had narrow cut-through streets, barely alleys, roads that a car—even a souped-up Mustang—wouldn't be able to traverse. She just needed to find one.

It wasn't more than a couple blocks before one such opportunity presented itself. It wasn't even a street, per se, but more of a driveway that narrowed into a dirt path into a backyard.

Shannon hit the brakes again on the bike and skidded into the driveway, carefully maneuvering the bike along a cobblestone path, before bursting into a grassy area behind a set of brownstones.

The Mustang couldn't follow her here, and no one from that middle-of-the-night rendezvous would be able to afford getting caught trespassing through private residence yards. She finally exhaled and cut the bike's engine to catch her breath. In the sudden silence, her own heartbeat pounded in her ears, drowning out the din of cicadas and crickets chirping. She walked her bike into the shadows beneath a large tree and waited.

She was out of sight now, but listened to the Mustang as it braked and slowed to a crawl as it passed the driveway, but after thirty seconds or so, she heard its engine pick up again and it drove away.

She waited for a full twenty minutes before daring to start her bike up again. Many of these housing units shared backyards, or had connected yards, so she puttered slowly and softly past a few homes until she found a safe exit point on the other street, that ran parallel behind the one she'd just exited. When she felt safe, she poked her head out an inch and scanned both directions. No Mustang to be found; they'd abandoned the chase.

She carefully extracted her phone from her pocket and dialed a familiar number for someone she knew would still be awake. He wouldn't be thrilled to see her, but she needed a place to sleep and they needed to plan next steps.

Chapter 4

Franklin spent a few minutes scouring his notebook for any connections or new revelations, but nothing jumped out at him. Maybe it was the lack of sleep. Or maybe the alcohol, but he couldn't make heads nor tails of the intelligence placed in front of him.

Best he could figure, the woman known as Phoenix — the apparent mastermind of the DC bombings, if not beyond that — had surfaced in the United States about a year before the attacks. No address, no family, not even a real name. The only thing anyone seemed to agree on is that she was ruthless. Her infamy centered around a particular penchant for violence and brutality. She didn't have a paper trail, but a trail of bodies had been left in her wake.

With help from Eve and Sloan, Franklin had tied over two dozen murders directly to her in the DC area alone and there were a few dozen in other cities stretching back to her first emergence in a town called Grozny, the capital city located deep in the heart of the Chechen Republic. The federal republic of modern-day Russia was ruled by corruption under a man named Ramzan Kadyrov.

Violence was commonplace in Chechnya — in fact in the entire Caucasus, from Dagestan to North Ossetia. Violence had a brutal history and near-mythic status among the people who created folk heroes out of anyone who stood up to Mother Russia. The First and Second

Chechen Wars, separatist conflicts aimed at seceding and building a new, ethnic-based state created hundreds of those heroes. And despite relative stability in the region since around 2000, there's still a strong militant undercurrent. No matter how stable the provinces appeared to be, they were always like a hornet's nest, quietly hanging from the eave of a house by a thread, but one wrong move and the whole thing would go up in a swarm of fury.

Somewhere in this mess of oppression, political confusion, and separatist ideology, Phoenix had risen. They'd tracked the first mention of a red-haired woman with a taste for cruelty to a survivor of a mini-massacre seven years ago. A mysterious woman had personally executed a half-dozen men, purportedly corrupt local officials. This man claimed to have witnessed the whole thing from a hiding spot in a closet and his description of the woman fit, from her ice-cold eyes to the slight curl of her lip as she gloated over her victims. From there, Franklin uncovered nearly one hundred kills, most reportedly by her own hand, a handful ordered to subordinates as she consolidated power and rose within the ranks of various criminal organizations.

It bothered him that they'd been unable to find anything further on her identity.

No family. No ID numbers. No immigration papers. No name. No past.

It was as though she didn't exist until seven years ago.

He groaned and rubbed his temples before knocking back yet another of those tiny bottles from the minibar. Suddenly, a shrill ring from his cell on the end table startled him and he cringed. The tone pierced painfully through the fatigue and his growing headache, interrupting his disjointed thoughts.

Who would call him this late? What time was it? 3:09am. That wasn't a positive sign.

The phone continued to ring. He stretched out an arm and snagged the device off his bedside table and yanked out the charging cable one-handed. Squinting at the bright screen in the dimly-lit room, he stabbed one finger and hit 'Answer.'

"Hullo?" he mumbled.

A sudden knock at the door interrupted Congressman Marcus Hartwell's meditation, jolting him back to reality. Irritated, he glanced at the clock sitting on his desk.

4:22am.

It was too early for his staff to have arrived. Even his main assistant didn't typically arrive at the office until five o'clock.

"Come in," he rasped before coughing. His voice was normally deep and resonant, one of the reasons his party often called on him as their face, the one picked to give speeches and answer questions to the press. But this morning, he felt a slight catch in his throat. Maybe he was coming down with something.

"Come in," he called out louder.

He watched as the knob turned and the heavy wooden door swung inward with a loud creak.

A muscular man in an ill-fitted suit slipped in, his alligator shoes squeaking with every step. Congressman Hartwell rose to his feet.

"Typhos, what are you doing here?" he hissed. "I told you we were never to meet at my office. We can't be seen together."

"My apologies, Congressman," Typhos growled and rolled his eyes as he uttered the title. "But you and I both know that isn't your call. We both answer to a higher power." He reached one hand inside his suit coat pocket and Hartwell instinctively flinched. But Typhos only revealed a small velvet bag, which he dropped onto the large mahogany desk with a heavy thunk. "Besides, I assumed you'd want to know we found what you've been looking for."

"At the cemetery?" Hartwell arched an eyebrow. He was skeptical. He'd been fooled before.

"Tucked in the old fool's arms like his most prized possession."

"Excellent!" Hartwell smiled, then laughed and snatched the bag off the desk. He undid the strap that cinched the bag closed and turned it upside-down.

A heavy gold ring landed with a dull thud on the desktop. Hartwell grabbed it greedily and peered. It was old, worn and scratched after many decades of use, but its high quality was still evident.

"And we're sure this is the one? From Alexander the Second?"

"As sure as we can be. It's his."

"Good, good. It's perfect," Hartwell crooned, as he slid the giant ring over his middle finger. It fit nicely. "This will solidify my standing. No one else has a relic like this."

"Sir," Typhos interrupted. Then again, "Sir?"

"Yes, what is it?"

"My payment. You promised…"

"Of course, of course. I have it all right here." Hartwell opened his bottom desk drawer and pulled out a duffle bag, dropping it on the desk. He slid the zipper open just enough to reveal the contents inside. "You're welcome to count it, but I assure you...it's all there."

"Counting isn't necessary. If it isn't enough, I know where to find you."

Hartwell nodded and waved his hand dismissively.

"Uh sir, there's one more thing," Typhos muttered, shifting back-and-forth on his feet.

"Yes," Hartwell didn't look up, his gaze lingering on the ring. "What is it?

"Well, you know the Rock Creek Park meeting tonight. The one you missed?"

Hartwell finally glanced up. Typhos was a stoic man, who barely showed emotion, but he kept biting his lower lip and fidgeting. Something was wrong.

"What happened?" he demanded.

"Well, someone else was there. A woman who was taking photos. She escaped on a bike. One of our men chased her, but lost her in a residential area near Columbia Heights. We aren't sure how much she overheard."

Hartwell absorbed the news with all the emotional demeanor of a statue. He had a suspicion about the identity of this mysterious biker, but either way, this was bad news.

Finally, he whispered, a hint of a tremble in his voice betraying a building rage. "I guess it's a good thing I wasn't there to be photographed. You will handle this," he ordered. "Find her. Destroy the camera."

"Yes, sir." Typhos nodded and departed.

The congressman took a deep breath to clear his head and put the escaped biker out of his mind. He shook his head; he'd told them an in-person meeting was too risky, but they'd insisted.

After a few seconds, he went back to staring at the ring. He couldn't believe it was his. After all this time searching, he owned the actual royal ring of Tsar Alexander II of the Russian Empire. Despite being known for his many reforms, the Romanov royal been the target of multiple assassination attempts. He'd survived a misfired pistol, an errant gun-wielding student, and a mistimed bomb, among others, but eventually had been taken out by an attack on his carriage by the anarchist group, the Narodnaya Volya.

No one quite knew how it happened, but the Romanov ring went missing that day. Long rumored stolen by the Volya, it remained vanished for nearly a century. Many suspected it had been smuggled out of Russia, but no one knew where until Hartwell tracked down its current owner, a wealthy Russian-American businessman living outside Detroit.

Hartwell twice tried to buy the jewelry off him, but he'd been refused. The man refused to even acknowledge his ownership of the ring. But he was old and without children, so when he passed, the treasure would be buried with him. And after ensuring a hastened passing and waiting for the man to be buried, all that stood between Hartwell and the Romanov ring was six feet of dirt. From there, it had been easy.

And now, having that ring would establish himself as worthy. Despite his status within the organization, he wasn't a true descendant like most of the other ranking members and that meant that to many, he was second class Volya. But not anymore. Now, he had a piece of Volya history—*the* piece of Volya history. With a piece of jewelry like this on his finger, he'd never have to listen to Phoenix or any of the others again.

They would have to take him seriously.

Chapter 5

Shannon rolled into the lot behind Franklin's motel in Fairfax ten minutes later and parked behind a row of bushes, concealing her bike from the main street. He met her at the door to the motel room, a corner unit on the second floor, and after a glance both ways, she slipped inside.

"Did they follow you?" he whispered.

"No, I lost him cutting through the backyards of some rowhouses," she muttered as she marched past him and took a seat in the armchair. She glanced around the room, noticing several empty bottles of alcohol littering the table—vodka, it looked like. She removed her camera from her pocket and placed it on the end table. "But my bike's probably useless. They'll have people watching for it now."

"I'm sorry," he moaned as he dropped onto the edge of the bed and stared at her. "Did they get a good look at you?"

"Not enough to identify me, I'm pretty sure. It was too dark." She wasn't as convinced of that as she insisted aloud, but it wouldn't matter. She was already on their radar at this point.

"What if they run the bike plates?"

"All faked. Eve worked up false registration papers a while ago," she shrugged and pulled out her phone. "If they track the license number, they'll turn up at a retiree's home in Arizona."

"Well, did you get anything useful?"

"Dozens of photos. I'm texting them to Eve, so she can cross-reference them with facial recog software. One man named Mark. Another named Andrew." She frowned and tapped on the screen of her cell, then paused and peered up at him. "Does the word 'Igloo' mean anything to you?"

"You mean like an Eskimo house?" Now it was Franklin's turn to frown.

"I don't think so. One man referred to Igloo as 'they,' and then a second later, as 'it.'"

"That...doesn't make much sense."

"I know. Maybe it's a codeword for something. Or a location? I'm not sure," she trailed off, focusing her attention on texting those photos. She needed to get these sent as soon as she could.

"We'll ask Sloan when he's back in the States. Maybe he'll recognize it."

"Maybe," she grunted, then continued, "but I'd like to have another crack at Graham O'Brian."

"O'Brian? But we haven't talked to him in over a month. He had nothing else to give us," he grumbled.

"I know, but I now have new information. New names. It's a long-shot, but we need something. We've been hitting our heads against a brick wall for too long."

Franklin sighed, but he knew she was right. It felt futile to keep returning to a dry well, but they needed to do something. Maybe the names would jog a memory.

"We'll run it by Sloan in the morning. Why don't you get some sleep?" he suggested.

"What about you?" she countered. She felt deep worry wrinkles appearing on her forehead, a genetic trait she'd gotten from her mother, and quickly shook her head to get rid of them.

"I haven't been sleeping much lately. I'll keep watch. And I can look through your photos from tonight...maybe something triggers a memory. Maybe I'll recognize a face from my time in the Brotherhood."

"Fair enough." She nodded, then yawned. Her nerves had been on high alert all night, but she felt them finally relax, as though his suggestion gave them permission to unwind. She stood and trudged over to the bed, allowed herself to collapse onto it.

She was asleep before her head settled on the pillow.

———※※———

"Franklin, wake up! Wake up!" Shannon's frantic whispering jolted Franklin from the stupor into which he'd fallen, head resting on the wooden desk. He wiped away a tiny spot of drool that dripped from the corner of his mouth and staggered to his feet. He glanced at the clock. 5:01am. So early. Too early.

"What is it?" he slurred.

"We have to go. Now." Her tone was firm, leaving no room for argument.

"Wha—why?" he stammered. He rose and began to stuff papers into a brown satchel he kept beside the bed. He shook his head to clear the tired cobwebs, but it was to no avail. The mental fog was stubborn; it was there to stay for now. "Did they find us?"

"I think so. There's someone on the first floor, dressed in a dark hooded sweatshirt, moving room to room. He drove up in a dark sedan about ten minutes ago. His engine woke me."

"Maybe it's motel staff." Even as he uttered it, he knew that wasn't right. He'd picked this motel mainly because they weren't nosy. They didn't check on their guests and certainly not at five in the morning. Many paid heavily for that level of privacy.

"With a gun? I doubt it."

"How'd they find us? You promised you weren't followed."

"I wasn't. I don't know. Maybe they caught the license plate number, started asking around, hacked into traffic feeds, tracked my bike's GPS…or maybe they tracked you somehow. I dunno. But we don't have time to figure it out right now. We need to MOVE."

Franklin slung his bag over his shoulder, stuffed his handgun into his waistband, and followed her to the door. A large window, which they'd kept covered with a heavy curtain, looked out over the parking lot. Shannon used one finger to open a slit and peaked out.

"Let's go," she directed and turned the rusted knob.

Franklin's heart began to race as she pulled and the door swung inward. He watched Shannon move a hand to the grip on her firearm, strapped to her waist, and he instinctively did the same. The two edged out onto the second-floor walkway.

No one was in sight, which only made Franklin jumpy. The motel wasn't large and it had been constructed in the shape of an 'L,' so if the man hunting them wasn't visible, that meant he likely searched directly beneath them.

"Where's your car?" Shannon whispered. "We can't exactly take my bike." Franklin pointed, indicating a gray sedan at the far end of the lot. He always parked as far from his room as possible so anyone stumbling onto the car wouldn't be able to identify his room, but that was feeling like a stupid rule at the moment. Being able to reach a vehicle and escape quickly seemed more important now.

Thankfully, Shannon didn't mention it and just nodded. Leading the way, she began slinking along the wall in that direction. Franklin followed.

They moved deliberately, but quickly, and reached the crux of the 'L'-shaped building in less than twenty seconds. Pausing here, Shannon peered over the railing at the rooms below. She nodded in the direction and Franklin leaned over to follow her gaze. A man dressed in all black was peering through the glass window into one of the rooms on the lower level.

From here, Franklin wasn't able to make out any distinguishing features. The man faced the other way and had a hood pulled over his head, masking his face, but it was clear Shannon was right. This man was no hotel staff. In his right hand, he held a handgun with a long suppressor tube screwed onto one end.

"We need to make a run for it," Shannon whispered and ducked away from the railing to get ready to bolt.

"Are you m-mad? He'll see us!" Franklin quavered. "What if he starts shooting?"

"Then we run faster," she glanced at him and flashed a half-smile before dropping into a serious frown. He didn't smile back. "You ready?" she asked.

Gulping, he nodded.

"Let's go. Stay light on your feet." With that, Shannon took off, running along the elevated walkway. Her footsteps landed nearly silently on the concrete; Franklin marveled at her ability to not make a sound despite the breakneck speed.

After a second, he followed, trying to mimic her quiet movements, but not succeeding half as well. His shoes clopped a little too loudly on the concrete, sounds that would attract attention.

He was right. About two-thirds of the way to the end, he heard a loud pop, followed by a sharp ping as a bullet hit the railing next to him.

Franklin yelped instinctively and ducked, but kept running. A second bullet splintered into the wood frame around one of the motel room doors.

"Jump!" Shannon called out from a few steps ahead. She'd stopped and turned back, gun raised. She fired a couple cover shots at the hooded figure.

Franklin reached the end of the walkway and dove over the second-floor railing with all the grace of a lumbering couch potato trying to make the Olympic swim team. He landed in a thick hedge of bushes, the kind with prickly leaves. It felt like landing on a pincushion, the sharp edges creating miniature scrapes across any square inch of exposed skin.

He floundered and flailed his arms for a second before rolling off the bushes into the mulch below. Shannon landed beside him much more gracefully, managing to miss the stabbing bushes entirely and staying upright.

She turned and fired two more shots at their pursuer as Franklin scrabbled in his pants pocket for his car keys. Finding them, he punched the unlock button and heard the car's locking mechanism disengage.

"Get in!" he called and yanked open the door, diving into the driver's seat. Shannon executed a quick, impressive roll over the hood and deftly slid into the passenger seat.

He turned the key and nothing happened. He did it again, while pumping the accelerator. The engine coughed a couple times, but refused to start. Panicking now, he tried one final time. This time, the engine sputtered, but at the last moment, it leapt to life.

He stabbed at the pedals, tore out of the spot and onto the main road.

"Which way?" he yelled.

"Any way you want," she directed. "Just get us out of here!"

"What if he follows us?"

"Not on a blown tire, he won't." She peeked over at him and smirked.

"You shot out his tire?" Franklin panted through a grin.

"I learned that lesson the hard way a few hours ago."

Franklin kept an eye on the rearview mirror, but Shannon was correct. No pursuit ever emerged.

Chapter 6

As they put distance between their car and motel, Franklin sensed his breathing relax and his heart beat slow. They were out of range for the moment, but there was still an edge of uneasiness that gnawed at him.

How had the Volya found them? If they could be found once, who's to say it wasn't only a matter of time until they were found again.

"Give me your phone," Shannon demanded, her words breaking through his thoughts, as they pulled onto the ramp for the interstate to head west.

"What? Why?" Franklin asked. "What do you need?"

"Just give it to me," she snapped.

He handed it over.

"Oh man, Franklin. Is your phone always this hot?" Holding it in her hand, she flipped it over and began to pry off the rear panel.

"It gets warm sometimes," he admitted. "It's old. Bad battery, I think."

"It's not the battery," she muttered as the panel snapped off with a pop and his phone came apart. She fiddled with the back, removing the battery. She poked around inside the device for a minute. "Here," she muttered, holding up her fingers.

Franklin glanced over. Between her thumb and forefinger, she held a small electronic device, like a tiny memory card, except a tiny antenna stuck off of it at a sharp angle. "Is that—?" he gasped.

"It's a bug," she explained. She pressed the button on her door to roll down the passenger window, then tossed the item outside and onto the shoulder of the road.

"They were listening in on my calls?" Franklin gasped.

"No, I think it was just a GPS tracking device. You were being followed. That's how they found us."

"I don't understand."

"It wasn't me that led the man with the gun to our door. They were tracking you, through your phone. That's why it's been running so hot. Bugs cause programs, namely location software to run in the background constantly. As though your phone was always on."

"But when did they have access to my phone?" he wondered aloud. "It hasn't been out of my sight in weeks. Months, maybe."

"I don't know. Could've been there for months. It wouldn't have taken more than sixty seconds to install. Maybe they wanted to track your movements, to document the places you frequented, to find all of us."

"But why use it tonight?"

"Maybe they're looking for me after the incident at Rock Creek Park. They figured we might link up after that near miss."

Franklin nodded and mumbled thanks, then they both fell silent as the rumble of the car on the cracks in the interstate asphalt provided a background beat.

Finally, Shannon spoke again, this time softly. "How are you doing?" she asked.

"I'm fine," he mumbled absentmindedly, as he flipped on his turn signal and merged into the left lane. "Tired."

"No, I mean about…about Joanna."

"Oh. That. I—" Franklin sighed. "It's been six months. I'm used to it."

"Used to it?"

"Like the pain is still there. It isn't getting better. I'm just used to it now."

"Ah, yeah. I know what you mean," Shannon assured him. She actually did understand too. It'd been several years since the murder of her fiancé on the eve of their wedding. And the ache was equally as raw today as it was then. Maybe less acute stabbing, more dull ache, but still excruciating. "People say time heals all wounds, but that's a lie. Not when it's something like this. Best you can do is learn how to cope. And pray to God that He allows you to keep moving forward."

"Prayer didn't work when Joanna's life was in danger," he muttered. "Why would it work now?"

"Maybe—"

"Don't say God did it for a reason," Franklin snapped. "Or that everything has a purpose. Just don't. If 'God' even exists, he certainly doesn't do much listening when we need something."

She'd clearly hit a sore spot. It hadn't been intentional, almost an offhand comment. She knew Joanna had been religious; she'd assumed Franklin was as well. Apparently, she was wrong.

"I'm just saying God doesn't work that way. He's not too busy—"

"God is always too busy," he snapped with a bite of finality to his tone that told her to stop pushing. "At least when it comes to me."

"Well, if you need someone to talk to about it…" she paused for a few seconds before continuing, "you know I know what you're going through. Better than most."

He nodded acknowledgment, but didn't say anything. He didn't even take his eyes off the road long enough to glance toward her. After a couple minutes of silence, however, he abruptly pulled the wheel to the right and the car descended an exit ramp off of the interstate.

"Where are you taking us?" she asked. "Director Sloan's still in Hungary, so we can't go to SISA. And we don't have any connections to the Bureau anymore either."

"To my father's," Franklin answered.

"You think that's safe?"

"As safe as possible now," he replied. "My father is more capable than most. He'll understand."

"Going there puts him in danger."

"More than he is already? Our entire families already may have targets on their backs."

"I know that. But these are legitimate terrorists. And for all we know, they're tailing us there now. That bug I found in your phone might not be the only one they're using."

"Well fine," he sighed. She was probably right; he knew that. "Do you have a better option?"

"What about Eve's?" she suggested.

"What makes you think she is more capable?"

Shannon knew what he was thinking. Eve Chase was a technological wizard; the things she could do with a computer routinely astonished the team. But she wasn't exactly cut out for a fight. "If they're on our tail, how much help do you think she'd be when the bullets start flying?"

"Not more capable. Just more aware. And you know her place is decked out with tech and cameras. We'll know if someone steps foot within a hundred yards of the place."

"Okay," he grunted after a second. "Eve's it is." He flicked on his turn signal again and made a U-turn. The rest of the ride was in silence.

Eve Chase's apartment was a ratty hole-in-the-wall place on the second floor of a building near the river. She owned one of those residences with no interior connection to the space on the floor below, but rather its own, private staircase that led up and around to a back door.

The entire unit possessed an aesthetic that would please a modern-industrialist designer. Exposed brick poked out from behind cracked Sheetrock and noticeable ductwork, but in this particular case, it wasn't intentional. It was just old and falling apart.

But that was exactly how Eve liked it. It kept the rent low and visitors scarce. She liked to say it had "character." Besides, she'd teched out the entire unit with some serious top-of-the-line electronic equipment, so the rundown nature of the building was offset by her lightning-fast connection speed and powerful processing capability.

The apartment wasn't large, but it suited her personality and her work. And Shannon was right about one thing. The technology served more than one purpose; it also served as quite the elaborate security system. It wouldn't protect them from pursuit, necessarily, but they would have sufficient warning if anyone came sniffing around.

Not five minutes had passed before Franklin pulled his car into a pothole-ridden alleyway and parked in a small lot behind the building, completely hidden from the main road. Still, they exited the car cautiously, eyes peeled for anything out of the ordinary.

High above, tucked in the eave of the roof, Franklin noticed a red blinking dot. *Eve's camera.*

Convinced no one was pulling in after them, Franklin led the way to a metallic door on the rear corner of the building. As they approached, the door emitted a soft click and the lock disengaged. Eve had seen them coming.

With a final glance behind them, the two slipped through the doorway and into the dark stairwell within.

"Come in, come in," Eve Chase's voice whispered out of the shadows as Franklin and Shannon approached her door.

"You saw us coming?" Shannon guessed as the two of them slipped inside.

"I was up late," Eve shrugged. "Or rather early, I guess. Depends how you look at it."

"Everything okay?" Franklin questioned, genuinely concerned. Eve was young and perky, but she looked a little rough around the edges. Tousled hair and bags under her eyes added years to her age and told him she was overwhelmed. Then again, they all were. He knew he looked ten times worse.

"Yes, yes. I'm fine. Just sleep-deprived is all." She ran a hand through her hair to untangle it, but the effort only seemed to make it worse.

"Why? Did you find something? I texted you some photos."

"I got them. But nothing usable. Not yet." Eve shook her head and glanced at the floor. She grimaced, frustrated with herself. "I've also got a dozen searches monitoring message boards and have reached out to several contacts, trying to dig up anyone who knows anything."

"Maybe you should get some rest," Franklin suggested. He glanced around her living space. A mess of computer equipment and wires lay on nearly-unusable surfaces. A barely perceptible hum whirred throughout the room.

"I will. I might. Maybe later." Eve bobbed her head with each statement. "So what brings you two here this early?"

Franklin and Shannon glanced at each other before answering.

"They found us," Shannon explained. "We were ambushed. Barely got away, to be honest."

"They found you? How?"

"We think they were tracking my phone," Franklin divulged with a grimace.

"They installed a tracker?" Eve's eyes widened. "When? How? Wait...you didn't lead them here, did you?" she sputtered.

"No, I got rid of the bug," Shannon interjected. "But we're all going to have to be more careful. We don't know when they got access."

"Ok, good," Eve breathed with a sigh.

Ding!

A sudden chime beeped from one of Eve's computers in the far corner and they all turned to look. Eve rushed over and dropped into the chair, nearly missing the cushioned seat in her haste.

"What...what was that?" Franklin sputtered.

"Your timing couldn't be any better. Because that," Eve began, "was a hit. I may have finally found something."

Chapter 7

Director Jacob Sloan chomped off the end of a cigar and lit up, using an old, battered Zippo lighter he'd bought at a corner market that morning and blew a cloud of aromatic smoke toward the ceiling of his hotel room. He stared out the open window, admiring the majestic city of Budapest laid out along the water, its lights striking against the night sky. The historic capital city of Hungary had been created out of the merger of several neighboring towns in the 1800s, most notably the cities of Buda and Pest. The Danube River ran through the middle of the city, creating spectacular views of the Buda Castle, the Hungarian Parliament, and the Chain Bridge from both banks. It truly was a stunning European metropolis, one of Sloan's favorites.

He'd flown in a few days ago for a major international conference in Hungary between the heads of dozens of intelligence agencies from around the globe, close to one hundred in all. The United States sent five representatives, the heads of the Federal Bureau of Investigation, the Central Intelligence Agency, the National Security Agency, a military intelligence woman from the Navy, and Sloan, who represented SISA—the Special Intelligence and Security Agency—as its Director.

The attacks six months ago shocked the world; no one had predicted it. No one even had it on their radar. Not the Americans. Not the Russians. Not the Chinese, the

British, the French. Not even the Israelis. And it'd created a bit of a crisis in the intelligence community. How could they have been so blind? What signs did they miss? There were always signs. And of course, the worst question of all, the one on everyone's mind: what's next?

Since that day, there had been three of these conferences. The first was a week after the attacks, in Brussels, and only involved NATO members. Because of the Russian connection of the terrorists, there had been some concern about whether or not they should trust Moscow. But it was deemed the Russian government was as shocked as anyone, so the GRU—foreign military intelligence—as well as the FSB and SVR—respectively, the internal and external intelligence agencies that report directly to the Russian President—all arrived at the second conference in full force.

That summit was held a few weeks later at the United Nations headquarters in New York City and mostly involved hours of arguing and accusations being hurled back and forth.

This conference in Budapest was different though. Cooler heads prevailed in the months since. A heavy fog of suspicion still hung over the meeting, but the raw anger and suspicion had dissipated.

Just a couple hours ago, Sloan had met up for a poker game with several of the old guard, agency heads who'd been in the business for as long as any of them could remember. Trust was a precious commodity in their line of work, but decades of work—even for different countries—created a brotherly kinship, a bond between them. There was no one else on earth who understood their jobs, their fight, and that'd built a weird brotherhood, or camaraderie, over the decades. And more importantly, Sloan knew them well enough to recognize when they were telling the truth.

He hesitated to call them friends; you don't make friends when you work in intelligence. But they were the closest thing Sloan had in this business.

As Sloan watched wisps of smoke from his cigar twirl in a gentle breeze flowing in through the open window, he mulled over their conversation.

"Well I don't care what the UN says. We can't trust the Russians," Rufus Hastings grumbled, the thick mustache on his upper lip quivering with each word. The head of the British Secret Intelligence Service, more commonly known as MI6 tossed his cards into the middle, folding the hand. "I'm still not convinced they weren't behind this." Hastings was grumpy; he'd lost of lot of money tonight. Then again, he was always at least a little grumpy.

"Both Moscow and St. Petersburg were attacked, Rufus," Jacob Sloan responded and pushed a few chips into the pot. "Are you still suggesting the FSB attacked their own people?"

"I wouldn't put it past them," Rivka Mizrahi chimed in with her trademark lilt, before raising the bet. She was one of Mossad's top directors. Former IDF special forces, she was among the first female pilots in the Israeli Air Force, but she really made her name in the industry after retiring from the military and entering Kidon, a mysterious branch of Mossad specializing in espionage and assassinations. She was famed as one of the greatest Israeli spies of all-time before settling into an adviser capacity with Mossad over the last decade.

"Please," Mostafa Barakat chimed in as he folded his cards. "This isn't the Cold War, anymore. The Russian FSB and SVR agencies might be assets in tracking this group. We all acknowledge the Volya's roots in Chechnya." The Moroccan

man was a high-ranking official in the Central Bureau of Judicial Investigation, often viewed as the most powerful intelligence agency in the Arab world. Barakat had gained a touch of notoriety as one of the masterminds behind the capture of the chief financial officer of the Islamic State just a couple years ago.

"Trust is earned, Mostafa," Hastings rebutted. "They haven't earned it."

"I agree." Omar Jameel interjected. "We may not be dealing with the Soviet Union anymore, but this new Russian leadership is every bit as untrustworthy as before." Jameel was the son of a wealthy and prominent Saudi construction tycoon and, despite the brutal reputation of the General Intelligence Presidency, or Saudi GIP, he'd earned his place at the poker table by showing a willingness to engage in more Western, or progressive measures. He'd even hired two female intelligence officers to work on his staff and was known for refusing orders that he found unethical.

"What do you think, Max?" Sloan asked, turning away from the game for a minute.

Max Moreau was the only member of their group not playing at the table. Rather, he'd settled in a chair across the room with a scowl on his face and deep lines etched across his brow. He was the oldest of the bunch, the least social, and not much for games. But the Frenchman was well-respected by all in the community. He'd spent his entire adult life in the intelligence business and remained well past typical retirement age, but no one minded. His mind was as sharp as ever.

Moreau sighed—more of a grunt, really—and stood. He shuffled over to the table and placed his glass of whiskey on the wood surface.

"I think," he began slowly, his voice a gravelly rasp that came from decades of smoking, "that we're going to need all the *help we can get. Treat the Russians with caution, if we must, but we need their intel."*

Hastings growled under his breath, but didn't reply.

"The better question," Barakat interjected, "is about Phoenix." At the mention of her name, the poker game paused and all players laid down their cards. "And any others in the organization at her level."

"That's true," Mizrahi agreed. "Others exist in the organization, but that women seems to be at the core of this. Her name is all over our intel. We even caught her on a security camera not far from the Knesset compound. We matched facial recognition to those images your people captured, Jacob."

"And we know she was in Great Britain at least twice in the past year too," Hastings chimed in.

"She may not be the puppeteer at the top, pulling the final strings," Moreau grunted, "but her fingerprints are all over this. She's someone important."

"But who? Who is she?" Sloan countered. "Who is she really? Do we have any clues as to her actual identity? She didn't appear out of nowhere one day like an apparition. She has a past somewhere."

No one responded.

"Nothing?" he continued. "How can someone just appear? Surely, there's a paper trail. A passport, a birth certificate, something."

"All of her documents we've managed to recover were forged. Expertly so, I might add. Always a different name too." Rivka Mizrahi stood from the table and paced over to the window. She tugged on the cord, making the old blinds clack and clatter as they lifted. "And as for a birth certificate, there's nothing. We think she's Chechen—you know about Grozny— but paperwork hasn't exactly been standard issue there, especially not decades ago. Plenty of people don't have any

documentation of their childhood. Endless fighting and rubble took care of that."

"Same here," Barakat added. "We're lost. She's a ghost."

"No one is a ghost," Sloan rebutted. "Ghosts don't exist. Everyone has a past and we need to find it."

The rest of their evening had consisted of Hastings losing everything at poker but his shirt and vague discussions of possible origins for Phoenix, but nothing concrete. The entire world was as stumped at her sudden emergence onto the world stage as the United States had been.

Of course, everyone implicitly understood the reason, even if it wasn't discussed openly. This new terrorist organization—a resurrected group from a century ago—had spies everywhere. They'd infiltrated extremely high levels in the American government and there was no reason to assume they hadn't done the same elsewhere. Not only did massive trust issues between countries now exist, but even within nations' own agencies, there was this sense of not knowing who you could turn to. Not knowing who you could rely on.

Sloan struggled with this within his own organization as well. He'd seen a half-dozen solid agents outed as members of Nasha Volya across the American intelligence community and that sparked what was quickly turning into a witch hunt. Shades of McCarthyism crept back into the public square and several key senators appeared to be vying to take on the Joseph McCarthy mantle once again, to investigate any hints of disloyalty among government employees. A member of the House of Representatives soon suggested re-opening the House Un-American Activities Committee, and it sounded like there may be enough support to pass that resolution and re-build HUAC. Even though it wasn't a communist organization, the explicitly-Russian ties and name of Nasha Volya had led many in the media to label this as the Third Red Scare. Other nations were following suit as well. And the public had bought into that narrative hook, line, and sinker.

But for those in the intelligence world, it was even more complicated. How could you hope to conduct true reconnaissance or trust a report if you weren't 100% positive the person delivering it was trustworthy? It was cutthroat and distrust ran rampant. Which was why Sloan leaned heavily on the few he did trust, those he could vouch for every aspect of their lives, and those who had been around long enough to prove themselves and would never risk ruining their legacy with extremists like Phoenix and Nasha Volya.

Best to keep your friend circle limited now.

Still, intelligence on the Nasha Volya proved remarkably scarce given how intricately woven into society they must have been. Paper trails were non-existent and electronic tracks had been expertly covered too. They were making progress, but it was a slow process. And every day without a breakthrough was one day closer to whatever Nasha Volya planned next.

"What is it?" Franklin asked. "What did you find?"

Eve didn't respond, instead tapping a few dozen keys in rapid succession. The screen kept flashing images and words and numbers too fast for Franklin to register, but she seemed to know what she was doing.

After a minute, she finally replied, "I told you I'd reached out to a lot of contacts, asking for any information about Nasha Volya, right?"

"Yes…" Shannon nodded. "And was that…?"

"Well, one of them just got back to me. He says he has something."

"What does he have?" Shannon leaned over the desk to peak at the screen.

"I'm not sure. He didn't say specifically. He just said, 'Let's talk.' I'm trying to get more information now." She typed furiously.

"Who is it?" Shannon probed.

"He's a…guy…" Eve trailed off, distracted by her monitors.

"A guy. That's invaluable. Thanks."

"His name is Heskovizenako Swanson." Eve rattled off the name quickly.

"Wow, that's…a mouthful," Shannon commented. "Heskaviz…what?"

"It's a Cheyenne name," Eve explained. "Means porcupine bear. But most people call him Hesko."

"Porcupine bear? What's a porcupine bear? And Cheyenne?" Franklin wondered. "Like the capital of Wyoming?"

"Like the Native American tribe," Shannon interjected. "They live all across that region of the country. Wyoming, the Dakotas."

"Right." Eve nodded. "And Swanson lives in South Dakota. Sioux Falls, to be exact."

"And he says he knows something about the Volya terrorists? How?"

"Well…that's the thing. Hesko is an…eh…an unconventional guy. Eccentric, you might say."

"In other words, he's crazy." Franklin grunted and crossed his arms. "Fantastic."

"No," Eve responded firmly and paused typing to turn and glare at Franklin. "He isn't crazy. He's actually brilliant. Perfect SAT score in high school. Graduated Harvard at 20. Earned a PhD by 23. He was recruited by every cyber-security firm on the Eastern seaboard, including the government ones. And he declined them all. To be honest, he might be a bit too brilliant for his own good."

"What does that even mean?" Shannon inquired.

"Hesko is...how do I put this delicately?" She frowned, but kept typing. "He's a little too caught up in his own thoughts. And well, he's an expert in conspiracy theories."

"Oh brother," Franklin rolled his eyes. "So he believes in UFOs and that the Queen of England is a lizard-person?"

"Yes to the first one, no to the second. As I said, he's not crazy. He's a whiz at tracking down information. And his brilliance means he often sees patterns other people don't. Sometimes, the patterns exist...but sometimes, well I'm not sure. Still, if anyone's capable of finding clues about the Volya, he's one who might be able to do it."

"So what kind of information does he have?" Shannon asked, getting back to the point.

"He won't say."

"Shocking. The conspiracy fanatic isn't helpful." Franklin closed his eyes and shook his head. "What a surprise."

"No, I mean he won't say by email. He's not the most open person...and he's suspicious of you, in particular, Shannon. He doesn't trust the government and feels he's been burned by them on multiple occasions. But because of the danger here, he's willing to talk, but only directly. I'll set up a video chat, if you're okay with that."

"I mean, I guess it wouldn't hurt." Shannon shrugged. "Let's do it."

"Yes, by all means, let's talk to the believer in aliens." Franklin threw his hands out, frustrated. This felt like a waste. Conspiracy nuts, as far as he was concerned, were all crazy. "Maybe the Volya is run by little green men. This is a strong use of our time," he deadpanned.

"Stop it, Franklin" Shannon chided him, making a clicking sound with her tongue. It reminded him of the sound his ex-wife would make when she was disappointed in him. He used to hate that sound, but hearing it now elicited a different reaction and he softened; he missed it.

Shannon continued, "We don't have any better options right now and if this...Hesko...if this Hesko can spot patterns as well as Eve says, maybe he can clue us in on things we've missed."

"Fine, fine." Franklin shook his head and sighed, then nodded to Eve. "Set it up."

"Ok. He's on board. Give me three minutes to create a secure connection and we'll be in business."

Chapter 8

The intelligence community summit had already begun the following morning as Director Sloan's taxi navigated the Budapest streets. He was late, having missed the entire first session and likely already into the opening speech of the 10am session.

It was only a couple mile trip, one he'd normally make on foot, but a brutal storm had descended upon the city. Turbulent skies had brought a driving rain overnight and turned to hail by the time Sloan left his hotel room. It came down in sheets and wind whipped all around, buffeting the cab, as blasts of golden lightning scorched across the horizon. The windshield wipers jerked noisily back-and-forth, making conversation with the driver impossible. But Sloan wasn't looking for someone to talk to.

As the car swerved out of traffic and whipped to the curb in front of their destination, Sloan threw some cash on the front seat, totaling over 2,000 Hungarian Forints, the local equivalent of about eight United States dollars. Then, mumbling to the driver to keep the change, he shoved open the door and tumbled out onto the sidewalk. He slammed the door and hustled into the building.

The conference was being held in a secure government center near downtown, normally used for Hungarian Parliament events, but there were few locations that could safely house this many important people. He moved quickly through the security process. This consisted of a metal detector, a couple Israeli guards employing their famous profiling techniques, and a local guard doing pat-downs of every person entering the building.

Normal United Nations meetings are strictly no-weapon zones; outside of a couple trained peacekeepers, no member was permitted to bring their personal handgun, knife, or anything else into the building. But this was different; this was no normal UN event. They recognized it would be near impossible to convince the best minds in the intelligence community to surrender their weapons and congregate all together in a semi-publicized meeting. It was too risky and everyone understood that. So the organizers found a compromise and banned anything larger than a basic handgun—no magazines with more than eight bullets and nothing over a 9mm. Which suited Sloan just fine.

As he trudged down the hallway to the meeting room, a low rumble rattled the windows as it reverberated along the corridor, but Sloan couldn't tell if it was a growl of thunder or merely the uneven pounding of hail and rain hammering against the exterior of the building. Reaching the door to the conference room, he opened it and slipped in the back. An official he didn't recognize was speaking, but the nametag in front of him on the dais labeled him as Molnár Rajmund, Constitution Protection Office.

Sloan recognized the entity as the Hungarian internal intelligence agency. The organization enjoyed a solid reputation in the industry, but was relatively new, having only been established in 2010, so didn't have a long history to draw on. Hungarians are one of the few European countries to put surname first, given name second, but Molnár wasn't a name Sloan normally associated with the agency. He assumed this must be a lower-level specialist, not the organization's intelligence director.

Taking a seat in the rear corner, he waved down an aide and requested a headset for translation. As he placed the device over his ears, the monotone voice of an English-language translator began to pipe through the speakers...

"...can't treat this like an isolated event. Now that this group is back, we must assume there will be more attacks. And we need to be ready."

Sloan had heard this all before. He'd even made that precise point in a brief statement at the first meeting in Brussels. After the attacks, some world leaders—possibly to placate their citizens—had insisted it was a one-time phenomenon. The new group had made their point and that was all they wanted. Now they'd stop.

However, the United States had led the way in pointing out flaws with that theory; namely, a group that spent a century underground strengthening itself and growing its ranks wasn't going to be content with a handful of attacks that ultimately changed nothing about the world order. They weren't going to stop coming, wave after wave, until they'd succeeded, until the oligarchical hierarchy—as they saw it—was toppled. Or until they were stopped.

"We must root out sympathizers, members in our governments, in society. Finding this Phoenix and the others should be a priority, but like the mythical Greek Hydra, cutting off the heads will only spawn more. We must destroy the body. Victory must be total."

This too was a rehashed argument from past meetings. Studies show a lot of people in the general population hold extreme ideas and beliefs, but only a handful ever act on them in a violent way. If you remove their inspirations, it was rational to assume the average person would never radicalize and the group would fade. This 'decapitation' strategy in counter-terrorism circles was hotly debated. In fact, killing terrorist leaders seemed to cause even more violence among religious extremists.

In Sloan's opinion, there was no universal silver bullet to stopping extremist organizations. As he'd been quick to point out, it'd been believed for a century that the Volya had been decapitated and destroyed, only to be proven wrong. But their hierarchy today did appear to rest on a set of specific keystones—or people—and removing all of them from the web just might cause an internal collapse.

Only half listening now, Sloan began to scribble ideas on a notepad. Phoenix was one of those keystones. There was a lot they still didn't know about the organization, but intelligence had identified four individuals as primary leaders, the ones around whom the organization revolved and followed. He believed eliminating them would result in the group collapsing like a house of cards. It was true they had leaders in high, governmental places, but Senators weren't exactly known for their courage and action. Take away their puppet masters and they'd shrink back to status quo.

The other three keystones were also known. There was a British man who called himself Hyde—possibly a reference to the evil persona in the famous Robert Louis Stevenson novella; a female in Asia who went by the name Mara—a demon of death common in Buddhism; and an African man referred to as Shango, after a god of thunder and lightning in West Africa. All three were on the run and in hiding. The Chinese were rumored to have a lead on Mara, who they claimed hailed from a family of Tibetan dissidents. Sloan suspected the public accusations had more to do with China needing a scapegoat to pacify the people than anything legitimate, but he didn't have any real evidence. Just a hunch that he wouldn't put past the Chinese government.

Sloan hadn't shared this idea with anyone yet, but he secretly suspected the existence of one more unidentified keystone. A fifth member. Possibly more powerful than the others; he wasn't sure. But no one had yet mentioned that possibility aloud, much less discovered an identity. He'd spent the last month trying to uncover that final person, or simply prove their existence, but had come up almost entirely empty. Best he could figure, that person had to be kept hidden for some reason.

Maybe they're waiting for something? But what?

He took a break from the doodled web he'd drawn to glance up, right as they were changing speakers. Recognizing the chief of MI6, Hastings, he laid down his pen, removed his unnecessary translation headset, and sat up to listen.

"Greetings. Thank you all for being here. Yet again." His gravelly voice carried well; he probably didn't need the microphone. "I know we're all still anxious. All still angry. I know I am. But we can't keep rehashing the same tired arguments. We need to do something. Do more."

Hastings had detailed his plan to Sloan and the others at the poker game the previous night, so Sloan knew what was coming. But he was more curious to observe the response in the room. It was going to be controversial.

"I want to propose further cooperation. But more than that, we need a team. An international strike force."

Hastings shifted his weight back and forth. "One that can operate across borders fluidly."

A quiet murmur began to emerge in the room, mostly from some of the Eastern countries. Sloan watched a couple of the Chinese officials leaning over to whisper among themselves.

"I don't mean more peacekeepers. The United Nations has plenty of those and they have proven to be often ineffective. We need soldiers who fight outside national laws." He scanned the crowd before quickly adding, "Still subject to an international body, of course."

At that, the murmur grew louder and Hastings paused.

"Counter-terrorism is an international problem and that requires an international solution. Even before the Volya, we saw spillover all across the Middle East, cells popping up in Europe and Asia, active extremist communities in Africa. And now, this new organization appears to have gone truly global. They operate across borders with ease and we need to be able to do the same. Otherwise, they will always be one step ahead of us."

At that, the room erupted. Sloan had expected this. A group like that would be incredibly controversial, operating outside national systems...it would create all kinds of problems. Who ran the group? Who would make up the members? More importantly, where did the power truly lie? And wouldn't it infringe on state sovereignty?

"Quiet everyone, please!" Hastings growled into the microphone. "Quiet!"

After a few seconds, the chatter had quelled to whispers.

"Thank you," Hastings remarked. "After the horrific attacks on 9/11 in New York and—"

He didn't get to finish the statement. A loud crack from the back of the room echoed and a red laser dot materialized on his suit jacket. Sloan's hand dove toward the gun he had tucked into his waistband, but he—along with everyone else there—was too late.

"Nasha Volya!"

A lone voice shouted above the din, a flash of light blinded him, and a split second later, a concussive force sent Sloan soaring backward into the wall. His head ricocheted off the plaster.

The room erupted in a scalding ball of fire.

Then it all went black.

Chapter 9

Jacob Sloan woke to a room in chaos.

For a few brief moments though, he didn't notice any of it. He couldn't move, couldn't think, couldn't breathe. He couldn't hear anything, couldn't see anything.

Then, like a tsunami, the memories hit him. He remembered a man running into the room, shouting something, and then a searing fireball. He remembered being knocked from his chair by the concussive blast. And he remembered smashing into the wall behind him before he lost consciousness.

The first sensation he became aware of was the sound. Bloodcurdling screams of the dying and injured mingled with the occasional burst of gunfire. Then the heat hit him.

Oh, the heat!

This wasn't over.

Slowly, his eyes fluttered open, but everything was hazy. He assumed his pupils needed to adjust after losing consciousness, but that wasn't it. The room itself was hazy. A black, acrid-smelling smoke emanated from a massive chasm in the floor in the middle of the room. The smoke, thick with wood shavings, Sheetrock, dirt, and dust, floated in a fog after the explosion and had yet to settle.

His tear ducts watered like fire hydrants as the cloud obscured his vision and irritated his corneas. Moving as fast as he was capable, he began a physical assessment. His arms ached, but both were operable. A gash along his ribcage was visible through a gaping hole in his shirt. It looked like a bullet wound, but it hadn't gone deep. Probably just a graze; it wasn't life-threatening. He could move his legs, but doing so sent fire through his right knee. Brushing aside shards of what he assumed was the desk, it became obvious the cause of the pain. A sharp metal bar penetrated into his thigh muscle an inch or two above the kneecap. Possibly a shattered piece of a table brace or a lever from his chair.

The bar wasn't long, nor thick—probably less than a centimeter across, but it had punctured the skin and embedded about an inch deep into the muscle. For a second, he considered attempting to remove it, but decided against that. As best he could tell, it hadn't severed an artery, but he couldn't take the chance. Pulling out the bar now might open vessels currently being blocked and he'd lose even more blood that way.

He ripped off a strip of cloth from his already-torn shirt and bound it tightly around his thigh to keep the bar in place. He'd deal with its removal later, when he could find a medical professional. Or at least out of harm's way.

Through the smoke and debris, he could make out the colossal hole in the middle of the room, the epicenter of the blast. Tables and chairs had been tossed and mangled, the floor littered with shards of splintered lumber and twisted metal. Sloan counted roughly a dozen unmoving bodies. There was movement around the periphery of the room, but he was having a hard time making out who they were and how many. In this haze, he was unable to even determine friend from foe.

The ceiling was shredded in the blast as well, leaving dangling wires and a shredded HVAC duct hanging into the room.

A suicide bomber, it had to be. That's how he'd been able to get as far as he did. No need for an escape plan meant you could get closer to your target and strapping the device to your body made it easier to conceal, especially under a rain jacket or heavy coat. *But how did he get past the metal detectors? The guards? There had to be an inside man, someone to help the terrorist evade security.*

Sloan mentally reviewed everything he remembered about suicide bombings. They weren't exactly a new phenomenon, but were rare outside of religious groups and Nasha Volya wasn't religious. In fact, the only major example of a secular terrorist group using suicide attacks that he could recall was the Tamil Tigers from Sri Lanka twenty years ago or more.

He began to struggle to his feet, but another salvo of gunfire sent him ducking for cover. Suddenly a thought hit him. *If it had been a suicide attack, the terrorist was dead. So why the continued gunfire? Unless...the bomber wasn't alone. There were still terrorists in the building! In the room...*

His hand instinctively moved to his waistband to retrieve his handgun, but it wasn't there. The weapon must've been dislodged in the blast, fallen from his hip the moment he'd been launched airborne. He scrabbled around in the debris nearby, but he couldn't locate where it'd fallen in the blast. Without it, he felt naked, exposed. More importantly, he was vulnerable.

Injured and unarmed, he would be no help. He had to get out of there.

Doing his best to avoid drawing attention and keep his injured leg straight, so as not to dislodge the metal shard, Sloan dragged himself toward a side door with 'Exit' emblazoned above it. After what felt like an eternity, he finally made it and tumbled out into a hallway. Out here it was quieter. And less smoky.

"Ja—Ja—Jacob?" A soft voice cracked. "Help—me—"

The monitor crackled and wavy lines danced around on the screen. But as the signal strengthened, a man's face came into view. He was a big man, but not muscular, dark-skinned with long, dark hair pulled into a scraggly ponytail. Chubby cheeks, a wide face, and a thin beard sat atop a thick neck.

"Hesko!" Eve laughed through a wide smile. "How are you?"

"Evie, my girl, you look wonderful." The man's voice boomed through the diminutive speakers on her laptop. It was deep and slightly hoarse. "I've been good. Good, good."

"You're up early."

"Up late. Life of a club owner. You know the drill," he chuckled…a hearty, genuine laugh.

Eve nodded, then turned to the other two. "Hesko, these are my friends. This is Franklin and this is Shannon."

Hesko's eyes narrowed and his tone deepened. "Which one is the government agent?"

"That would be me," Shannon chimed in with a little wave.

"But she's fine, Hesko. She's a friend, like I told you," Eve chided. "No need to get agitated. She's working the Nasha Volya case. The bombings."

"Oh yes, I'm very familiar with the Volya," Hesko boasted.

"You are?" Shannon asked.

He hesitated and Eve broke in again, "You can trust her."

After several long seconds, he muttered, "Ok. Any friend of Evie is a friend of mine. If she's willing to endorse you..." he trailed off for a minute, as though losing his train of thought, before sputtering, "So what do you want to know?"

"Anything you can tell us," Franklin chimed in, speaking for the first time. "You said you're familiar with the Volya."

"I am. I presume you already know all about the Narodnaya Volya, the group from the late 1800s."

"Yes, we do know. Anarchist group out of Russia. Assassinated one of the tsars, but ultimately they all—or at least most—were hanged. The group supposedly died out."

"True, true. But by now, I'm sure you've realized that isn't the whole story." He spoke with the authority—and oversized ego—of a college professor lecturing his freshman seminar course.

"Obviously." Shannon nodded, throwing a quick glance and roll of her eyes at Franklin.

"Right. Much like Kennedy being assassinated by the mob, Area 51's experiments on aliens, or the CIA testing LSD on American citizens, there's a lot more the public doesn't know about," he trumpeted, a smug look on his face.

"The—the what?" Franklin stammered.

"I told you," Eve interrupted. "He's a bit of a..." her voice dropped to a whisper, "...conspiracy nut."

"I can hear you, Evie," Hesko responded with a slight chuckle.

"The LSD one is actually true," Eve added. "He's into a lot of conspiracies, but Hesko's legit. He's a little nutty, but he's no crackpot."

"Wait, wait...the CIA did what now?" Franklin sputtered, incredulous. He'd never heard of this.

"Project MKUltra," Hesko confirmed, his head bobbing like a pigeon's as he spoke. "The CIA was testing to learn what chemicals or other methods would weaken people and get them to confess crimes. They basically sought to induce mind control. Hypnosis, abuse, torture, sensory deprivation, and yes...drugs, including LSD."

"And that—that actually happened? In real life?" Franklin stammered.

"Look, can we focus here for a moment?" Shannon interjected. "You can research LSD and the CIA later, Franklin. Let's get back to Nasha Volya."

"Right. So there's more to this story we haven't been told. As you know, the group didn't die out. The original Narodnaya Volya was kept alive through descendants like the Perovskaya family, but it only persisted deep underground. The ideas continued to thrive and were passed down, whispered in back alleys, for decades. But over time, those original anarchy concepts morphed. It started out anti-tsarism, but became more global. They claimed an elite class was rising, one that oppressed the people, and it was happening all over. Europe, America, China, etcetera. The group perceived large income gaps, informal caste systems, little class mobility, the same families always in power. They became anti-oligarchy and wanted to return the power to the people. It was still anarchical, but with a...different bent."

"Right, but how did they manage to stay hidden all these years? And how did they infiltrate governments, but still remain underground?"

"Ahh, that's where the story gets a little more complicated," Hesko faltered, his voice cracking. "And a lot more mysterious."

"What do you mean?" Franklin asked.

"Well, most people believe it hid in plain sight, with sympathizers posing as collectors or historians interested in the topic. And so they passed messages out in the open, identifying one another with those coins you found. But I always believed there was more to it. There still must be physical locations, probably scattered across the globe. Places where they could speak more openly, where information was stored, where the orders originated. Maybe even publicly, hidden in codes. Old school spycraft...hidden messages in newspapers," he hypothesized, shrugging.

"I agree," Shannon frowned. "Carrying around ancient coins doesn't explain how the attacks were planned so meticulously. They must be communicating another way. There had to—has to—be some centralized headquarters."

"Precisely," Hesko nodded vigorously. "I still haven't figured out the communication part. Private social media accounts, burner phones, hidden email servers. Maybe all of the above. Or maybe they're doing it old school with dead drops and coded messages in newspapers." He shook his head and shrugged.

"So what about Phoenix? What do you have on her?"

"Well, that's where it gets tricky..."

"It wasn't tricky before?" Franklin scoffed, hiding his frustration in a fake cough.

"Well, up until six months ago, Phoenix was believed to be a myth. The name was bandied about on message boards, but the stories seemed too fanciful and too numerous to be true. Even true believers seemed unsure. Personally, I suspected it was an amalgamation of several people."

"Clearly, it's a real person. It's a she," Shannon insisted.

"Yes, clearly. And that's changed the way I look at those references. If we assume the information about Phoenix refers to one person, that paints a very different—and more terrifying—picture."

"What do you mean? What kind of picture?"

"Well, keep in mind a lot of this is speculation, bordering on folk lore. But Phoenix is likely Chechen, by heritage, and carries a long history of violence. Parents were butchered in the Chechen wars when she was a child. Grew up on the streets with a younger brother, I believe, but he also died young. Got entangled with a street gang by the age of six, who raised her, but she worked hard and climbed the chain of command quickly. She impressed the bosses with her lack of emotion; she's a classic sociopath. She derives joy—her version of joy, anyway—through killing. Death followed her throughout her life and, as best I can tell, she's the direct suspect in over one hundred murders. And those are the ones with evidence. Her real body count is probably at least triple that. Maybe more."

"So she had a family? We haven't been able to create a paper trail," Shannon interrupted. "Anyone still alive?"

"No, not that it'd help if she did. I told you her brother died young. Many have theorized his death wasn't an accident. She doesn't feel loyalty like normal people."

"She—she murdered her own—" Shannon stammered.

"I didn't say that. I don't know. It's a theory. But she's been alone a long time."

"What about a name? A birth name?"

"No, sorry," he sighed with a sad shake of his head. "Whatever her name was, she abandoned it long ago. Probably only reminded her of her family she lost and wanted to make a clean break."

"I see. Well that's more than we had before. What about other family? Uncles, cousins, that sort of thing?"

"None anyone knows about."

Shannon nodded. "So let's get back to those physical locations you mentioned. Where are they?"

"Ah...that—well, I'm not positive about that either," he stammered. "But I do have theories. Best I can gather after the attacks, there'd need to be at least five central hideouts. But there may be more."

"Get to the point," Shannon prodded. Franklin could tell she was getting impatient. "What are your theories? Where are they?"

"That's the good news. I have strong evidence to suggest one of them is here."

"Here where?" Shannon pondered. "In America? Sioux City?"

"First, it's Sioux Falls. Sioux City is in Iowa," he smirked. "But I actually meant South Dakota."

"Where?"

"I—" he cut off and abruptly glanced over his shoulder toward the door. "I'm not sure I feel comfortable saying over a channel like this." When he turned back, there was a weird look on his face. He tugged at the collar of his shirt and his body stiffened.

"We're secure, Hesko," Eve broke back in. "You know me. Would I ever set up a non-secure link?"

"I know, I know," he stammered and crossed his arms across his chest. Something was wrong.

"What's wrong?" Shannon asked.

"I—I'll tell you. But only in person." His words were shaky and clipped. He tried to force a smile, but his grin came out lopsided, as though his brain couldn't settle on the right expression. He leaned in close to the monitor and whispered, "I've gotta run. It was nice to see you, Evie." And then he was gone. The image on the screen was replaced by the dancing, wavy lines again.

"In person? We have to go to South Dakota now?" Franklin grumbled.

"If he's correct about the location of the Nasha Volya headquarters, then you'll be going to South Dakota anyway," Eve countered.

"That's a big if, Eve. He sounded a little—" Shannon trailed off.

"I know he's a bit out there," Eve responded, nodding. "But he's not crazy. I'd trust him. I promise."

Shannon didn't respond, but glanced at Franklin. He didn't know what to say. Gallivanting halfway across the country to South Dakota on the word of a conspiracy loon wasn't his idea of a good use of time. But he trusted Eve and she trusted Hesko. At long last, he sighed and nodded.

Shannon smiled grimly, "Then I guess we're going to Sioux Falls."

Chapter 10

"H—he—help me, Jacob," Mostafa Barakat choked out the words.

Sloan's head snapped up to notice his friend propped against the far wall. He hobbled the dozen or so feet over to Barakat and struggled to kneel beside him. The Moroccan had a nasty head wound and blood streamed over his face and across his chest. His skin had turned several shades too pale. A piece of shrapnel had lodged in his side as well.

"Mostafa, are you alright?"

"Jacob," Barakat reached out and grabbed Sloan by his shirt. "Rufus is dead. That first shot went straight through his heart. I saw it."

Sloan hung his head and took a deep breath. Rufus Hastings was one of his oldest friends in the community; they'd known each other for at least thirty years. He'd hoped the bullet had only caught Rufus in the shoulder, but it apparently had been far more deadly than that.

"The others? Rivka? Max?"

Barakat shook his head. "I don't know. I got out of the room as fast as I could."

"It's not over, Mostafa. There are gunmen too. Backup, I think. And they're still active. I lost my gun in the blast or I'd still be in there. But we have to move before anyone follows us out here. But first, we need to work on that wound." He pointed to the piece of metal lodged below Barakat's ribcage.

Barakat agreed and put both hands on the shrapnel.

"No, stop!" Sloan exclaimed. "Don't remove it. Not yet. Let me take a look." He bent over it to get a better look. "Ok, it doesn't appear to be too deep and I don't think it's hit any major arteries. I think we can remove it. But we'll need something to stanch the blood."

He looked around, but the hallway was bare. Thinking fast, he grabbed his own tie and ripped it from his neck, then whipped off his belt. He squished the tie into a ball and handed it to Barakat. "Here, as soon as I pull out the shard, press this into the wound immediately. Got it?"

Barakat nodded, so Sloan reached out and placed one hand on the metal, bracing himself against the wall with the other.

"Three...two...one!" With a single smooth tug, he slid the piece of shrapnel out of the wound and Barakat replaced it with the balled-up tie. Sloan tossed the metal to one side and rushed to wrap his own belt around Barakat. He cinched it tight, holding the ball of cloth in place.

"There. That won't last long, but it will suffice for now. Long enough to get somewhere safe." He placed a hand on Barakat's shoulder. "Now, let's get out of here. Quickly."

"And here I was led to believe the great Jacob Sloan didn't believe in running," Mostafa chuckled, then groaned in pain. His attempt at a joke made Sloan smile though.

"I don't," he retorted. "But I don't have a weapon and I prefer running to dying."

Barakat grinned and nodded, then attempted to push himself upward. He struggled until Sloan caught ahold of his arm and pulled him to his feet. The strain sent waves of pain through Sloan's leg, but he ignored them with only a small grimace. He'd had worse injuries. Sloan snagged a couple long jackets off a nearby coat rack. They would mask their wounds and avoid unwanted attention. Then, Barakat threw an arm over Sloan's shoulders and the two of them limped and stumbled out a side exit door and into the busy sidewalk. An alarm blared as the exit door swung open, adding to the chaos.

"Where are we going, Jacob?" Barakat groaned. He struggled to keep up and Sloan felt a little extra weight on his shoulders with each passing step, forcing more and more stress onto his injured leg. They needed to find somewhere close by.

"We need to go to ground for a day or two," Sloan responded. Barakat would know what he meant by that; it was a near universal phrase in intelligence for going into hiding, or going dark. "I'm taking you to the Gypsy. He'll help us find a safe house quickly."

"A safe house? Why not the embassy? Or at least to a hospital? Neither one of us is in good condition."

"Think about it, Mostafa. How did the terrorists get into the meeting? They had help. Help from the highest levels. People can't just waltz into an intel community powwow. Someone opened the doors, greased some wheels. And until we know who that was, we have to assume anyone may've been turned. That includes embassy personnel. And, unfortunately, hospitals won't provide the security needed to avoid government officials."

"And the Gypsy can be trusted?" Barakat's voice wavered. He was weakening.

"He's paid well enough to be. And with his history, there's no way he's gonna trust the Volya. His parents were murdered by terrorists—Communists—years ago." Sloan gently directed his friend to turn left and the two men hobbled down an alleyway, away from the main hustle-and-bustle of the big streets.

"Fine, fine." Barakat coughed. "To the Gypsy it is, I suppose."

As Shannon called the airlines to book last-minute flights for that afternoon, Franklin took the opportunity to slip outside and get some fresh air, but kept to the back lot—out of sight from the road—just to be safe.

It was hard to tell inside Eve's compound because she kept the windows blocked by metal blinds and a thick curtain, but it was already seven in the morning. The sun had risen. Birds cheerily twittered about in the trees along the rear of the building, the poor creatures living their lives in blissful ignorance of the jeopardy the world faced. He envied that ignorance, that freedom. Even to be a normal citizen was enviable, at this point.

Obviously, the public knew about the bombings, the witch hunt in government. But they were unaware of its extent. Blissfully unaware of its danger. Even his own family seemed content to continue their daily routines as though nothing had happened. His father still opened and ran the bookstore every day. His brother helped with research early on, but he continued to teach university classes.

They didn't know. Didn't understand.

His brother...Jeremiah...Jay... Franklin found himself thinking about his brother a lot lately.

They'd had a tumultuous relationship over the years, but ever since Franklin helped save the life of Jeremiah's young son, KJ, from Phoenix the brothers had been on better terms—even though Franklin was the reason the boy had been at risk in the first place.

But it wasn't all roses. One moment—albeit a powerful one—didn't undo years of bad feelings between the two siblings. But it was a step forward. Maybe several steps forward.

Still, Franklin worked hard to keep his family away from danger, especially lately. He'd lost too much already and he wasn't about to lose anyone else. Not his father, not his brother, nor his brother's family.

He had to continue the search for Phoenix and the Nasha Volya, to avenge Joanna's death. He didn't feel he had a choice. So to protect his family, he'd pulled away. It wasn't ideal, but until this was over, he couldn't risk bringing dangerous people to their doorstep.

They didn't truly understand, which made it harder, though it was for their own good. Especially his brother, who kept pushing for a closer relationship; he didn't seem to grasp the peril and had, on more than one occasion, chided Franklin for his lack of connection.

But on the eve of their first real lead in months, Franklin felt he should reach out, to tell his brother they were getting closer.

It was early, but Jeremiah was a morning person; he liked to get in a five-mile run before showering and arriving at his campus office by eight. So he pulled out his cell and dialed a familiar number.

The phone rang three times before Jeremiah picked up.

"Hello?"

"Hi Jay," Franklin said. He was the only one allowed to call his brother Jay. It was his childhood nickname for Jeremiah, a callback to when Franklin was first learning to speak, but unable to pronounce the complexity of 'Jeremiah.'

"Frankie!" his brother exclaimed. He sounded out of breath. He must still be on his run. "Good to hear from you. How have you been?"

"I'm fine," Franklin responded. "Tired." He chose to leave out the part about nearly being killed and running for his life. No need to worry his brother.

"It's been a while, Franklin. Is everything okay?"

"You know I have to keep my distance, Jeremiah. Last time I didn't, KJ..."

"Family is still important, Frankie," he interrupted. "And we're better prepared now."

"I know," Franklin grunted, annoyed. At a certain point, he'd learned it was simply easier to just agree with his brother and move on. "Listen, I wanted to tell you something."

"Ok...what's up?"

"We have a lead on Phoenix. It's nothing concrete, but there's a man we found who claims she's hiding out in South Dakota."

"That's great! So what next?"

"Well the first step will be to go to South Dakota. I'm leaving—we're leaving—for Sioux Falls this afternoon to talk to the source. After that, we'll have a better handle on what to expect next."

"Is it gonna be dangerous?"

Franklin sensed the concern in his brother's voice. "We're talking to some nerdy conspiracy theorist. It'll be pretty tame." He wasn't sure if that was the truth, but he figured if he didn't know, it didn't count as a lie.

"But what about after that? When you know where she is?"

"*If* that lead pans out—a big *if*—that'll be up to Shannon. She's the expert."

"I know that, but she's a bit...cavalier...isn't she? She knows you aren't trained for this, right?"

"Stop worrying, Jay. I'll be 100% safe," Franklin promised, unconvincingly.

"You're never 100% safe, Franklin. Don't lie to me." Franklin could hear his brother's growing frown through the phone.

"I said stop it, Jay! I'll be fine!" he exploded.

"I'm your older brother, Frankie...I just want to keep you safe," Jay chastised him.

"You're a college professor, Jay. An academic who's never been in a fight in his life. You couldn't keep me safe today any more than you did as kids."

It came out far more harshly than Franklin intended and he recognized immediately he'd crossed a line. He hated when his brother patronized him, but anger wasn't the appropriate response. But rather than apologize, he stewed for a few seconds before hanging up. As he did, he heard his brother's faint "I'll pray for—" before he was cut off.

"Franklin!" Shannon's voice sliced through the morning fog in the parking lot. "Get in here! There's been a problem."

Franklin shoved the phone back in his pocket. He couldn't dwell on it. Couldn't let a brotherly squabble distract him. He needed to be single-minded, driven by one desire. To find Phoenix and capture her—or, if not that, take her out himself.

And the path to that outcome went through South Dakota.

Chapter 11

Congressman Hartwell stood near the window as the sun crept over the horizon, but he wasn't watching its majestic rays poking their way through the fluffy clouds, creating a brilliant tapestry across the sky. No, he was focused elsewhere.

Rather, his eyes were directed inside, glued to the television. A field journalist—a portly man with a bad comb-over—was reporting on the terrorist attack in Budapest, Hungary from the day before. Hartwell had hardly been able to tear his gaze away from the screen ever since news first broke.

He'd been flipping between multiple channels, trying to soak up every bit. Most images were taken outside from the street, showing the exterior of the building where a suicide bomber had burst into the meeting, pledged allegiance to Nasha Volya, and blown himself to kingdom come. Flames and smoke poured from every window. Even after fire crews managed to douse the inferno, ash still hung in the air like wafting snow, casting a gray pallor over the whole city block. It was reminiscent of New York after 9/11.

But a couple stations were brave enough to send a camera inside. The sight in what was once a conference center was gruesome, with the worst bits blurred for viewers. But no amount of blur could hide the blood, the charred body parts. Experts estimated roughly a dozen of the world's brightest intelligence minds died instantaneously in the blast.

But the real damage had been the second wave. Four more terrorists had stormed through the room in the smoke and chaos, wielding AK-47s and cutting down anyone who tried to escape.

Forty-three people had been killed in total, the reporter announced, but another two dozen still fought for their lives in the ICU at the local Budapest hospital. Many weren't expected to make it.

They were still in the process of identifying the victims, but already names and faces of the confirmed victims flashed across the screen. Most notably, Rufus Hastings, the head of MI6 was dead. London was reportedly in an uproar, accusing Hungarian officials of not doing enough to protect their people. Other deaths included two members of the Italian delegation, the Canadian leader of CSIS, a half dozen Asian intelligence agents, and the head of the Brazilian Intelligence Agency.

One of the American intelligence leaders, Director Jacob Sloan of SISA, was still missing and presumed dead. And he wasn't the only one.

Hartwell recognized the name of Sloan. He had led the team that exposed and arrested Graham O'Brian and Nathan Hook over at the FBI. While Hook had eventually escaped, O'Brian rotted in a cell and Nasha Volya had lost one of its most powerful insiders; it had been a major blow to their operation.

But not for long, Hartwell mused. *Soon there'd be another, in a more powerful position than even the FBI. Soon, the Volya would have someone in the White House itself.*

He smiled and strode over to his desk, picking up a piece of paper that lay in the center of his workspace. His announcement speech. The one where he'd reveal his candidacy to the country in two days' time. It wouldn't be a shock, of course. He'd been predicted to enter the race for months now, but he wanted to wait for the appropriate moment. And now was it. The time was close.

Most people would discern his announcement as standing strong in the face of a national security attack, like President Bush's speech in the rubble of the World Trade Center towers. And it'd lift his approval rating, as it did for Bush.

Hartwell was already a well-known and fairly well-liked congressman and the sympathy vote as a Volya survivor, in the wake of more attacks, would skyrocket him up the polls. He'd be viewed as a powerful symbol of a victim and a nation fighting back against terror. But he would know different. He would be showing solidarity with the Volya itself, promising to finish what they started.

The flight into Sioux Falls was uneventful, which Franklin always felt was the best kind of flight. Flying in a metal tube at thousands of miles per hour, high above the earth, was the last place you wanted to suddenly become 'eventful.' They'd had a very brief layover in Minneapolis, which didn't give them enough time to scarf down any dinner before rushing onto the one hour flight into South Dakota, so Franklin's stomach was starting to complain.

Shannon had spent most of the flight linked into the plane's Wi-Fi network, trying to learn about the attack in Budapest. News stations had yet to confirm anything useful, but she'd recognized the building as the same one where the international intelligence conference was taking place.

She'd been unable to get ahold of Director Sloan, so they both feared the worst. The casualty count was around two dozen so far, but expected to rise. They'd briefly entertained the idea of flying to Hungary, but there was nothing either of them could do.

The Sioux Falls airport was small, with only seven gates, so deboarding the plane and exiting the terminal was quick and painless. They rented a car with no trouble—they were the only ones in line—and headed straight for the club where Hesko Swanson worked. Crazy conspiracy theorist aside, he operated a mildly successful nightclub in town called Tatanka. Sioux Falls wasn't exactly known for its nightlife, but they did have a few hot spots. They weren't scheduled to meet with him until the following morning, but Shannon convinced Franklin they needed to scope out the location. And take a night to relax.

Shannon informed him that Tatanka was a Native American word, meaning 'buffalo,' from the Lakota people. But given that Hesko himself hailed from the Cheyenne tribe, his use of a Lakota word was probably incidental. Tatanka was also the true name of one of South Dakota's most famous residents, the native leader Sitting Bull and the club's website seemed determined to capitalize on that, with a photograph of the man front and center.

The nightclub wasn't far from the airport, so twenty minutes later, Shannon pulled the car into the parking lot of an unassuming building.

Tatanka didn't look like much from the outside. Someone had graffitied the Lakota word on the side of a building in a tribal-looking script, but no windows, no decorations, and no advertisements adorned the exterior walls. If you didn't know what it was, you'd probably assume it was a warehouse. But the lot itself was packed with roughly thirty cars. Shannon took one of the last few empty spots.

"Popular place," she commented and turned off the engine.

Franklin nodded. The two remained in the car for a minute and watched. Two men, one clearly a native and one Caucasian in a gargantuan cowboy hat, sauntered past and entered the club, but otherwise, it looked like everyone was already inside. When the door swung open to allow the men inside, a cacophony of voices spilled out into the lot.

After a few minutes, Shannon moved to exit the car and Franklin followed suit. It had been a warm day, but the air temperature was cooling, making for a comfortable evening. A slight breeze rustled, tossing about a few papers, and carrying the unmistakable smell of grilled barbecue and...was that hamburger? Franklin's mouth began to water.

Franklin held the door for Shannon, as they found themselves tucked in a small entryway—a vestibule—sandwiched between two doors, but they were halted just inside by a beefy man in a leather jacket. His heft spilled over his belt and he struggled to stay balanced on the stool.

"IDs?" he grunted.

"IDs?" Shannon marveled, a slight smile on her lips. "Do we *look* under 21?"

"Sorry, ma'am," he smiled, revealing a messy array of yellowed teeth. "Club policy. We ID everyone."

"Fine," she responded, chuckling as she reached into her pocket. She paused for a second, as though reconsidering something, then switched pockets. She pulled out her traditional driver's license, not her federal bureau badge and identification. Franklin assumed she didn't want to make a scene.

The man peered at both of their licenses, but after a few moments, he waved them through with that same toothy grin and a friendly 'Have a nice night!'

They passed through the second door into the bar and were quickly greeted by a larger-than-life, wooden statue of a Native American man. Two feathers stuck up from his head and he wore his hair in long braids that hung over either side of his chest. A chiseled sign labeled him as 'Tatanka, Sitting Bull,' the bar's namesake.

Edging around the large sculpture, Franklin and Shannon found themselves in an Old West saloon-style bar. It felt like stepping backward in time. Wood-heavy decor, with animal pelts and antlers, adorned the walls. Crude chandeliers had been fashioned from old wagon wheels.

Along either side wall ran long high-top counters, behind which a single barman—one on each side—was filling drink orders. A wide array of bottles of all shapes, sizes, and colors lined the walls. Scattered throughout the middle of the establishment were a series of low tables where a few young women in low-cut blouses, corsets, and skirts served food and drinks. Immediately to their left sat a small gaming area. Two poker tables were full of a rough-looking biker crowd and a couple was playing darts behind them.

Everything was low-key and calm, except for the back of the bar. Here, the furniture had been cleared for a dance floor and a couple dozen people were line dancing to some truly-terrible live music from a band that looked like they'd passed their prime decades ago. Inset along the far wall was a traditional set of swinging saloon doors that appeared to lead into a series of offices.

It was loud, but not so deafening you couldn't be heard, a fact Franklin learned when Shannon leaned over and pointed, "There he is." He followed her finger to their left and, sure enough, Hesko leaned over one of the poker tables, deep in conversation with a couple of the bikers. It looked like bad blood had boiled over during the game and needed cooling down and Hesko was handling mediation.

Franklin took a step toward Hesko, but Shannon put her hand on his arm and held him back.

"Let's get a drink," she suggested. "Let him work."

Franklin nodded. Tonight wasn't about the conversation. They would talk to him tomorrow morning, in detail. And he wasn't expecting them tonight. For now, all they needed to do was observe. There was no need to make their presence known. And Franklin wasn't one to reject a drink. Vodka. Bourbon. Rum. A beer. It didn't matter what. He just needed something alcoholic.

She pointed again, this time to two empty stools along one of the bars, and the two of them crossed room, weaving between tables, to take a seat.

"What can I getcha, folks?" A hulking bartender in plaid moseyed over and addressed them. He was young and of native heritage, maybe Sioux, like the town's namesake, but he sounded like a Midwesterner. He had the classic 'Minnesota' accent that was so common across this part of the country, lengthening the letter 'o' in folks.

Not as exaggerated as the popular movie *Fargo*, but every bit as distinctive.

"Just a Coke for me," Shannon replied, then eyed Franklin.

"A beer," he added. "Something local."

"Sure thing, you betcha," he drawled and turned to grab two mugs from a shelf on the wall behind him. He filled them from the tap and placed them on the counter. "Your Coke, ma'am. And this here is Possum Belly from Monks, right here in Sioux Falls. A tad unusual for a pale ale, but it's one of my favorites to recommend."

"Thank you," Franklin replied, eyeing the reddish-amber liquid greedily.

"You two aren't from around here," the bartender noted. "What brings ya to town?"

"Business," Shannon answered vaguely. "We're looking for someone." Her tone was friendly, but carried an undertone that told the man to drop it.

"94490082054962231894443," he grunted, but took the hint. "Sounds serious. Well, I hope you find this person. Ya let me know if you need anything more."

As the bartender wandered away to refill the mugs of a cluster of patrons at the other end of the bar, Franklin grabbed his glass and took a big sip. The man was right. A hint of citrus, a taste of malt sweetness. Different, but tasty. He took another swig and closed his eyes.

"Take it easy, Franklin," Shannon's voice broke his focus and snapped him back. "We're here to scope out Hesko, not sample the local booze."

"We can't do both?" he asked, only half-joking.

"You have a problem, you know," she replied. "I haven't said anything because I know it's been hard, but…"

"But what?" he snapped, interrupting her mid-sentence.

"I'm not saying I understand, but you weren't the only one to lose someone..."

"You're right. You don't."

She fell silent, clearly choosing not to push the point, and turned her attention to the patrons at the bar. She nodded in the direction of the swinging doors near the back. Franklin followed her gaze and spotted Hesko again. He'd just exited the offices. He looked concerned, upset even. They watched as he stomped over to the bartender and whispered something in his ear.

The bartender's eyes widened and he gaped at Hesko, who nodded as if to confirm what he'd said. The two immediately turned and headed for the back room again.

Shannon and Franklin watched and waited for half an hour. A different bartender soon took the place of the one who'd disappeared with Hesko, but their target never re-emerged.

Chapter 12

The Gypsy was not a real gypsy. Not the kind portrayed in the movies, anyway. But he was Romani, a member of the normally nomadic ethnic group frequently called gypsies. But many Roma, including this particular asset, hated the term; they considered it pejorative. But as a cover—a codename—it worked well. And would often dispel any suspicions about him, if anyone ever accidentally overheard his name.

Neither Sloan nor Barakat knew the Gypsy's real name. It was quite likely the U.S. government didn't even know it for sure. He'd gone by so many monikers, changed his name so many times, it was impossible to keep track of which was real and which ones were invented. Hence, they called him the Gypsy.

He managed a bookstore on the east side of Budapest, thankfully only a couple blocks from the attack, so it didn't take them long to stumble to the shop.

The outside of the establishment was dingy, with grime-laden windows, covered by a set of dirty, wooden blinds, and a tacky neon sign greeting them. Upon entering, the hinges squeaked loudly and they found themselves standing beneath a bare lightbulb, burned halfway out, and hanging from a string.

"Hello?" Sloan called out.

"Who is it?" A boorish, heavily-accented voice croaked from a hidden spot off to their right. After a couple seconds, a scrawny man stumbled out into the open. Sloan had only met the Gypsy once, many years ago, and it took him a moment to recognize this wreck of a man as the same person. Where he'd once been a clean-cut businessman trying to make a legitimate name for himself, this was an entirely different person standing before him. Balding, unkempt hair sat on a puffy face and led into sideburns so thick, the man resembled a bargain bin knockoff of Ambrose Burnside.

He was dressed casually in a ratty pair of blue jeans, a red V-neck sweater over a white T-shirt—both a size too large for him—and dirty tennis shoes. Hardly a business professional look for a shop owner. In one hand, he held a lit cigar and in the other a half-empty bottle of Pálinka, a potent brand of Hungarian fruit brandy. *That didn't bode well so early in the afternoon,* Sloan worried.

"Who're you?" the Gypsy grumbled, slipping into Hungarian. "Mit akarsz?" He didn't seem to recognize Sloan, nor notice that his two new visitors were wounded. Maybe this wasn't such a good idea.

"We're looking for a copy of *Bésy*, by Dostoyevsky," Sloan initiated the contact by using the predetermined code phrase, specifically using the Russian title for the work rather than its more common English title, *Demons*. The book was one of Dostoyevsky's masterpieces, an allegory of the consequences of nihilism, a trend that had been rising and disastrous for Russia in the mid-1800s.

When the agency created this asset decades before, they'd created a set of statements to ensure identity; if anyone arrived asking for formal help, but hadn't begun the conversation with those precise words, the Gypsy was instructed to respond as any normal shopkeeper and pretend he had no idea what they were talking about.

And if the Gypsy responded incorrectly, that meant something had become compromised and they were to leave immediately.

The Gypsy paused and blinked a few times in rapid succession. Sloan could almost see the gears whirling in his head; he likely hadn't been contacted as an asset for the agency in a long time and he hadn't expected official company.

"I haven't had anyone request that book in years..." he began, but after several seconds, he finally he gave the correct response, "I believe I have the Maguire translation in the back." For the first time, he seemed to have noticed the blood and injuries of his guests. He turned and set the bottle of brandy on the cashier's desk with a trembling hand.

"We would really prefer the 1945 Magarshack," Sloan dutifully continued the script. This was the key line; it contained an intentional mistake, as David Magarshack's famous translation was actually published in 1954.

"I—I apologize. I don't have that one." His alcohol-induced slur was disappearing as well; the seriousness of the situation appeared to be sobering him up fast. "Why is man unhappy?" the Gypsy proposed, his question a slurred mumble. It was a paraphrase of a quote from the book.

"Because he doesn't know he's happy," Sloan answered correctly. "It's only that."

That completed the pre-arranged script.

"That's right," the Gypsy nodded and staggered to the door. He flicked off the neon sign and turned the deadbolt. "We're alone. Now, what the hell happened to you two?"

"You haven't heard? There was a terrorist attack. All the intelligence heads in the world in one place. A bomb followed by gunmen."

The Gypsy's face paled. He obviously hadn't been watching the morning news. "I heard…something. Thought a car backfired. Casualties?"

"Yes." Sloan swallowed hard. "Many."

"Basszus" the Gypsy trailed off.

"Now, can you help us? My friend here is badly wounded. And I could use medical assistance myself." He nodded at his leg, where an inch of steel still protruded from his thigh.

"Yes, yes of course." The Gypsy glanced down, apparently only just now noticing the metal shard. He beckoned them through a curtain behind the counter. "Let me get you settled. Come with me."

$$\sim$$

As they pulled out of the parking lot to the club, Shannon turned left and drove through the downtown area of Sioux Falls, a few block stretch of Phillips Street that gave off a very small town, 'everyone knows your name' feel. As they passed shops and restaurants, Franklin felt his mind drift.

This wasn't his first time to the state best known for Mouth Rushmore. His mother had grown up in the state, in a tiny town out in the country, and the whole family traveled to visit her hometown when Franklin and his brother Jeremiah were children. But this was his first time here as an adult. And despite the less-than-favorable circumstances, he'd looked forward to seeing it again. Seeing where she'd lived wouldn't bring her back, obviously, but somehow simply being in the state had sparked something in the part of his heart where he kept the memories of her. In some strange way, it was as though she was alive again in him.

It was already dark, so they didn't get to observe much of the hustle and bustle of the city as they drove through. The sun had long since disappeared below the horizon and darkness swept across the day like a cloak. He'd have liked to stop in a local store or simply walk the street, just to feel the ambiance, but because of the time, all of those options had long since closed.

So at Shannon's recommendation, they chose to head straight to the hotel for some shuteye. Franklin had left the overnight booking to her, an error he soon regretted as she pulled into the lot of a dirty, run-down motel that looked like one of those pay-by-the-hour places depicted on true crime shows. The type of place where dead bodies liked to show up.

The lobby of the motel was all but deserted. A bell above the door rang as they entered, catching the attention of a night clerk behind the counter and he glanced up for a second. A small, gangly man with a wiry body and the face of a rodent, he was watching a Mexican telenovela on one of those old portable TVs with large rabbit-ear antennas. He handed Franklin a key for a room near the end of the row, not bothering to request his license or other form of identification.

Franklin and Shannon could've been fugitives, mass murderers for all he cared. But that was okay. They didn't want anyone asking too many questions. It was probably an unnecessary precaution, but Shannon insisted on the anonymity, just in case. They couldn't be sure who knew they were there, so every little bit of protection they could afford themselves would be useful.

The room itself was unassuming, but it would do. Two twin beds sat against one wall and a simple wooden desk with a beat-up chair sat along the other. The bathroom tile was stained, as was the tub, but it appeared clean. Well, clean enough. The air in the room gave off a faint hint of stale cigarette smoke and mold. But they wouldn't be here long enough to matter.

Shannon sank onto the nearest bed, which protested with a loud creak. She pulled out her phone and glanced at the screen, but after a sigh, tossed it aside.

"Still nothing from the Director. I don't know about you, but I'm exhausted," she moaned. "I'm gonna get some sleep. It'll be an early morning. We need to get there when it opens. And maybe we'll hear from Sloan by then too."

"You go ahead," he grunted. "I'm going to stay up a while longer. Maybe read through your notes."

"You sure?" she asked. "It's already after midnight. And you look dead on your feet as well."

"I know," he mumbled through a yawn. "But I didn't get to study the dossier on the plane and I need to at least skim it while I still have a couple synapses firing up here." He tapped the side of his head with a tired smile.

"Fair," she yawned. "Fair enough. But I'm gonna shut my eyes." She kicked off her shoes, but didn't bother changing clothes. She crawled under the sheets still fully dressed, asleep before her head hit the pillow. Within a couple minutes, Franklin could hear a faint snore through shallow breathing.

She was out like a light.

He removed the manila folder from Shannon's bag that held all they knew about Swanson. But the truth was,

Franklin didn't need to brush up on his case file. Shannon had already given him all the particulars he needed. And she was going to be the one running point; she was the expert. He was just a tag-along.

He'd lied about needing to read the dossier. Really, he wanted to be alone. The room they booked had a tiny porch, so he slipped outside. A rickety folding chair sat propped in one corner and he settled into it. He placed the file on the ground beneath the chair, then leaned forward, his shoulders hunched and head resting in his hands.

He was grateful for the darkness that enveloped the city at this late hour. It felt more and more like a familiar embrace. The silence and blackness of the night swallowing his pain. It'd been weeks, months since he'd felt anything other than pain, the sting of loss. The questions kept coming, night after night, and they wouldn't have allowed him to sleep anyway. He'd smuggled one of those miniature airplane bottles of alcohol off the flight, but he knew that wouldn't touch his insomnia.

As a dog barked nearby, breaking the silence, Franklin found himself thinking about his family.

About his mother and father. His mother had passed away a couple years ago and he missed her. The two of them were like peas in a pod, so identical in many ways. And it didn't help that his father was sort of...prickly. He'd retired from the military, with the personality stereotype to match. He'd softened since retirement, more since his wife died, but Franklin and his brother Jeremiah were still just now getting to know their dad.

Then there was Jeremiah.

Jay.

Why had things fallen apart again? Why had he lashed out on that call? Were they falling into their old patterns again? Franklin didn't know. He didn't understand. Things were just starting to get better, but then his brother had to bring up the faith issue again and Franklin snapped.

Sure, he'd prayed a couple times recently. Once over his ex-wife, once for his nephew. But while they'd saved his nephew, Joanna had still died and prayer with fifty-percent effectiveness just didn't seem worth it. He might as well have flipped a coin.

Franklin knew he needed to call Jeremiah back and apologize for what he'd said. For the accusation. It was the right thing to do. Even a text apology would help. But that would require deep self-reflection to understand why he'd said those words in the first place and he didn't have time for that. He didn't even know how to go about it.

So rather than apologize, rather than send his brother a text, he did nothing.

Instead, he stood and rested against the rusty railing, looking out over the alley. If he leaned out a few inches and peered to his left, he could make out Falls Park, through which the Big Sioux River ran, creating the town's namesake. He remembered seeing the waterfalls as a kid. They were impressive, not for their height—this part of South Dakota was remarkably flat—but for their length and beauty. If only he'd been here on vacation, he'd have a chance to go witness their greatness. To sit at their edge and enjoy the scenery.

But time was short. The clock was ticking and they wouldn't have time.

After a while alone in the darkness, he turned to head inside. Sleep was elusive, but he'd need to get some if he planned to function tomorrow.

He grabbed the manila folder off the concrete—the folder he hadn't cracked open—and slipped back inside. Placing it quietly on the desk, he kicked off his shoes and crawled into his bed. There, he slid the bottle of airplane alcohol from his pocket and, with a quick glimpse over his shoulder to make sure Shannon was asleep, chugged it in a simple gulp. Then he closed his eyes and waited for the liquid drug to take effect.

Chapter 13

They both awoke the next morning before the sun did. The first whispers of light on the horizon were just beginning to make their appearance, but neither Franklin nor Shannon could stay in bed any longer. Franklin had eventually managed to squeeze in a couple hours of sleep, but insomnia and nerves prevented him from getting any more. He yawned and stretched to ease the stiffness that had settled in his joints. Every morning was the same. He moved slowly, painfully, until his body finally shook loose his tired muscles.

Shannon, however, seemed on edge this morning, like a tangled ball of barely-contained energy. She'd nearly catapulted out of bed like she'd found a spider in the sheets. As he clambered upright and perched on the edge of the bed, he watched her flit back and forth from the desk to the bathroom, hairbrush in one hand and file folder in the other.

She seemed eager to get moving, to talk to Hesko Swanson. And he didn't blame her. It'd been months since they'd come across a lead as solid as this one.

In the bathroom, he avoided the mirror. He knew what he'd see if he did and he hated that image. He threw on a shirt and pulled a pair of jeans over his boxers. Shannon had taken a shower and the steam from the hot water still hung in the air, but he eschewed the cleaning himself. Instead, he ran his hand through his messy hair a few times, taming it into something mildly presentable.

By the time he'd finished and walked out into the main room, he found Shannon standing out on the porch, talking on the phone. Seeing him, she quickly hung up and joined him inside.

"You ready to go?" she asked.

He nodded. "Who was that?" He pointed at her pocket, where she'd stored the cell.

"On the phone?" She waved her hand dismissively. "Just leaving another message for Director Sloan." She paused. "He still isn't answering. And Eve hasn't heard from him either."

"Still?"

"No," she said with a slow shake of her head. "They apparently recovered his ID and security badge in the rubble. But they've started naming the dead and his name hasn't popped up yet, so it's possible he made it out."

"You think he's okay?"

"He's one of the most capable at that meeting. If the initial blast didn't kill him—and I guess we won't know for sure until they finish identifying bodies—then he may just be laying low in case he's targeted again as a survivor. Hopefully, his wallet and badge were simply knocked loose in the blast."

"What will he do? Is there some sort of...procedure or something?"

"When a cover is blown or you're targeted in the field, protocol dictates you go to ground."

"What does that mean?" he asked. Shannon had a tendency to slip into industry speak.

"It means he'll find safety, change his appearance, and break out a fake ID to get out of the country."

"Interesting."

She nodded. "Now...shall we?" She moved toward the door.

He waved a hand for her to take the lead, then followed her into the hallway and then to the car.

The drive to Hesko's bar was uneventful and when they arrived, they found him waiting at the front door for them. The club sat largely empty this morning, save for a few employees cleaning and one customer who had passed out, slumped over on one of the stools.

"Come, come," Hesko beckoned them passionately to follow him into the back. "Please hurry." He didn't seem as big up close. Franklin towered several inches taller than him. But the man still outweighed him by at least twenty pounds. *Short and stout, like a hobbit,* Franklin thought. His ponytail hung unbound and long hair fell past his shoulder.

They moved to follow him and, after stopping to place two fingers on the neck of the man to ensure he was simply unconscious, they were led through the swinging doors and into a dark hallway.

"You have some information for us?" Shannon requested, once they'd all taken seats in his office. The room was cramped and a distinct mold smell made Franklin's nose crinkle.

"Something happened," Hesko's voice was at a whisper, as though delivering some big secret.

"What do you mean?" Shannon said, her eyes narrowing.

"When we spoke earlier—yesterday—there was a noise. At the door. Like a scratching."

"Ok..."

"When I went to investigate, I found this." He reached into his shirt pocket and withdrew a crumpled sheet of paper that looked as though it'd been torn out of a spiral notebook. He handed it over to Shannon and she carefully unfolded it, holding it out so Franklin could read it as well.

Keep your mouth shut. - P

"I tell you, that scared the daylights out of me. Didn't wanna talk to you feds anymore, but Evie convinced me I should. Said it was the right thing to do and you'd be able to keep me safe."

"P..." Franklin muttered. "You think that's Phoenix?"

"I have no idea," Hesko conceded.

"Did you see anyone? Anyone who might've left this note?" Shannon's questioning was a little forceful, like an interrogation.

"No, no one."

"What about security cameras?"

"Here, I'll show you," he waved them around the desk and pointed at the screen, indicating a tall man in a long coat. "I have a half dozen cameras on the property and not a one got a good look at his face."

"Coincidence?"

"Not at all," Hesko shook his head. "Here, look." He sped up the video, fast-forwarding thirty seconds. "You see he angles his head awkwardly, tilts his cap, as though he knows exactly where the camera is."

"So he had inside knowledge of your security system."

"Right, but I don't know how he could have. Several of the cameras are hidden and I installed all of them myself. Not even my employees know them all."

"Can you zoom in? We can't see his face, but maybe there's something else we can learn."

"Sure," he tapped a few keys and the image enlarged.

The trio found themselves staring at a fuzzy image of a man in a dark coat, his face obscured by shadows and a baseball cap.

The resolution on the image was pretty low, but they could make out a short beard and round glasses. That was the extent, however, of any identifying clues. No distinguishing words or marks stood out on his clothing, nothing that stood out as remarkable, at all. And the best shot of his face was a blurry profile, not enough for any facial recognition tests. This was likely a dead end.

"Can you make us a copy of this?" Shannon asked.

"Why?" Franklin interjected. "There's nothing here."

"I'd still like Eve to take a look at it. She might be able to pull something."

"Sure thing," Hesko nodded. "I'll send a copy directly to her."

"Ok, so other than this, what do you have for us? You implied on the video chat that you knew something about the Volya, that they were in South Dakota."

"Right, right. Let me show you." He stood and stepped over to a file cabinet. He tapped the side of the box, then grabbed the handle on the bottom drawer and pulled. It slid open with a rusty grating noise. He stuck his full arm inside to pull something from the back and, after a few seconds, his hand emerged holding a manila folder. He dropped it on the desk and flipped it open, revealing what looked like a satellite image of mountains.

"Where is this?" Franklin blurted.

"This is a 250-square mile area in the western portion of the state. And you see this here?" He pointed to a series of brown, dome-like structures in one corner, nestled in a valley. Their coloring helped them blend into the surrounding land, but as soon as you knew where to look, they became obvious.

"What are they?" Shannon asked.

"They're weapons storage, technically. Or they were. Built during World War Two, they were designed as munitions storage and maintenance facility for the Army. But they served a number of purposes...chemical weapon storage, holding facilities for prisoners of war. I suspect they were also built as bomb shelters...bunkers for when the big one hit. But when the war came and went, they languished for a couple decades, but then went abandoned and were ultimately re-purposed to sell to citizens afraid of Armageddon. Or a nuclear holocaust. Or a zombie apocalypse. Whatever your fear is. And while many are still abandoned, many now belong to private citizens. Kind of a refuge for the uber-rich, in case the whole world starts to go to hell."

"Fascinating," Shannon said, leaning in for a closer look. "How did you get these?"

"Satellite." He muttered under his breath, without elaboration.

"What kind of satellite, Hesko?" Shannon pushed a little harder. "I've seen photos like this before...this has the markers of a military intelligence device."

"It's amazing what you can do with a computer and an Internet connection." Hesko eyed her closely and shrugged, but didn't offer details. "Here's an enlarged image." He slid aside the one photo to reveal another underneath, zoomed in on the brown domed structures. Franklin started to count, but quickly lost track. Easily hundreds of the bunkers, all lined up in neat rows, dotted the landscape.

"And you think the Nasha Volya holed up here? Why?" After a moment's pause, Shannon shook her head She'd clearly decided not to push the satellite issue.

"Well, it makes sense, doesn't it? An underground group in a literal underground bunker."

"We're gonna need a little more than that to fly across the state on a wild goose chase..."

"Of course, of course," Hesko's head bobbed furiously on his neck as he nodded. "I have a friend in Deadwood..."

"Like the TV show?" Franklin suggested.

"Yep, that's the one," Hesko continued. "Real city. It's not far from these shelters. My friend's a blackjack dealer in a casino there and says there's been a lot of Russians frequenting the place the last year or so, way more than there used to be. They don't get many Russians in Deadwood, ya see. But the accent stands out."

"How far is Deadwood from these bomb shelters?"

"About two hours through the Black Hills, by car."

"Two hours?" Franklin scoffed.

"Two hours is nothing out here. Sometimes you'll drive that far just to get to the next town."

"What are the Black Hills?" Shannon asked.

"It's a mountain range," Franklin jumped in with the answer. "Largely covered in evergreen trees, which gives it a 'black' appearance from a distance. It's where Mount Rushmore is located. And the Crazy Horse Memorial."

"Interesting," Shannon mused, nodding. She turned her attention back to Hesko. "So is there any more?"

"More?" Hesko raised a bushy eyebrow.

"This seems promising, but an increase in Russian tourism to Mount Rushmore doesn't mean they're Volya terrorists."

"They're definitely not tourists," Hesko protested. "They're regulars. Familiar faces over and over. Real shady folks too, according to...my friend. Probably KGB."

"Well, the KGB doesn't exist anymore. Replaced by the FSB and SVR. But that's interesting. If that's true, this could be them," Shannon said. "But I dunno...it still feels like a long shot."

"He also said there's a woman with them. Fits the description of your gal too."

Shannon's eyes widened and she exchanged a knowing look with Franklin. That changed things. *If it was her...* He nodded. "We're gonna need to talk to this friend."

"You—I—what? I can talk to him for you."

"Oh no, he's not an anti-government conspiracist like you, is he?"

"No no, not at all. He's just...cautious..." Hesko spoke slowly, measuring his words carefully. "Around government folks..."

"In other words, he's a criminal," Shannon interrupted. "Look, we don't care about whatever scams he's running in Deadwood. We only need to know about the Volya."

"Tell you what. Give me a few hours to touch base with him. Can you wait? If he's open to talking, I can give you his information then, after I've spoken to him."

"Fine," Shannon nodded and stood. "We'll be back this afternoon." She stuck out her hand to shake Hesko's. "Thank you for your help."

"You're welcome." He took her hand gingerly and shook it. "So what next?"

"What do you mean? I thought you were gonna—"

"For my protection. Evie promised you'd protect me. And after that note…"

"You want a special government detail? Surveillance outside?"

"No, no… I don't—I don't trust—"

"What kind of protection are you hoping for?"

"I hoped maybe you'd stay…"

"You're going to be fine, Mr. Swanson," she began. "You seem well protected here. Do you carry?"

"Sure do. Got a Taurus on my ankle at all times. My bouncers are armed too."

"Then don't worry. If your information pans out and we feel you're in any real danger, I'll send an agent or two out here to help. But let's take this a day at a time."

She turned to exit and Franklin followed. Hesko grunted once, apparently in protest, but dropped it.

"We'll be back soon," Franklin added. "Thank you for everything. You've been very helpful."

Shannon paused in the door, as if an idea just hit her. "What are these bunkers called, Hesko? Do they have a name?"

"They go by a lot of names. Formally, it's the Black Hills Ordnance Depot. Some call it Doomsday, South Dakota. But locals call them 'Igloos' because of their construction. They have an unusual shape, you see…"

"Igloos?!" Franklin sputtered and grabbed Shannon by her elbow. "Isn't that what you said—?"

"Yes, I did," she answered quietly. "That's what the man in the meeting at Rock Creek Park called it."

"This has to be it," Franklin declared.

"I agree," she nodded. "Hesko, if you could hurry…"

"I'll send a message to my friend right now. I'll have something in a couple hours."

"Excellent. This just might be our lucky day..." She turned and left, leaving Franklin to toss out one final 'thank you' to Hesko, who'd already started typing on his keyboard. In a few hours, if all went well, they might have a lead on a precise location—down to the individual bunker, or bunkers, they're occupying—but also faces, or even names of its occupants.

For the first time in six months, Franklin felt a surge of hope and he did something he rarely let himself do nowadays.

He allowed a hint of a smile to escape.

Chapter 14

The Congressman's aide reached over and tightened his tie. She patted him on the shoulders, dusting off a few flakes of dandruff and smiled up at him, from ear to ear.

"How do I look?" he grinned, staring into her baby-blue eyes. Lydia Fisher was barely twenty and interning with his office for the summer, on break from her studies at Rutgers. She was young, strong, and idealistic—not yet encumbered by the cynicism that so many in Washington become afflicted with. And more importantly, she looked up to him, respected him; in her eyes, he did no wrong. Much better than the sniveling man-child who'd interned last year.

"Perfect, Congressman Hartwell," she replied, her normally high-pitched voice bubbling over with excitement.

"It's been months now, Lydia. You can call me Marcus." He nodded, as he fiddled with the Volya ring, placed carefully and conspicuously on his right middle finger. He'd been asked to give a live television interview—along with his colleague, Congressman Lawson—on the attack in Budapest and this felt like the appropriate moment to debut his possession of the ring.

Both he and Lawson had been in the building six months ago when Nasha Volya set off a bomb at the Rayburn Congressional Office Building. In the ensuing firefight, one of their own—Republican James Holgate of Tennessee, a frequent sparring partner of Hartwell's on the congressional floor—had been killed. So naturally, any time there was an update on the Nasha Volya, Lawson and Hartwell both saw their office phones ring with appearance requests.

As was the norm, the two congressmen had been shuttled off site into a room frequently used for news interviews. It was little more than a trailer, but the inside had been decorated with several different backdrops, like a mini Hollywood set. Hartwell sat in front of one built to resemble an office. Lawson was seated across the trailer, with his own camera crew, in front of a background that looked like the White House lawn. It was silly, but the optics made for good television. Or so they said.

Hartwell crossed his legs to create a more natural demeanor and plucked a tuft of lint off his suit trousers, flicking it off camera before flashing a winning, toothy smile right as the camera's red light blinked on. They were live.

The interview began simply enough. The host—a petite blonde woman with a bad haircut and a worse dye job—introduced the story by showing images from the attack, with the gruesome bits blurred, then transitioned into the initial bomb blast at Rayburn six months ago.

"Here to discuss this recent attack, we are joined by Congressmen Howard Lawson and Marcus Hartwell, who had both been present—possible targets—of the Nasha Volya six months ago." Hartwell had given them the line about possibly being victims. He liked that. It shifted blame further away from him and created sympathy. She continued, "Gentlemen, how are you doing today?"

As discussed before going live, Lawson answered first.

"Thank you, Kendall. Like most of America, and the world, today, I am saddened by news of this cowardly attack in Budapest. It is a painful reminder of how unprepared we are—we still are, months later—to deal with this new terrorist threat in the world."

"It is incredibly sad," the show's host interjected. "We are seeing reports now of over fifty dead and many more still in critical condition."

"Unfortunately, that death toll will inevitably rise as well, Kendall," Congressman Hartwell stepped in. "My sources in the intelligence community have informed me those numbers only include the identified victims."

"So tragic," Kendall nodded. "So Congressman, what exactly does this brazen new attack tell us about this group, the Nasha Volya?"

"It tells us a few things," Hartwell responded. "First, this organization is still far more powerful than we gave them credit for. To gain access to such a high-security meeting is simply unprecedented."

"Do either of you suspect this might be an inside job?"

"That is certainly possible," Hartwell responded. He reached up and scratched his nose, flashing his ring. His hand trembled ever-so-slightly as he did. To most of the world, the ring meant nothing, but to the right people, it would mean everything. His place of power had just gotten a whole lot stronger. "But we don't know for sure. All of the attackers were killed, unfortunately, so we won't be able to interrogate them."

"Possible?" Lawson interrupted. "I know it was an inside job. It had to be. How else do you explain it?"

"All I meant," Hartwell replied calmly, "is that we don't have proof of that yet."

"True, that's true," Kendall jumped back in. "Do you think this mole is another American?"

"Of course!" Lawson sputtered. "One of our own colleagues, Senator Ferguson from Vermont, was already exposed. And Director O'Brian over at the Bureau. The chance of another, yet-unrevealed mole is high. We must be on full alert."

"What do you think, Congressman Hartwell? Do you agree?" Kendall pivoted to him.

"It's obviously conceivable," he spoke slowly, choosing his words carefully. "But I think it's rash to jump to conclusions. My esteemed colleague may indeed be right, but I have to wonder if anyone would be able to still remain hidden through the new investigations. Personally, I suspect the mole to be foreign. We have a tendency here in America to view everything through a red, white, and blue lens, but these attacks were global. They targeted a dozen cities around the world and it is logical that moles exist elsewhere as well."

"That makes sense. Well, what can we expect going forward?" Kendall asked. "How will Congress respond?"

"I think we need to take a step back," Hartwell responded. "Regroup, reunite, and focus outward. We need to build better infrastructure, stronger welfare programs to help victims and their families, and return to our roots of what made America great once…its people."

"I agree," Lawson nodded. "But I'd also add that I plan to propose a bill to raise the budget for our military as well, by the end of this week. We need to feel safe again and the United States is in a unique position in the world as the most capable of handling such an endeavor. We are a hegemonic power, the world leader, and it's time we started acting like it."

"Excellent ideas, both of you. We're up against a commercial break, so thank you both for coming on the show. I'm sure we will have you back on the show as more developments emerge."

"Thank you, Kendall," both Congressmen echoed. Hartwell's microphone went dead, but he could hear the show's anchor keep talking. "As of right now, they have not listed any Americans among the victims, but we do know at least three attended the meeting. We all hope and pray that we'll hear of their survival soon. And I'll be back in a few minutes to discuss how this is impacting our alliances abroad."

Hartwell cursed under his breath and tugged on his ear. He still hadn't heard any word about Director Sloan's status. That had to mean he had survived. Jacob Sloan was too smart to have sat in the middle of the room. He'd have taken a seat along a wall, keeping him far from the blast.

If they hadn't identified Sloan's body by now, they wouldn't.

He'd escaped.

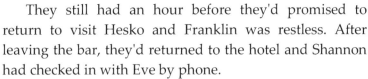

They still had an hour before they'd promised to return to visit Hesko and Franklin was restless. After leaving the bar, they'd returned to the hotel and Shannon had checked in with Eve by phone.

Director Sloan hadn't yet been identified as one of the casualties, so there a little hope still burned. But that hope was dwindling. Surely, he'd have tried to get in touch by now, to let them know he was alive, or at least to give them information on the attack.

Eve hadn't been able to ping his cell phone through the SIM card, but it might've been turned off, or dead, or damaged in the blast. Shannon and Franklin must've called him two dozen times as well, but it kept going straight to voicemail.

Neither wanted to pass the time in the seedy motel room, so had gone out. Shannon stopped in a local sandwich shop and posted up in one corner of the restaurant to examine the map from Hesko.

Franklin, though, chose to get outside and get some air.

His walk took him along Phillips Avenue of Sioux Falls, a charming two-lane road with diagonal parking on either side that reminded him of when they used to visit Joanna's parents in North Carolina. Wide sidewalks were lined by restaurants with outdoor seating, sculptures, and other art displays on every corner.

One such art display drew his attention. A sculpture of two people, abstract enough that Franklin couldn't recognize a single identifiable feature. They could be anyone. Their bodies twisted, encircling one another, yet never actually touching. Two people whose whole beings revolved around each other, but never connecting. There was something alluring about it. Tragic, yet purposeful. Two lives so devoted to one another, yet either unable or unwilling to admit it.

As he stared, his mind began to drift. It didn't feel so long ago that he'd visited Joanna's family for the first time in a town north of Charlotte, much like this. She'd taken him to visit her grandmother, a once-strong woman who had been in the throes of a powerful dementia. It would be the only time he'd ever meet her; she passed before the wedding. But he owed so much to that woman...

They entered the Alzheimer's facility through a security door, the kind that required a nurse to enter a code for the doors to open. Normally, a security door was installed to keep someone out of a place, but here, it had the opposite purpose. This one was designed to keep the patients in.

Dementia patients, Joanna explained, were prone to wander and could easily get lost. It was for their own protection, she said.

They strode past multiple rooms—doors wide open—and Franklin paused to glance into the other 'apartments.' One man lay asleep in his bed. The woman in the room next to him stared blankly at a TV screen playing re-runs of 'I Love Lucy.' They both were alone, their rooms empty and stark with few personal adornments and Franklin couldn't help but feel a tear form at the corner of his eye.

Eventually, they reached the room of Joanna's grandmother. Her door—like all the others—sat open, so they slipped in before she noticed them.

The woman was sitting in a chair by the window, watching birds flit back and forth to a feeder someone had installed outside her room. With the sunlight streaming through the glass panes, her hair—thinning now—lit up as snowy white. Her head bobbed in near-constant motion, as if agreeing with thoughts and ideas no one else was privy to.

Unlike many of the other rooms they'd passed, photos covered nearly every surface, reminders of family and friends, most she'd long-since forgotten.

To one side though, a large photograph stood out, situated in a place of honor on a dresser. A black-and-white wedding portrait.

Franklin was struck by the image, drawn to it. The groom stood tall, proud, smiling and next to him, a full head shorter stood the breathtaking bride, holding a beautiful bouquet of flowers.

As her grandmother heard their footsteps and turned to greet her visitors, Franklin's eyes flicked between the youthful photo and the aging woman. He was reminded of the old song by B.B. King:

Time is a thief
That will rob you of your years
And never return only yesterday

To hear Joanna and her family tell it, this woman had once been a powerful matriarch. So much had been stolen from this woman by time. Her youth, her health, her strength, even her memories…

"Grandma, it's Jo," Franklin's then-girlfriend began. "I want you to meet someone." She beckoned Franklin forward. "This is Franklin, my boyfriend."

"This is who?" Joanna's grandmother croaked.

"Franklin. Franklin Holt. He's my boyfriend."

"Humpf," her grandmother grunted, but didn't say anything further. She returned her gaze to the birds outside, but her face still brightened at their presence.

The two of them took seats and for the next half-hour, Franklin sat mostly in silence as Joanna spoke with her grandma, telling her all about her life. Franklin felt confident the woman only understood about ten-percent of the story, if that, but her head bobbed along. Most importantly, though, a wide smile spread across her face when the two joined her and hadn't left since.

Franklin's mind had drifted, but he snapped back to the present when Joanna said, "Talk to Franklin for a few minutes. I need to go to the restroom."

And then she left the room, leaving Franklin alone with her grandmother.

"So..." he began, unsure what to say to the woman.

"She's a good girl, you know," she suddenly interrupted, cutting him off. "The girl who was just in here."

"Joanna? Jo?"

"I—I don't remember her name." She furrowed her brow for a moment, as though trying to recall a fleeting memory. Like a computer trying to open a corrupted file; it was there...just not accessible. "But I remember I love her. And she's a good girl."

"Yes, I know," Franklin smiled and nodded. "She is."

"You treat her well," she insisted. "She deserves that."

"Yes, I plan to."

"Good. Good." She nodded. "That's good."

For years, Franklin remembered that brief conversation. The rest of the day was a blur, but in that one brief moment of lucidity, Joanna's grandmother being so sure of Joanna's character, if not her name, stuck with him. And that was the day he'd decided; he would marry her.

It had taken him another month to admit it aloud, even to himself, and another three months before he actually proposed. But that moment...deep in his heart, that was when he knew.

He was shaken from his reverie by a buzzing in his pocket. He wiped away a tear as he retrieved the device. Shannon was calling.

It was time to visit Hesko again.

Chapter 15

Jacob Sloan didn't recognize the face staring back at him from the mirror. He avoided mirrors, normally. He always looked older than his years; decades of stress and life in the intelligence community had taken a heavy toll on him.

What little hair he had left—which ringed his head like a halo—had turned gray, and deep wrinkles had set in across his forehead and around his eyes. Heavy jowls framed his jawbone and he'd packed on more weight than was healthy since he'd retired from field work.

But this morning's attack was something different. Even his normal appearance was hidden under a coating of ash, dirt, and blood. He looked haggard too.

Not worn-out, just worn-down.

Sad, almost.

The Gypsy had gotten him and Mostafa settled into a safe house a block away. It was an American site, typically off limits to foreign agents.

But desperate times…

Sloan dressed and closed Barakat's wounds using a new zipper-like medical device stocked in the safe house. It was easier to utilize and less invasive than suturing. Then, he dosed the Moroccan with painkillers, and let him fall asleep on the bed.

When he awoke, Barakat would be able to clean himself up, get dressed, and they could discuss next steps. But while he was passed out, it was Sloan's turn.

He started by splashing water on his face. Simple, but necessary. It took off the outer, superficial layer of dust and ashes, but more importantly, it served to refresh him. He learned in training that a splash of cold water triggers a host of nerve endings to fire all at once; this caused the brain to administer a dose of adrenaline and induces the mammalian diving reflex. It leads to a whole host of benefits, including slowing down one's heart rate and redirecting blood flow to the heart and brain, clearing his mind and calming his emotions.

Panic in times of crisis was contagious and self-perpetuating, but so was calm. He noticed the impact immediately and his pulse began to relax.

A shower came next, during which he carefully cleaned his wounds as best he could. The metal in his leg hadn't left as big of a gash as he'd thought, so closing the wound with that zipper or sutures wasn't required, but he did bandage it pretty tightly. He needed to be able to move around without risking it bleeding again with every step.

Each safe house the United States keeps abroad is stocked with all kinds of supplies, from medical kits to listening devices.

But Sloan went straight for the disguise bags. A disguise bag contained everything a spy might need to disappear…wigs, hair-dye, false facial hair, scissors, new clothes, and more.

It might be overkill, but if a conference like that could be infiltrated, he wasn't sure whose eyes he needed to hide from while still in Budapest. Best to be on the safe side and disappear for a day or two.

Sloan didn't have much hair to work with, so shaving it wasn't going to be particularly effective.

But maybe if he dyed it black?

And ever since the Lincoln Memorial attack, he'd been growing out a scruffy spade-shaped beard. It was as gray—nearly white—as his hair, but darkening it would take twenty years off his appearance.

He added a pair of prescription-less glasses—rimless, very modern—and slipped a device inside his mouth that pressed against his gum line, designed to slightly alter his jawline and speech pattern. A pair of colored contact lenses turned his eyes a dark green and he dabbed a slight bronzer on his skin to darken it.

Thankfully, the bag had multiple different sizes of clothes, as Sloan squeezed into the biggest pair of jeans and hooded sweatshirt it had. A pair of shoes with lifts to change his height completed the transformation. Finally finished, he studied himself in the mirror once more.

That should do it, he speculated.

He wished he was in DC, where their specialists could add fake wrinkles, moles, and more, but this would be enough to fool most people.

At least at first glance.

Thankfully, Hungary had joined the European Union, which meant they could escape into another country without needing to go through passport control. Which meant they wouldn't need false papers.

Budapest was too hot right now; clearly someone from that conference was in on it, so they couldn't trust anyone. They couldn't risk being recognized there. They might make themselves a target. But once they'd left the country, they could shed the disguises and get out of the EU on their own identities.

It was time to wake up Mostafa.

———

Shannon and Franklin drove all the way to Tatanka and pulled into the parking lot without saying a word, but the buzz of excitement was tantalizing. Neither wanted to jinx anything by talking about it, but they felt like they were getting close. If Hesko's friend in Deadwood agreed to meet, they might finally have a chance at uncovering Phoenix. And finding Hook again, bringing them both to justice. This felt right.

Shannon practically leapt out of the car when the vehicle jerked to a halt outside the club. The parking lot was already filling up for the lunch hour and they followed a couple clad in leather jackets into the club. Inside, about half of the tables were already occupied and most of the bar stools were filled with patrons.

Shannon quickly flagged a petite hostess and inquired about Hesko.

"Sorry, miss. I haven't seen him in an hour. He's probably in his office. I can get him for you." The young girl seemed flustered.

"That's no problem, hon. We'll find him," Shannon demurred the offer and allowed the poor girl to return to her job.

The two picked their way through the mess of tables and reached the back where they were met by a large man with a ponytail, who informed them Hesko had ordered him to bar anyone from entering the offices. A quick flash of Shannon's badge, though, and he moved aside.

Hesko's office door was closed when they reached it, so Franklin knocked.

"Hello? It's Franklin Holt and Shannon Faye. We're back." No answer, so he knocked again.

Still nothing. They exchanged a look and Franklin tried the doorknob. It was unlocked, so he slowly turned it and pushed the door inward.

"Hesko? Are you in here?"

After a beat, Shannon gently tapped Franklin on the shoulder and gestured for him to take a step back. She removed her weapon from a shoulder holster, holding it loosely at her side. Taking the lead, she nudged the door open further and edged inside. Then she screamed.

Franklin rushed into the room, colliding with her as he did, but he barely noticed the impact.

The limp body of Hesko Swanson lay slumped over his desk. He could be sleeping, if not for the pool of blood that coated the surface and dripped to the carpet below.

Shannon carefully stepped forward and touched two fingers to his wrist, checking for a pulse. After a second or two, she shook her head. He was dead.

"Stay here," Shannon commanded and straightened. Her whole demeanor had changed. The friendly smile gave way to a steely glare and she strode out of the room with purpose. It was a familiar face, the same face Joanna wore while at work. He heard her yelling at the guard. *How did you let this happen? Who else came back here? Are you an incompetent boor?*

Franklin was hesitant to move—he didn't want to disturb any possible evidence—but he took the opportunity to glance at Hesko's desk. There wasn't much on it. The surface had been cleared off. And it looked like—he leaned forward for a better view—yep, the killer had stolen Hesko's hard drive from where it had been tucked in a corner under the desktop. A ghostly outline of dust and a mess of unconnected cables was all that'd been left behind.

Well, there goes our lead, Franklin fumed, then immediately chastised himself. He took both a literal and a figurative step back. A man was dead—almost certainly because of them—and he was worried about his own mission. This man may have been a bit of a conspiracy nut, but he seemed to be a nice, genuine guy…a successful businessman…and he didn't deserve this.

Wait…

His step backward had given him a different angle and a new flash of white paper caught his eye. It lay fallen between the desk and the wall. It appeared fresh, not covered with dust yet, like everything else in this office.

Maybe…just maybe…

Franklin peeked over his shoulder toward the door. He wasn't sure if he should wait for Shannon to return, but the angry strains of her shouts still echoed from the hallway. And as he listened, he heard the faint sounds of a siren. One of the workers must've called 9-1-1. The police were almost here.

That made his decision for him. He trusted Shannon, but this was bigger than the local Sioux Falls crime squad. If that paper was important, he couldn't let it fall into the hands of a local police department, where it would sit in an evidence lock-up for weeks. He needed to see what was on that sheet. And if it turned out to not be important? Well, then it wouldn't matter if he touched it anyway.

Besides, I'm not an agent, so I can't be held to the same standards as Shannon, he reasoned.

Franklin crouched against the wall—careful not to touch anything else—and slowly tugged the sheet out from its resting place. It had become bent when it slid into this crevice, so he straightened the scrap and began to read.

At first, it didn't make much sense. The top line read: *Friendly Furs Pet Salon.*

A pet salon? Franklin puzzled. *Was Hesko researching a new place for his dog to get a haircut? Did he even have a dog? That had never come up. Maybe this actually was irrelevant.*

As he stared down the sheet, it made even less sense. This wasn't a list of pet services or hours or any details a normal customer would want. It appeared to be a photocopy of the financial history for the business. Total intake and profits by month, amount of cash outflow in overhead. That sort of thing.

What in the world—?

An address at the bottom listed the business as existing on Main Street in Deadwood, South Dakota and Franklin stiffened.

Deadwood...that's where Hesko said... he mused. And then it hit him. *Was this connected? But how? What would a doggy hairdresser have to do with Russian anarchists?*

The door burst open all of a sudden and Shannon emerged. He stuffed the document into his coat pocket right before a police detective followed her into the room.

"Sir, we're going to have to ask you to step outside."

"Yes, yes of course," Franklin nodded and followed Shannon's lead into the hall.

"They're going to want you to give a statement, Franklin, but I've already covered most of it with Lieutenant Burns here."

Franklin nodded. He wanted to tell Shannon about the dog salon document, hopeful she'd make more sense of it, but the detective was too close. He might overhear.

She turned to a mortified member of the staff who stood nearby, hand over her mouth. She was young, mid-twenties, with a shock of pink in her hair. "Excuse me…excuse me…can you get us some water?"

"And maybe a shot of vodka," Franklin added.

Shannon gave him a pointed look, her pencil-thin eyebrow arched, but didn't comment. Finding a dead body was as good of a reason as any to have a drink, he rationalized. And it would help him calm his nerves.

The waitress mumbled something in response and shuffled off to get the drinks.

Forty-five minutes passed before Lieutenant Burns finally pulled him aside to talk. They settled into chairs in a separate room adjacent to Hesko's office. Crime scene technicians were already combing through the office, photographing everything, dusting for fingerprints, and processing the scene.

"Franklin, is it?" Burns began. He flipped out a small spiral-bound notebook and removed a pen from his suit jacket pocket. He clicked the top by pressing it against his chin. He sported a bristly Vandyke moustache and gritty stubble on his cheeks.

Franklin nodded.

"Your partner said you two found the body together. Is that right?" he asked, his voice deep and gravelly.

"I mean, she went in and noticed him first, but yes, we were together."

"Can I ask why you were here? Was Dr. Swanson expecting you?"

"Doctor?"

"My records show he has a PhD from the University of Minnesota. Political Science."

"I didn't—wow." Eve had briefly mentioned Hesko had a PhD, but in Franklin's haste to judge the nutty conspiracist, he'd completely forgotten. For some reason, that put Hesko's ramblings in a different light for Franklin. He'd never given conspiracists much credence— they didn't seem the intellectual type. Maybe he'd been a little harsh.

"Mr. Holt...I asked you a question. Why were you here?"

"Didn't Shannon already tell you all of this?"

"She did. And we're aware of her Bureau affiliation. But we're just double-checking stories for consistency. It's standard procedure, don't worry. You aren't a suspect. Not right now, anyway." He added a wink that did absolutely nothing to assuage Franklin's nerves.

"Hesko was helping with a Bureau case."

"Was he? What was the nature of that assistance?"

"You'll have to talk to Shannon about that," Franklin deflected. "It's a classified situation." He actually wasn't sure about the classification status of the Nasha Volya investigation—nor even, honestly, if it was an official case for Shannon—but he knew he wasn't supposed to be discussing details with anyone, much less a newcomer like Burns. The detective seemed nice enough—and competent—but he was still an unknown. And he'd seen enough to know you can't trust strangers, no matter how nice they seemed.

"I see," Burns nodded, scribbling in his notebook. "For that matter, what's your role in this? I understand you are not an agent with the Bureau."

"I'm…a consultant," Franklin began. He wasn't sure how Shannon had described his presence there, so he wanted to choose his words carefully. "I have special experience with this case. And she thought Hesko might be more willing to talk to someone who wasn't a federal G-man, you know?"

"Uh huh," Burns murmured and continued writing. "Interesting."

"I'm sorry. I don't know what my relationship to Agent Faye and the Bureau has to do with anything."

"Did you touch anything in Dr. Swanson's office?"

"Not that I—" Franklin's mind raced, trying to think. The only thing he'd touched was the paper…he thought. But he struggled to remember. "I—I—I touched the doorknob."

"Ok, but that's it?"

"Oh wait! We were here earlier this morning. I touched his desk then."

"I see." Burns nodded. "Well, we're going to need to fingerprint you."

"Me? Why?" Franklin held his breath. A strange tingle that electrified his spine reminded him of his days in the Bratva.

"Exclusionary purposes. We're dusting the office for unknown prints and if we have yours, we can rule out those prints and focus elsewhere."

"Oh," Franklin exhaled in relief. "That makes sense."

"Do you know much about Dr. Swanson's… extracurricular activities?"

"His what?"

"His non-restaurant business, I mean."

"I—can you elaborate?" He assumed Burns meant the man's conspiracy studies, but something about the way he said it gave Franklin pause, like there was something more he should know.

"Hmm," Burns heaved a sigh but hesitated—as though contemplating what to say—before finally answering, "You know, his...aliens..."

"Oh, you mean he's a conspiracy theorist," Franklin acknowledged with a tilt of his head.

"Theorist is one way to put it," Burns snipped. "A nice way. So what do you know?"

"Not much," Franklin answered honestly. "I know he had some unusual beliefs, but that's it..."

"I see," Burns scoffed. After more scribbling in his notebook, he stood. "Well, that's all I have for now. You're free to go."

"That's—that's it?" Franklin wasn't complaining, but he'd expected something more. He wasn't sure what...but just...more. Maybe Shannon's credentials really had smoothed over the process.

"That's it. Thank you for your time. We'll let you know if we have any further questions we need from you."

Franklin made a hasty exit from the room. He wasn't going to give Burns a chance to change his mind. And he needed to find Shannon. That piece of paper was burning a hole in his pocket.

Chapter 16

"You bumbling fool!" Phoenix's voice crackled with electricity, even over the phone. "You may have just cost us everything!" She'd seen his stunt with the Volya ring on television.

Congressman Hartwell scowled as blood began pounding in his ears, but allowed her to keep ranting.

"You're lucky I'm halfway across the country or else I'd kill you for being such an idiot."

"You don't get to threaten me," Hartwell exploded, a heat flushing throughout his body. "We're equals in this organization. Except now I have the ring and you have...what was it? Oh right, you have nothing. Which I guess makes me more equal than you." He paused to cough and Phoenix took the pause as an opportunity to interject.

"The ring?! The ring is nothing but a trinket. You report to me."

"There's always another rung above you in the food chain. But you're so well-known that you have to skulk in the shadows, hiding! I get to live out in the open, thriving." Hartwell crowed with a haughty laugh, He slowly clenched, then unclenched his fist. "Who has the real power?"

"You're only in the open because we still need an asset in government. You're an asset. A pawn, Marcus. Nothing more." Her voice turned unnaturally calm, but there was an acid that dripped from every word. "You and the buffoon you call a bodyguard, Typhos. I could end you both with the snap of my fingers."

"I don't have to sit here and be bullied by you," he growled. He'd never liked Phoenix much, but the truth was she did intimidate him. She never spoke much about her past, but it was clear she'd lived a rough life. The kind where she had to fight to survive, kill or be killed. He'd never gotten his hands dirty and there was pride in that kind of power, but pound-for-pound, he knew she was tougher than him. Still, the ring sitting on his finger gleamed and it gave him energy to feel fearless. "Besides you know Agent Faye and Franklin are in your backyard, don't you? They booked a flight to South Dakota."

"I've got it handled," she snapped, mocking his tone. "I always handle your messes. But your little stunt on TV with that ring might be hot water too deep to get out of. You better hope no one recognizes it. We can't afford to lose all the work we've put into getting you into position."

"I did what I had to do. To get respect. From you and the rest of this organization"

She snarled through the phone before whispering, "The instant we don't need you anymore, I'm going to—" She cut off, letting her words hang in the air like a million tiny daggers.

"I won't be intimidated," he fumed, then hid a gulp.

"You will be. Soon enough."

The line went dead and Hartwell replaced his phone in his jacket pocket. He cracked his neck from side to side and grabbed the armrest of his chair until his knuckles turned white. Technically, she was right. She possessed the background, the know-how, and she'd been calling most of the shots. But he was the face. The most important piece of the puzzle. He got whatever he wanted. And he didn't intend for that to stop anytime soon.

The organization would follow him over her, if it came to that. His role carried more importance. Less replaceable. But even if they tried to replace him, that's what the ring was about. He was Volya royalty, with the jewelry to prove it. She had nothing but lore and stories. She claimed to be a direct descendant, but only he possessed a direct relic. And that would mean something to the rest of the group. He knew it.

In a fury, he grabbed his computer mouse and chucked it across the room where it hit a wall and shattered.

He wouldn't play the Volya ring card unless pushed, but he *would* play it if he needed to.

Finally free from Detective Burns, Shannon grabbed Franklin by the arm and forcefully dragged him into a corner, away from the prying eyes of the police presence.

"Well?" she demanded, her voice an octave lower than normal and her brow furrowed.

"What—?" Franklin rubbed his elbow where she'd dug her fingers into his skin. "I didn't tell him anything. I promise."

"Not that, you buffoon. The paper," she insisted, leaning forward until Franklin was uncomfortable with how close she stood. "I noticed you stash it in your coat as the detective came in the room. You found something!"

"Oh, you caught that?" Franklin eyed the restaurant patrons over her shoulder to make sure no one was looking their direction before he removed the crumpled paper from his pocket. "I was going to show you."

He handed the document to her and she quickly smoothed it out.

"It's some financial document for a dog hairdresser in Deadwood. I think Hesko was investigating them, but I don't know what I'm looking for."

"I do." Shannon's eyes widened as she scanned the paper. "These numbers are crazy."

"What do you mean? I never took any economics classes."

"I mean, this document says thousands of dollars in business flow through this salon each week."

"So what?" Franklin wondered, confused. "Is that not normal?"

"No, that's not normal. That's a heckuva lot of poodle cuts. There aren't enough pets in all of Deadwood to justify this level of cash flow. Maybe not even in all of South Dakota."

"You mean—you mean it's a front?" His mind whirled through the implications of that, causing a flutter of hope to take flight in his stomach. A pet salon was innocuous enough to not spark interest from local law enforcement. They could move large quantities of money without anyone noticing.

"Bingo," Shannon's face glowed, failing to hide her burgeoning grin. "I don't know where Hesko got this information, but he obviously suspected the same thing. They're using this pet salon in the middle of nowhere to whitewash thousands of dollars in dirty money."

"So we have a place to start!"

"Exactly. Hesko paid for this information with his life, but it won't be in vain. We still have our lead." She stashed the paper in her jacket and stared up at Franklin. She gently bit her lower lip along a sharp exhale. "Good work finding this."

Franklin smiled.

"Now, let's clear it with Sioux Falls PD for us to get out of here and we can hit the road to Deadwood. If we hurry, we'll be there before nightfall."

Chapter 17

Disguises complete, Jacob Sloan and Mostafa Barakat exited their safe house. They'd waited until darkness had fallen, but Sloan was pleased with their new looks. They would be difficult to recognize unless someone knew exactly what they were looking for.

He pulled his sweatshirt hood up over his head and walked with a slight hunch to hide his face. Barakat had opted for a baseball cap tugged low over his face and a leather jacket. It was too late in life for them to ever be mistaken for 'young,' but with the clothing and dye jobs, Sloan felt they could still pass for someone a decade their junior.

The most difficult part was hiding their injuries. Barakat's side made it arduous for him to bend or turn and Sloan struggled to conceal his limp. Baggy clothing helped with physical ailments and masking the bandages, but the pain and limitations forced them to move slowly, which he worried might draw attention.

But their worrying was for naught. So few people were out that late and the mayor of Budapest had warned everyone to stay indoors because of the attack, so as long as they stuck to the shadows, there was virtually no chance of being spotted, much less recognized.

Sloan and Barakat chose not to risk the airport, where security agents readily checked IDs, and their appearances didn't exactly match their passports right now. It'd be difficult to explain and more likely to be noticed. A bus station was closest to their location, but Sloan chose to avoid that as well. Buses were slow and more easily stopped. Plus, they were notoriously unreliable; way too many were canceled and he couldn't take that chance.

Rather, the two men headed for a train station a few blocks further away. The European railway system was leagues ahead of the American trains. Clean, on-time, with a vast network that could get you anywhere you wanted to go with ease. Utilizing the secure Internet connection at the safe house, Sloan had booked two tickets under fake names. After some discussion, they'd ultimately chosen a destination a couple countries away. It would take nearly fifteen hours and one transfer, but by the time they debarked, they'd be in Milan. Italy was an easier country to fly back to the States. More flights and friendlier customs.

The Budapest Keleti railway station had been designed with a mixed architectural style. It looked like some architect had been unable to settle on one style, so threw different designs together in eclectic fashion. But it was most noted for its massive semicircular glass window at the main entrance, flanked by large stone statues of two men whom Sloan presumed were influential in the history of the train. Or maybe the city. He wasn't sure.

Once inside, Sloan and Barakat worked their way around to the tracks and quickly found their train. Like many places of rail transport, no one checked their tickets, so they managed to get aboard without having to show their faces or IDs to anyone.

This was a EuroNight train, meaning it came equipped with several cars that offered beds for travelers to sleep while the train rumbled across the continent through the night. Sloan had booked a private rail room with two beds for privacy. They locked the door and Barakat headed straight for the bed, without hesitation. He was asleep before his head hit the pillow. But Sloan couldn't sleep. His mind raced. Besides it made sense for one of them to stay awake at all times. Getting out of Budapest made them safer, but it didn't eliminate the danger. He wouldn't feel secure until he sat in his office chair in Washington once again.

The previous twelve hours had been chaotic and painful, and he hadn't had time to check the news to find out what the media was saying about the attack. The train was scheduled to leave shortly and they had many hours until the transfer, so it felt like an opportunity. The go-bag he'd taken from the safehouse included a cell phone with Internet capabilities, so he quickly connected and started searching. He didn't dare log into any secure sites or Google his own name...these train Wi-Fi connections possessed virtually no online defenses and as secure as the phone was, he didn't want to draw attention with unusual searches. But soon, he was buried in articles from several prominent news stations discussing the attacks.

The rental car—a two-year-old Honda Civic—was silent, except for the steady hum of the road passing between the tread of its tires. Shannon had drifted to sleep and Franklin was left with his thoughts. He wasn't thinking about anything in particular, just doing his best to remain alert on the road this time of night.

Finding Hesko lifeless and lying in a pool of his own blood had been demoralizing. Neither of them dared say it aloud, but both knew his death was their fault. If they hadn't contacted him, if they hadn't flown to South Dakota to meet with him…he'd still be alive. And worst of all, Shannon had promised Hesko they'd protect him, that he'd be safe. And she'd failed—they'd both failed.

Shannon's credentials sped along the process with police, but it was still several hours before they'd been allowed to leave the bar, return to the hotel to get their things, and hit the road. Deadwood was a five-to-six hour drive from Sioux Falls, so they were getting their money's worth out of that rental vehicle. Franklin had volunteered to drive…it felt like the chivalrous thing to do, but really, he knew he wasn't going to be able to relax, much less sleep. He might as well let Shannon relax. And besides, he'd always had a special affection for open road and countryside, so driving gave him the opportunity to enjoy the scenery while Shannon slept.

From his time there as a kid, he'd remembered South Dakota as an unpopulated state, but he was still struck by just how desolate it could be. Once they'd left the Sioux Falls area, towns became few and far between.

There was something peaceful about it. The rural 'flyover states' were blessed with a certain quaint beauty that so many Americans never experienced.

The isolation had a secondary effect on Franklin as well; it allowed him to think. Clearing the mind of visual distractions calmed him and, as he passed a sign for the town of Winner, Population 2897, it wasn't long before he found his thoughts drifting.

"Are you ready?" his mom asked softly from the doorway.

Franklin stood at the window in his childhood bedroom, looking into the backyard at the swing set he used to spend hours playing on. He didn't answer. Didn't even turn to look at her. Not because he sought to be rude or ignore his mother. He just didn't know the answer, didn't know how to begin an answer.

"I know what you mean," she continued, proving that — once again — she could read minds. "I'm not sure anyone is ever truly ready for this."

"Was Dad ready?"

"Your father? Ha," she chuckled. "Your father was terrified when he asked me to marry him."

At that, Franklin turned around to face his mother. "He was? He always said he knew you'd get married from your first date."

"He was sure. But being positive of something doesn't make it less intimidating. In fact, it can be even more so. Being together forever is a lot to process, even when you know it's meant to be. It's okay to be nervous about it."

"Were you nervous?" he asked.

"Of course I was!" she exclaimed. "But that's not even the right question. It's not 'are you nervous' or 'are you scared.' What matters is your love and commitment to one another."

Franklin was startled out of his reverie by a sudden vibration of the car and loud growling that told him his car had drifted out of the lane. He'd hit the rumble strips.

"Wha—? Is everything okay?" Shannon was soon awakened by the noise and sensation as well, but he quickly assured her everything was fine and she soon drifted back to sleep.

And he soon drifted into another memory from the same location, this one less pleasant.

"Are you sure?" His mother's warm voice sounded from that same doorway where she'd stood many times. And Franklin stared out the window as he'd done many times before. He hadn't been home to visit his family in a long time, but when Joanna broke the news to him that she wanted a divorce, that's where he needed to be. In his childhood bedroom. With his parents.

"No. I'm not," he replied, his voice trembling so slightly that only a mother could detect it. "But she is."

"I'm sorry, honey."

"I always thought we'd be together forever."

"I know, Frankie. I know." She entered his room and walked over to where he stood. Slowly she wrapped an arm around his waist and leaned her head against his shoulder.

He turned and rested his head on top of hers, a lone tear escaping his eye and rolling over his cheek until it dampened her hair.

"Franklin?"

Startled, he blinked a few times and the memory faded.

"Are—are you okay?" Shannon's voice was nearly a whisper from the passenger seat.

"I—I'm fine," he stammered. "Why?"

"Well, you're crying…" She pointed at his face and he instinctively touched his cheek with his hand. Sure enough, wet with tears. He quickly wiped them away with his shirt sleeve and swallowed hard, buffering himself against more tears.

"Just thinking," he mumbled. "About my mom."

"She was from this area, right?" There was a softness in her tone he'd never heard before. A tenderness that didn't fit her typically steely exterior.

"Yeah." He nodded. "She was there for every major moment in my life before she passed. Both good and bad."

"And you miss her."

He nodded again. "Yeah...I do. We actually passed the sign for her hometown a few minutes ago."

"How about we make a stop on the return trip to Sioux Falls? For a bite for lunch?"

He smiled and turned slightly to look at her.

"That would be great."

Chapter 18

"What are you doing, Jacob?" Mostafa Barakat's voice startled Sloan. He hadn't expected the Moroccan official to be awake yet.

"I just hung up with Omar," he replied. He'd made the decision to reach out to his old friend while Barakat slept. Omar sounded elated to hear they'd survived and were, for the moment, safe. "He and Max escaped with only minimal injuries. And Rivka is alive and critical, but still in the hospital. But Rufus…wasn't so lucky." Sloan shook his head. He'd known Hastings a long time. It was almost unthinkable that the man was gone.

"Good, good. Wait, you called Omar?" Barakat bolted upright and pursed his lips as he spoke. "What were you thinking? Did you tell him where we're going?"

"Relax, Mostafa. I used a burner cell. It can't be traced or tracked."

"That's not my concern, Jacob." Barakat's voice wavered. Sloan couldn't tell if it was pain or fear. "Aren't you the one who said you don't know who we can trust? At least one member of our community betrayed us."

"And you think it was Omar?" Sloan frowned and tilted his head to one side to stare at the man. The muscles in his jaw tensed as he spoke.

"I don't know who it was. Probably not. But it's possible."

"I've known Omar for well over a decade. Going on two. He's as solid as they come."

"You Americans," Barakat spat. Sloan hadn't seen Mostafa this angry in many years. "You've always had a blind spot when it comes to Saudi Arabia. When oil is involved, you refuse to admit even the potential for bad."

"That's not what I'm doing. And you know that." Sloan scoffed and rubbed the back of his neck. "Omar is no more likely to be the mole than Max. Or you for that matter."

"But you admit it's possible?" he demanded, his tone sharp and hard.

"I—I suppose," Sloan rolled his eyes and crossed his arms across his chest. He was normally the paranoid one. Maybe the pain was affecting Barakat more than he let on. "It's possible...I guess..."

"As long as there's even a small chance, we need to be more careful."

Sloan snorted, but didn't say anything right away, allowing Barakat's words to flow over him. And after a beat, Sloan sighed and nodded, forcing himself to relax. "Fine. No more phone calls." He hated to admit it, but his Moroccan counterpart wasn't wrong. As unlikely as it seemed, he couldn't rule out the possibility that the mole was one of them. But—as he'd just come to realize a moment ago—if no one was above suspicion, then Barakat wasn't either. His injuries didn't exclude him from suspicion. He'd need to keep his eyes wide open from now on.

"Now, how much further?" Barakat asked.

"We'll transfer to the next train within the hour, when we get to Prague. From there, about four more hours to Milan."

"And no one other than Omar knows where we'll be?"

"Unless you told someone."

Barakat sighed and closed his eyes. "I apologize for snapping. I, too, doubt Omar's involvement. My nerves are just a bit worn right now."

"Mine too," Sloan nodded. "Mine too." He leaned back in his chair, but for the first time, he eyed Mostafa through a different lens.

———

By the time they pulled into Deadwood, the sun hung low in the western sky. Long shadowy fingers stretched across the rustic downtown, adding to the Wild West aesthetic. They entered the town through an arched sign announcing their arrival onto Historic Main Street.

Shannon had read aloud information she found online about Deadwood as they drove, but Franklin wasn't prepared for how historic the town still appeared. Early settlers had discovered gold deposits in the area, which led to a major gold rush in the mid- to late-1800s and much of that era's architecture was still preserved. In fact, it was so well-preserved, the entire city had earned the distinction as a National Historic Landmark District.

Deadwood wasn't a large place, with only about 1,200 residents living there, but the street was lined with dozens—nay, hundreds—of motorcycles. Bikes of all shapes and sizes were parked up-and-down the street, a sight only surpassed by their larger-than-life riders, who wandered the sidewalks in leather jackets covered in pins, bandannas, and colorful tattoos. A large poster placed prominently in the window of a shop proclaimed "Welcome Sturgis Motorcycle Rally Riders" in a bold font.

A quick online search revealed the Sturgis Rally was an annual event where hundreds of thousands of riders descend on the nearby town of Sturgis, South Dakota for special stunts, races, rides, and other events. Apparently, many bikes spilled out of Sturgis into all the nearby towns.

The poster claimed tomorrow was the final day of the rally, so numbers had declined from the peak earlier in the week, but there were still more motorcycles in one place than Franklin had ever seen.

It was such a sight that for a couple minutes, Franklin forgot why they were there. As they cruised through town, he didn't know which direction to look. On one side of the street, a swinging set of double-doors led to an old-timey saloon famous for being where the infamous outlaw Wild Bill Hickok had been shot and killed in 1876. On the other, several hefty bikers waited in line to enter a flashing casino that sat next to a jewelry store advertising their genuine gold products.

It wasn't until they passed a sign for *Friendly Furs Pet Salon* that he was jolted back to reality and their purpose for being here.

"There!" He pointed out the unassuming shop, nestled between a bar and yet another casino.

"I see it," Shannon said and flicked on her turn signal. "Do you want to go tonight?"

"We can walk past, but it's already 8 o'clock. They're closed."

"We should do that," Shannon acknowledged. "Get a feel for it before going there in the morning."

"Agreed."

It took nearly twenty minutes to find a parking spot with all the motorcycles clogging the side roads, but eventually they found one at the end of town.

The pet salon was dark and dingy, definitely not the type of place you'd expect to be doing thousands of dollars in business every week. But blinds had been pulled, so they weren't able to learn much that night. A sign on the door claimed it opened at 10am every morning, so they agreed to come by as soon as its doors opened. Several posters decorated the windows of the shop, advertising various local events and other shops.

One such paper caught Franklin's eye and he directed Shannon's attention to it.

"This is odd," he commented.

"What is?" Shannon asked. It was an advertisement for the casino next door and included a coupon you could tear off for 20% off food and drink there.

"That symbol at the top. It's a Russian letter."

Shannon leaned in close. The symbol he pointed to looked like two capital 'K's' placed back-to-back.

"You're right," she agreed. "That's the 'zhe' sound, isn't it? There isn't a good English letter it correlates to."

"What are the chances two businesses in the tiny South Dakotan town of Deadwood, both owned by Russians, are unrelated?" Franklin raised an eyebrow.

Shannon took a step back and eyed the next-door casino. "You think...uh...The Firebird is also owned by our favorite Russian terrorists? Why would they need a second business for their money laundering?"

"Well, if I remember correctly, the Firebird is a Russian myth about a magic, glowing bird. It's a lure for people seeking fame and fortune...seems appropriate for a casino, I'd think?"

"Firebirds aren't exclusively Russian though, right? I mean, that sounds a lot like the Phoenix. And those myths are also common in other cultures too... Egypt, Native Americans..."

"Native American was actually the Thunderbird. But you're right. Still, it's as good an explanation as any. Their ad has a firebird logo *and* a Russian letter. It makes sense."

"You're right, you're right." Shannon assented, nodding her head. "And it's open tonight. Let's check it out."

Chapter 19

"Lydia!" Congressman Hartwell called out from his desk chair. It was late and he was ready to leave the office. But he had one final thing to do first.

His assistant bustled into the office, arms full of papers. She never left before he did, though he'd never ordered her to stay. She was dedicated. To service, to party, to government, but most of all, to him.

"What can I do, Congressman?" She smiled, then winked. "Or, should I say, Mr. President…"

"Let's not get ahead of ourselves just yet," he cautioned with a wave of his hand. He began gently tapping his ring against the desktop with a rhythmic cadence as he spoke.

"Oh, I just know you're going to win though," she sputtered in excitement.

"I haven't even announced my candidacy yet," he said with a smile. The cadence of his ring on the desk sped up, matching his heart rate as he imagined it. "But I appreciate your enthusiasm."

"Did you need something?" she chimed.

"Ah yes," he pushed his chair back and stood. "Actually, I need to schedule that announcement. Can you set up a press conference?"

"Absolutely." Her head bobbed furiously in agreement. "Somewhere back home? In our district?"

"A nice idea, Lydia. Truly. But I was thinking somewhere bigger."

"Bigger?"

"The steps of the Lincoln Memorial."

"Sir? Wouldn't it still be better to do it in your district? It helps establish your candidacy as a man of the people."

"That's true. But that would primarily get votes in my district. I need the country's vote. And imagine the optics. On the same steps where the Nasha Volya executed a terrorist attack in the heart of our nation's capital. It will show leadership. Strength through power. I'll be a media darling by the end of my speech. And by the time they realize it's a Presidential race announcement, I'll have them eating out of my palms."

Lydia's eyes widened as he spoke. She truly admired him, which only fed his ego.

"Perfect!" she squealed. "That's much better!"

"So can you get it done? Get that conference on the books?"

"I have a better idea," she gasped. "The six month anniversary of the attacks. It's in two days. I can get you on the docket to speak at the memorial celebration."

"Excellent, Lydia. That sounds absolutely perfect." He turned to look out his office window at the setting sun. "Get it done."

He listened as her footsteps skittered out of the room and he smiled. He wasn't sure how he'd forgotten the upcoming ceremony—he was undoubtedly too busy—but the more he pondered it, the better he felt. It truly felt perfect, the perfect time for such an announcement.

While Lydia made the call from her desk in the outer lobby of his Congressional office, he reached for his own phone to make a very different call. He had one more thing to set up, a surprise no one would predict. Not even his own staff. But one he was confident would propel him to within a stone's throw of the Oval Office.

It was nearly time.

The marble-floored entryway to the casino was dark and reflective, almost disorienting. The rug—a plush Persian blend of ruby and sapphire threadwork—seemed to hover over a void beneath them, floating, supporting their weight, like the magic carpet from Aladdin.

Above them hung a silver chandelier with flame-shaped bulbs. They were frosted, which softened their glow, but cast the entire foyer in a mildly hazy light. To the right, a help desk sat, with a disinterested worker sitting behind it who barely glanced up when they entered. And off to the left, a wooden staircase rose and twisted around a corner into darkness. But ahead of them lay the doorway to the main floor of the casino.

Franklin took the lead—he was no stranger to the hallowed halls of a gambling den—and pushed the gold-gilded doors inward and they swung open.

It took a few seconds for his eyes to adjust to the lighting inside the casino. The whir of slot machines and the mumbled voices wafted through the thick, smoky air, but the dominant sound that hit Franklin first was the desperate whisper of lost money. Lost livelihoods. Lost hope. Over and over, the yank of levers followed by the whir of machines, and finally a heavy sigh, only to be repeated again. Music to a casino's ears, it was also the most prevalent melody in gambling meccas across the world...Las Vegas, Reno, Atlantic City, and Macau.

The two shuffled slowly through the aisles of flashing lights and people on stools cursing the failure of machines to give them what they craved.

"What are we looking for?" Franklin whispered, unsure why he felt the need to lower his voice.

"Anything that tells us we're in the right place," Shannon answered.

"Like what?" Franklin asked. "It's not as though they're going to be flying a flag with 'Nasha Volya' emblazoned across it."

"I'm not sure. Just keep your eyes peeled."

Franklin nodded confirmation, but not understanding. He turned right and headed past a diagonal row of blackjack players, heading for a cluster of tables in one of the back corners. He recognized the game immediately, Texas Hold 'em. His favorite.

After watching a couple rounds, he shrugged and decided to take a seat at the table. What harm was it to play a few hands? He didn't even know what they were supposed to be looking for. And Shannon had disappeared into another part of the casino.

He placed some cash on the table—a couple hundred dollars, the amount he'd been able to retrieve from his bank account before going underground—and the dealer handed him a stack of chips.

He quickly folded his first hand, an unsuited three and seven, and watched a cowboy in full hat, frilled shirt, and boots win a big hand.

The second hand looked more promising. Ace of spades, eight of clubs. He called the blinds and waited. Four other players stayed in for the flop. Other than that same cowboy, there was an African-American man who appeared to be one of the bikers from the motorcycle rally, a businessman in his mid-to-late forties with rolled-up sleeves and a loose tie hung around his neck like a noose, and a young woman with a bronzed complexion who Franklin wondered if she was even old enough to be in the casino. *Maybe a student at the local college*, he mused.

The flop came and paired Franklin's ace with the ace of clubs. High pair wasn't an amazing hand, but it was enough to stay in. The cowboy brushed a hand through his sandy-blond hair and placed a small bet, enough to wash out the businessman and the biker. The college student called and Franklin followed suit.

The turn card was useless for all of them. The cowboy placed another weak bet, hoping to force the others to fold, but both Franklin and the student weren't deterred.

The river card—the final one—landed and Franklin stifled a smile. Eight of spades. Two pair, aces and eights. Unless someone was slow-playing pocket aces, this hand was his.

The cowboy again placed a bet, but Franklin countered with a much larger one.

The student blinked a few times and scratched her nose but, after a beat, folded her hand.

Action moved around to the cowboy who didn't seem to have a read on the newcomer.

"You bluffing?" he drawled.

Franklin shrugged.

"I think you're bluffing," the cowboy added.

"Then call me," Franklin countered.

The cowboy smirked, unable to tear his gaze away from his chips. He seemed to be counting, seeing how much of his stack he was risking.

"You're bluffing," the man said, after a long silence. "I call." He pushed his chips into the middle of the table to equal Franklin's bet.

"Fascinating..." A new voice interrupted the game. "He wasn't bluffing."

Franklin spun toward the source, finding himself staring upward at a tall, muscular man with an angular face and shaved head that sat atop broad, square shoulders, like those of Olympic swimmers. His eyes were a dark, chocolate brown, behind which there was no emotion, no light. They were, as Franklin had come to recognize, the eyes of a killer. Lifeless, emotionless, stony.

"Mr. Holt here...is not that good of a liar," the man said, a hint of a nasal Russian accent creeping through.

"Who are you?" Franklin faltered, his voice betraying a hint of a tremble. He glanced at the table and for the first time, he noted the unique design on the playing chips...a bear-like creature that strongly resembled those familiar Rosomakha coins the Volya used. A wolverine!

"Why don't you come with me?" the man said. It wasn't a question. "Don't worry, your winnings will be held for you."

Franklin didn't respond, but the man placed a strong hand on his shoulder and roughly yanked him out of his seat.

"This way," he directed, pointing Franklin toward a door in the corner with a shove.

"I—but—I—" Franklin stammered, pointing to the table and his pile of chips.

"They will still be here when you're...back," he smirked. "We've already got your partner too. She's waiting for you."

Chapter 20

Jacob Sloan awoke from a restless sleep. He and Mostafa had successfully transferred trains in Prague and were now on their way to Milan. They'd gotten different cabins on this leg, allowing Sloan to relax enough to close his eyes. But they didn't stay shut for long.

Mostafa's comments about trust had left him shaken; even hours later, the Moroccan's words roared through his mind with the force of waves pounding the shoreline. Over and over. Of course, Mostafa was right; they couldn't trust anyone. Not after Budapest.

How could he have been so stupid to contact Omar?

He silently cursed himself, then did it out loud. It wasn't that he distrusted the Saudi official—Omar Jameel had been nothing but honest and straightforward with him—but clearly someone was responsible for the attack in Hungary. Someone who had the audacity to launch an attack on a room full of armed intelligence specialists. Someone on the inside. And he didn't know who. He doubted Omar had been behind it, but what if Mostafa was correct? What if he blindly trusted Saudi Arabia because they were friends with the United States?

It had been years since Sloan had truly operated in the field. He'd led the occasional domestic raid in his time as Director of SISA, but never anything on this scale. And he felt rusty, out of shape.

His body ached, and not just because of the shrapnel wound. His muscles had been strained in ways they hadn't in a long time.

He rubbed the sleep from his eyes and sat up on the edge of the bed. He attempted to stretch, but found he was unable to touch his toes. He sighed, ashamed at what he'd let himself become. There was a time when the name Jacob Sloan was revered in the intelligence community; he had been the best in the world at what he did. He was feared, even.

But this version of himself, this rotund, pudgy middle-aged man was not the same person.

As he beat himself up over letting his body deteriorate since getting a desk job, another worry hit him.

What if it wasn't just his physical body that had lost a step? What if his mind, his reaction time, his instincts were also a step slow?

He hated to think that, but he couldn't get Mostafa's words out of his head. He'd made a mistake calling Omar and how else would you explain it? He'd lost his touch in the field.

Sleep eluded him all night.

That thought carried him all the way to Milan.

Eve Chase hung up the phone, her face ashen. A man who called himself Cypher in the hacking—'social engineering,' as they preferred—community had broken protocol with that call; in their world, computers were the sole mode of communication, but this was important. It was too big.

Heskovizenako Swanson was dead. Murdered at his desk, left lying in a pool of his own blood.

Cypher had been one of Hesko's closest friends, so he'd taken it upon himself to let everyone know. According to local reports, Hesko had been discovered by two unnamed individuals—rumored to be G-men—and the Sioux Falls Police Department was investigating the case as a typical burglary, maybe even a robbery gone wrong. Cypher wasn't buying it. Skepticism was a personality trait with him.

If this was a simple burglary, why was he discovered by FBI spooks?, he'd hypothesized. *That can't be a coincidence. There's a cover-up here. And I'm gonna find out what it is.*

Cypher often went too far with his skeptical ideas into wild conspiracy theories. The wilder, the better.

But his questions weren't misplaced in this case. Eve didn't let on that she knew the identities of the anonymous 'FBI agents,' nor that she'd been the one to send them to Hesko. But Cypher was right. They must be connected to his death.

And she felt responsible.

She sat in silence for a solid minute. Sixty seconds to mourn a friend whose death in which she unwittingly played a part. It felt like the appropriate thing to do, given the circumstances.

Then she acted.

Cypher's call hadn't only been about Hesko's death, though obviously that was primary. He'd also mentioned one other detail that meant a lot in her world.

"I don't know if you've had any contact with Hesko lately," he'd begun. *"But rumor is his hard drive went missing at the scene. Whoever killed him took it."*

"What did they want with it?" she'd asked, but her mind was already whirling. No doubt they'd use it to track his contacts.

"No idea, but I'm taking precautions. And you should too."

She knew what that meant. And he was right. She needed to take precautions. Major ones. Hesko was uber-careful with his online activities; he was a technical genius. Everything had been heavily encrypted, password-protected, and as anonymous as possible. She doubted he'd used his work computer for anything incriminating. But if they were after his work computer, it wouldn't be long before they grabbed his home network too, if they hadn't already.

It was a dirty secret on the dark web, but no system is ever un-hackable. Even a hacker's. Unless it's been pulverized with a hammer or otherwise severely damaged, the information hidden in its memory is there for the taking, for anyone with enough skill and patience. Eve even knew one hacker with a penchant for dissolving hard drives in acid to avoid that.

If someone desperately wanted to find out the contents of Hesko's hard drive, they would eventually. And once they got in, it wouldn't be long before they tracked that back to Cypher. And to Eve.

She was as well protected as anyone in the industry, but nothing was iron-clad. And if someone was willing to kill Hesko—a low-level conspiracist in the community—she was confident they wouldn't hesitate to go after her as well. Especially once they started tracing his communications back to her. They'd know her identity, but worse, they'd know who she'd been helping. And that would turn deadly in a hurry.

It was time to go. And to cover her tracks

She owned too many hard drives to bring with her, but she had a failsafe built in. One she'd hoped to never use, but it was something all of the best implemented, in case they were ever caught. Her preference involved a series of computer viruses, locked away in a folder on her hard drive. They weren't complicated, by any means, but allowed to run rampant through a computer system, they would do immense amounts of damage in a short period of time. And they wouldn't merely corrupt the code either; she'd programmed this particular cocktail of malware to overheat the system until the hard drives themselves fried. The physical damage ensured no one would be able to piece back together any code that managed to escape even partially unscathed.

She'd named the destructive program Order 66, an homage to her favorite sci-fi series, but also because it worked in much the same way the infamous *Star Wars* order did. Upon execution, it was coded to trigger a couple dozen sleeper files to activate, essentially behaving like miniature assassins, taking out all aspects of her system from different angles.

It certainly wasn't an ideal solution and every cell in her ached at the mere thought; she'd lose her entire set-up, a system she'd spent years building. She'd need a new identity, new papers. But when a threat bangs down your door, you need something to ensure any incriminating information would never be recovered. And she could rebuild; a woman of her skills didn't need much more than an Internet connection. She just needed to make sure her tracks were covered when she did.

Before she executed her version of Order 66 though, she hastily pulled a small—yet powerful—laptop out of a drawer and connected it directly into her system. A few folders dragged and dropped and she had everything she needed to set back up in a new location. That took nearly ten minutes to transfer, but as soon as it finished, she disconnected the cable. She took a moment to look around her apartment. It had been home to her. A tear welled up in the corner of her eye at the realization that it was home no longer. Then, with that tear running down her cheek, she leaned over and clicked 'Run.' Thirty seconds from now, her system would be toast. And it was too late to stop it.

Lastly, she ducked into the large Faraday cage — disconnected from the rest of her network — and tapped a handful of keys to bring up the same 'assassination' program here. She took a deep breath, pressed 'Enter' and closed the cage. With one final backward glance, she grabbed a go-bag she'd stashed in a cabinet near the door, stuffed her travel laptop into a sleeve on the side, and stepped out into the hallway.

It was official; she was never coming back.

Chapter 21

The Russian casino man deposited Franklin in a lounge area where he found Shannon waiting. It was actually a pretty nice room, with oblong couches, dark wall panels, and a long wooden table. It had the feel of a conference room.

He took a look around, taking in an ornate, antique chandelier that hung over the table and a series of glass-enclosed bookcases lining one wall, stocked with dozens of ancient books. Tucked in the corner, but propped on one of those golden floor stands, was a large Russian flag with the famous bands of white, blue, and red. A potted plant Franklin couldn't identify stood in another corner.

There was only one exit, the door through which they'd entered, and no windows. Despite the posh nature of the room, there was something isolating about it. Claustrophobic, even.

The goon eyed them both, looking them up and down, his nostrils flaring as he leered at Shannon.

Then the man left, leaving the two alone in the room.

"Well…" Franklin began. "I guess there's no doubt now that we're in the right place." He smirked. In spite of their situation, he enjoyed a touch of pleasure in being right for once. That didn't happen often with Shannon.

"Shut up," Shannon snapped. She stood and paced along the far wall, her forehead creased with worry. "We need to find a way out of here."

"If they wanted to kill us...or even to hurt us...they'd have done so by now. Instead we're relaxing on comfortable couches in a room full of mahogany. I think we need to let this play out."

"You know these people, Franklin. You really think they're just going to release us?"

Franklin didn't respond, and a few seconds later, their conversation was interrupted by the sound of the door opening.

A young man appeared in the doorway. Really more of a boy, he couldn't be more than eighteen years old. He was slim, almost scrawny, and dressed in all black. Peach fuzz spotted his cheeks where he clearly struggled to grow a beard.

He glanced nervously both ways as he entered. The door closed behind him and he stared at Franklin and Shannon, but didn't say anything.

"Who are you?" Shannon asked softly.

The boy didn't reply, instead fidgeting in place and shifting his weight rapidly from foot to foot. His eyes roved the room, as if too afraid to land on any one thing for too long, but always flicking back to the two of them.

"Can we help you?"

"Why are you here?" the boy stammered. He spoke flawless English, without a hint of a Russian accent.

"What's your name?" Franklin inquired.

"It's—it's Alec." His breath hitched a little as he spoke.

"Hi Alec, I'm Shannon. And this is Franklin," Shannon began. She stepped over to the boy and reached out to touch him on the shoulder, but he jerked away. "Are you okay?"

"You—you have no idea what you're into here. You need to leave."

"Leaving isn't really an option, Alec."

"These people will kill you, if they have to," he spat out, spittle flying in every direction.

Franklin and Shannon exchanged a look, each a little confused.

"Wh-wh-why are you h-here?" he stuttered, his voice boyish and squeaky. "Are you looking for Mercury?"

"What's Mercury?" Franklin demanded. "Or who's—?"

"What's—you two, you're in over your heads," Alec interrupted, then glanced behind him at the solid wooden door, as if he expected it to open any second. "If you don't even know Mercury…"

"What is it, Alec?" Shannon added. "Can you tell us, so we know what we're facing? Is Mercury a person? Like from Queen? Is it a place? A plan?"

"I—I—I can't. I have to go. If you leave now, you can escape. Right now. There's no one—." His voice petered out, then he mumbled something so fast it was unintelligible, glancing over his shoulder at the door every other second.

"I have to go." On a dime, he spun and darted out of the room, leaving both Franklin and Shannon staring at the door as it swung shut after him.

———◦◦◦———

Milan's city centre was bustling. They'd pulled into the train station early that morning and checked into a budget hotel to wash up and rest. Neither had slept much on the train, so used the opportunity to close their eyes for a couple hours. Sloan booked a flight for the two of them out of Milan Malpensa International Airport, the first direct flight out with an open seat. They had to cut across the city a handful of blocks to get to the shuttle stop for a direct-line bus to transport them to the airport.

There was some festival going on in the city this weekend...it reminded Sloan of a farmers market, but mixed with a raucous party. The central square was decorated and busy; at one end a mariachi band played something fast and cacophonous, and at the other, booths sold freshly made tacos and quesadillas. Crowds of people—a mix of locals and tourists—drifted between food stands. A handful staggered as they walked, already drunk despite the early hour, yelling friendly curses at anyone who crossed their path. Anyone who would listen.

Music blasted from speakers that amplified the mariachi band and inspired several dozen festival-goers to start a sort of frenetic dancing in the middle of the square. A handful of children—the oldest couldn't be more than six or seven years old—danced joyfully in front of the mariachi band. More like jumping, or bouncing actually, but they were excited.

Sloan paused to watch them. One young boy caught his attention. His dark, bushy hair and slender build reminded him of his own son. Ben was older now and living with his mom. He rarely saw either of his children these days—Ben or his older sister Tracy, who was in school at the University of Pennsylvania—but Sloan cherished the memories from those early years.

Little Benji had the same dance moves too, he chuckled.

After a moment, Barakat tugged at his elbow to get moving again and Sloan reluctantly turned away. He made a mental note to call Ben—both of his kids, actually—as soon as he was home, safe and sound in the United States.

As they weaved their way through the crowd, he allowed his gaze to drift across the square, taking in the city.

Sloan had spent a bit of time in Italy in his younger days. Before he settled into a desk job with SISA, before he'd gained that last fifty pounds, and back when he still had all of his hair, he'd traveled the world as a covert operative. One of the best, in fact. Among certain circles, his exploits were well-known, his name whispered, and his reputation had gained a legendary status that was only partly undeserved. Removing himself from the field and landing in an office hadn't been his decision; his cover had been blown on a mission and he'd been extracted on the spot. He retired, settled his scores with any intelligence enemies he'd made, and took on a new role back home.

But he'd always missed the travel, the excitement of being on the run, the danger. And Italy had been the site of a few of those trips, including one in Venice that still made him nervous to show his face there again. But Milan was three hours from Venice by car and a world away in terms of culture.

Milan was an unusual city for Italy; in some ways, it held the title as the least 'Italian' city in the entire nation. The Second World War had devastated and destroyed much of it, so upon rebuilding, Milan grew into a new-age European cosmopolitan center. If Rome was 'old world Italy,' then Milan was definitely 'new world Italy.' Noted for style and fashion, it mixed modern architecture alongside its famous Duomo and the Dominican church that housed *The Last Supper*.

As he marveled at the aesthetic of the city, he sensed another tug at his elbow. Barakat was impatient and Sloan didn't blame him. They'd been through a lot in the last day and a half and the crowd surrounding them was a mixed blessing. The horde allowed them to blend in, but also made it difficult to react if anything went sideways. Not that he expected it to; they were in a foreign country, many miles away from where they'd been attacked. There was no sign they'd been followed and the list of people who even knew what city they were in was extremely limited.

Still, you couldn't be too careful. So Sloan nodded at Barakat and refocused. The shuttle stop was only another two blocks; soon they'd be on their way to the airport and, not long after that, they'd be on their way to the United States and safety.

Chapter 22

"**W**ell, you heard the boy," Franklin finally said. "We need to move now. Let's go."

He half-walked, half-ran across the room to the door. Placing his hand on the knob, he glanced over his shoulder at Shannon, who hadn't moved yet.

"What—what is it?" he pleaded. "Alec said we need to move now."

"I'm—I'm not sure. What if it's a trap?"

"A trap? By that kid? He was so nervous he was shaking like a leaf."

"He might've been faking." She shrugged.

"Weren't you the one who was just saying we need to, and I quote, 'find a way out of here'? You said that right before Alec stumbled in." He turned the timeworn knob, but didn't push yet. "Now's our chance to do just that."

"Right, right. I know you're right," she shook her head and joined him at the door. "That was just so…strange."

"Besides, if it is a trap, then we're right back here, where we started. What would be the purpose?"

"I said you're right." She placed her hand on the door and pushed. "Now let's move."

The door swung open into the hallway and for a split second, Franklin panicked. *What if it WAS a trap?*

But the hall was empty and he breathed a short-lived sigh of relief.

"This way," Shannon whispered, grabbing him by the elbow. She yanked him left and they quickly found themselves stumbling back onto the main casino floor.

As they headed toward the front door, Franklin suddenly froze and pulled Shannon into one of the aisles of slot machines. The guard who'd accosted him at the poker table was guarding the exit. They hadn't been spotted yet, but there was no way they'd get past him without being recognized.

"What do we do?" Franklin mumbled.

Shannon pointed and he followed her finger. A gift shop was situated along one side of the store. It took him a second to understand her point, but then he noticed the merchandise.

They each snagged a hat off the rack and pulled the brims low over their face. It wasn't much, but it kept their faces better hidden.

"This won't be enough," Shannon whispered. "What else?"

"We need a distraction."

"But what? It won't be long before they notice we're missing and then everyone will be on the lookout."

Just then, a siren blared in the casino, causing Franklin to nearly jump out of his skin.

"Relax," Shannon ordered. "That's our opportunity." She nodded at something behind Franklin who turned to catch a glimpse of a woman jumping up and down at winning a slots jackpot. The machine blared and strobe lights flashed, as coins poured from a slot into her bucket and onto the floor.

All eyes turned toward her.

In the cacophony of people cheering and moving closer to get a better look, Shannon and Franklin moved slowly along the wall. After ten seconds of leading the way, Shannon paused and turned toward Franklin, a smile on her face.

"One final thing," she smirked.

Then she reached out and grabbed a fire alarm. She yanked downward and everything seemed to explode around them. Extinguishers from the ceiling began spraying water, a new set of alarms went off, and people began to panic.

The chaos also triggered one of the most basic human emotions: greed. Other customers started grabbing at poker chips, blackjack chips, and a dozen or so moved in to grab handfuls of coins from the jackpot winner's haul.

The woman fought back and started throwing punches.

A free-for-all brawl broke out, interspersed with gamblers running for the doors and others still trying to loot in all the mania.

It wasn't long before the two guards at the front entrance abandoned their post to break up the fight. The casino had given way to lawlessness and bedlam, which required their attention.

As soon as the guards abandoned their posts, Shannon and Franklin made their move. Walking briskly, but not running and drawing extra attention, they dodged the turmoil and soon found themselves crossing the threshold and stumbling outside into the night.

A few minutes later, they were in their car and driving to a hotel in silence.

They'd made a mistake coming here tonight. They both knew that. But it was too late to change that decision now. Their plans had to change. If the Russians hadn't already, they now knew Shannon and Franklin were coming.

And they would be ready.

―――――◦◦◦◦――――――

"Scusami! Mi scusi, signori. Che ore sono?" A woman grabbed him by the wrist and Sloan spun toward her. She was dressed as one of the Romani, the gypsies who lived in many communities across Italy. A colorful headscarf wrapped around her head, with a long braid that escaped the covering and a shawl draped across her shoulders, despite the heat. A long skirt, with a ring of shiny bangles, coins, and jewels hung nearly to the ground.

Milan itself was noted for the Roma people, with a large camp of thousands not far away. They had reputations of being con artists and thieves—a reputation that, while wasn't entirely unearned by a small segment of their population, was certainly exaggerated.

"Signore? Che ore sono?" The woman repeated herself, his arms gesturing wildly. Italian was a beautiful language and for a moment, Sloan simply enjoyed the ease with which it flowed from her lips. Sloan had forgotten how much Italians talk with their hands, their entire bodies. He hadn't been in Italy in over a decade and his grasp of the language had faded, but he recognized the simple question. *What time is it?*

The woman tapped at her wrist impatiently.

"Sorry, sorry," Sloan mumbled. He shook his arm free of the sleeve and glanced at his watch. "It's—it's ten. Dieci. It's dieci."

"Grazie, signore." The woman's head bobbed in thanks, her hair bouncing with each bob, and she turned to leave. Sloan watched her go.

What an odd woman.

After a few seconds, Sloan lost sight of her as she disappeared into the crowd of the festival.

"What an odd woman…" he mused aloud, turning back to Barakat. "So—"

He stopped speaking as he realized he was talking to himself. Mostafa Barakat had disappeared. Sloan spun, his head on a swivel, but the Moroccan had vanished.

"Mostafa!" he called out. Then louder and more strained, "Mostafa, where are you?" But no response came back; only the cacophony of festival-goers singing, dancing, and chatting returned.

He rushed ahead, thinking he must've just fallen behind his friend on their way to the station. But the further he went, the more worried he became. Barakat was injured and not exactly young anymore; he wouldn't have been moving fast. There was no way he could've gotten that far ahead.

Only a few explanations existed for his disappearance and none of them boded well.

He swatted at a mosquito on the back of his neck, pricking at his skin. Italy had become known for their Asian Tiger mosquitoes—a Zanzara Tigre—the same species that carried the famous Zika virus that made headlines not long ago.

It took him precisely three seconds to realize that prick wasn't a mosquito. But by then, it was far too late.

A pair of strong arms grabbed him by each elbow, propelling him forward. His vision was already fuzzy and his mind was close behind. He tried to protest, but it was as though he'd lost free will. His legs stumbled forward at the insistence of the men propping him upright on either side. He vaguely heard one of them mumble 'ubriaco' to a concerned passer-by, and then 'Ha preso una scimmia.'

Sloan tried to insist to people they passed that he hadn't been drinking, that he was being kidnapped, but as his vision began to shrink, he could only mumble a string of unintelligible gibberish.

They ushered him along as if friends taking care of a drunk comrade until they reached an alleyway. A windowless van awaited. Sloan knew he should try to identify make and model, or maybe a license plate, but his vision was too blurry; he didn't even register its color.

Out of sight of the crowd, he was unceremoniously tossed into the back, landing with a thud on top of another body.

"Ja—cob—?" Mostafa's voice cracked from beneath him.

Then everything went black.

Chapter 23

The dingy alleyway below their hotel room balcony was lined by a long row of garbage cans against one brick wall and obscene graffiti scrawled across the other. A bare fluorescent bulb cast a sickly, flickering bluish light over the cans. The shadows that danced with each flicker were dark and purple, like a day-old bruise.

As Franklin watched from his perch, a man in a heavily-stained kitchen apron pushed open a screen door on one side of the street, staggered out, and perched on one of the garbage can lids. He didn't notice Franklin watching as he rolled a joint, stuck it between his lips, and lit up.

As he drew in the smoke, his eyes closed and he leaned his head back.

"Franklin, get in here!" Shannon snapped from inside the hotel room. Obeying, he left the porch and closed the door behind him. He was hit with the smell of carbolic soap and bleach; he tried not to think what foul odor that combination was being used to conceal.

"Relax," he sighed. "It's just an alley. No one saw me."

"Our cover was blown tonight because of our mistake. They're going to be looking for us." She marched over and poked him in the chest with an accusatory finger. "We—no you…you need to be more careful."

"I said no one saw me."

"This time." She shook her head and ambled over to the edge of one of the twin beds in the room. The room was dingy and tattered, with bare-bones furnishings. Two twin beds, a dresser with one missing drawer, and a small desk with a chair that threatened to fall apart at any moment. She slumped into the chair and rested her head in her hands for a moment before looking up at him. "This might be our chance. The one we've been waiting for. We have a chance to get Phoenix. And Hook."

"But you know it's gonna be a setup," Franklin cautioned. "There's no way they'll be there after tonight."

"But what if it's not a setup?"

"If it's not? Then she made a mistake."

"And that's a mistake we need—no, we *will*—take advantage of."

"And if it *is* a setup?"

"Then we get out of there," she nodded. "Quickly."

"I don't care about speed." Franklin sat on the adjacent bed and paused to look over at her before adding, "I just care about being alive."

"Then we get out of there alive."

"That's easy for you to say. You're a federal agent. You're trained for dangerous situations."

"And you weren't? Franklin, you were a part of this group."

"Not *this* group," he quickly corrected her.

"Well, no…but before the Brotherhood became a tool of the Volya. You were a getaway driver for the Russians in DC. That's a dangerous job."

"I guess," he acknowledged with a half-hearted shrug. "That mostly involved me staying in the car though."

"Don't worry, I'm going to protect you."

He stood and lumbered over to the dirty, cracked mirror that hung above a tilted sink. He tried, but couldn't dodge the gaze of his own solitary form staring back. "You aren't afraid we're going to be caught in a trap and get killed?"

"Of course I'm afraid," she sighed and stood. She strode over and stood behind him, staring over his shoulder into the mirror as well.

"You don't show it," he said, turning to look at her.

"Franklin, our lives have been in danger ever since you and Joanna came to me that night at the Lincoln Memorial and told me about the Brotherhood and Phoenix. If your life's in danger and you're not terrified, that makes you a liability. It makes you reckless. But you can be afraid and still do your job. That's what courage is; it's being afraid and forging ahead regardless. For Joanna. For Silas. For your dad and brother, who still need protection. For everyone else too. I can't take you tomorrow if you're going to cower in fear, but I don't think that's you. I think you're capable of being brave for those you love. Am I right or am I wrong?"

"You don't know me very well," he cracked a fake smile, but his joke didn't land. "I—I mean..." he stammered, "you're right. You're right."

"Good. Now stay in the room and get some sleep. We're going to need it tomorrow."

She reached up and tapped him on the shoulder, a light touch, a momentary touch, but a meaningful one that gave him confidence and this time he smiled for real. Then she turned away and disappeared into the bathroom, leaving him staring at their hovel that dared to be called a hotel room.

After several long seconds, he shambled over to the bed, kicked off his shoes, and crawled inside, not bothering to take off his clothes.

It didn't seem worth it and morning would arrive soon enough.

———

Sloan jolted awake, his face doused in water. He sputtered at the deluge, a mist spraying from his lips. He tried to wipe his face, to dry his eyes, but his arms had been bound at his sides by a version of duct tape. A quick check revealed his feet were bound to the chair in similar fashion.

"Oh good, you're awake," a thick, throaty voice snarled.

Sloan blinked several times to clear the liquid from his eyes and glanced around the room to find the source of the voice, until he locked in on a wiry man standing in the corner, a cigarette balancing precariously between his lips. The two of them were alone.

The man leaned against the wall, observing his prisoner with the concentration of a hawk tracking its prey. The man was dark-skinned, his face pocked and scarred, the knotty evidence of murders, street brawls, and near-death encounters. And the corners of his wide, thin-lipped mouth turned up in the familiar loathsome smile that felt both condescending and obscene.

"You are Jacob Sloan, yes?" the man asked. He straightened and plucked the cigarette from his mouth, flicking it aside. It landed a couple feet away and he ground the burning ember into the carpeted floor below.

Sloan snorted, half in derision and half because his nostrils were still drenched, but he didn't answer.

"Qualunque," the man finally snorted after several silent seconds. Sloan recognized the word. *Whatever*. "We already know who you are. Your reputation precedes you." He sauntered over to Sloan until he stood directly in front of his prisoner, gawking down at him with a look Sloan couldn't quite decipher. Part curiosity, but also a strong element of scorn. "I wasn't expecting you to be such a…how do you say…a cicciobomba." He chuckled and made a mockingly-round motion around his waist, indicating Sloan's girth. "Age has not been kind to the amazing Jacob Sloan, I see."

"Who are you?" Director Sloan asked.

"My name is unimportant," the man replied, shaking his head.

"You clearly know mine," Sloan retorted. "It feels a little unfair."

"If you insist, you may call me Mario."

"Mario?"

"Yes, like the video game you Americans are so fond of. You play?"

"Is that your real name?" Sloan ignored Mario's comment, but he was very well acquainted with the mustachioed, Nintendo character from afternoons with his son; racing cartoon characters was one of the few activities he shared with Ben on his court-appointed weekends with his kids.

"Does it matter?" Mario laughed and pulled out a cigarette carton from his back pocket. He pulled one out of the package and lit up.

Sloan noticed a long-barreled handgun hanging at Mario's side.

"That's a Welrod. World War II British pistol. Impressive choice."

"You know your guns, yes?"

"Unusual choice, though. Less than 15,000 were ever manufactured. There can't be many still around, much less operational. How did you get one?"

"Operation Gladio. Are you familiar?" He didn't wait for Sloan to respond. "Some years after the war, Western countries created paramilitary groups to stay behind in enemy territory to act as resistance movements. NATO itself ran several clandestine units all throughout the Cold War. When they were finally dismantled due to public outcry—and an EU resolution—many arms caches ended up getting left behind, including in Italy."

"And Welrod's were part of those caches," Sloan nodded. He'd heard of Gladio, but didn't know Italy had been a part of that. "Still raises the question of why you'd choose to use one today. Surely better handguns exist for your purpose. Ones more easily concealed."

"If my purpose were concealment, you'd be correct."

"Ah...but you're more concerned about noise." It clicked. The Welrod was one of the quietest firearms in existence. Less than half the decibels of a typical gun, even when suppressed. "We're somewhere where someone might hear and report a gunshot, aren't we?"

Mario frowned, but didn't answer. He likely wasn't expecting their banter to reveal something important about their location.

They wouldn't keep him captive in a highly-trafficked area, Sloan mused. *That's too risky. Maybe a warehouse district? He couldn't hear typical city noise, so it likely wasn't a commercial area. An old office building would make sense. Renting an entire floor would serve their purposes for avoiding nosy neighbors coming and going, but a loud bang would still raise suspicion from neighboring floors.*

"What do you want with me?" Sloan shifted gears. "And Mostafa?"

"We considered killing you both. Finish the job we failed to complete in Budapest. But you're an American. And Americans pay for their people."

"The United States doesn't negotiate with terrorists," Sloan snapped, then held his tongue from saying more. Intentional or not, the man had just confirmed he was Nasha Volya. Obviously, that was expected, but men with histories like Sloan's have a lot of enemies. Knowing the affiliation of his captors might provide useful.

"That was the policy years ago, yes." Mario nodded before adding, "but we both know America has constructed deals with a variety of groups lately. Prisoner swaps and the like. Your President, did he not swap several Taliban members for one of your own not long ago? A deserter too. And you're important. My boss thinks we can get a pretty penny for you."

"Your boss is wrong. You might as well kill me."

"Don't worry, my friend," he taunted. "That option isn't off the table yet either."

"Where's Mostafa?" Sloan took a deep breath. If he was going to get out of here, it would require a clear head.

"Mostafa Barakat still lives, if that's what you're asking. For the moment, anyway. But he's not nearly as valuable as you. I'd be more worried about your own fate."

"Just let Mostafa go." Sloan spoke with an even, non-threatening tone. "How did you even find us?"

"We have eyes and ears everywhere, Jacob. But don't take this so personally. This is merely a business transaction, at this point. And I'm not in the business of hurting people."

"A minute ago, you said you planned to kill us."

"True, but we did some shopping around. Turns out Hezbollah in Lebanon has a standing offer of two million American dollars for any captured U.S. serviceman. And they aren't the only ones."

"I'm not a serviceman."

"You're right, you're not. But you're better." The Italian began to pace around Sloan. "You see, your reputation precedes you. We know who you are. You're not just a chief of intelligence in America. You're not even just Special Forces. You're a Midnight Agent."

A Midnight Agent.

A term unknown to the general public and only whispered about in hushed reverence in intelligence circles, it was deeply familiar to him. The Midnighters had been a clandestine, off-the-books, black ops team that ran missions during the 70s and 80s around the world. A cooperative effort by many anti-Soviet powers, with agents from a half-dozen countries. Their operations were stories of legend, exaggerated over time as many things are, but impressive in their own right. They were untouchable for nearly two decades.

Until it all blew up, that is.

The Midnighters had been called back to their respective countries, their missions deeply classified, and given cushy jobs to never talk about what happened. Sloan landed in a desk at SISA and had been there ever since. He hadn't even been abroad again until the last few years, after his promotion to the Director's chair. And he hadn't spoken a word about those years to anyone since.

He sure wasn't about to start now.

"No matter if you won't admit it," Mario finally said. "Your government knows who you are and won't want you and your secrets in the hands of Hezbollah or anyone else. They'll pay."

Sloan bowed his head, chin to chest, and refused to say anything more. Deep down, he realized Mario was probably correct.

Unless he did something, they would pay.

Chapter 24

Franklin was roused by Shannon long before the sun finished peaking its head above the horizon. Faint colors had barely begun to streak across the sky and he groaned. He'd drifted in and out of sleep all night, never unconscious for more than thirty minutes at a time.

"Here." She handed him a mug. "I picked this up downstairs for you."

How long had she been awake? He took a sip and cringed. Hotel coffee, an insult to the black elixir so many depended on to function. It tasted…dirty, almost. Burnt. He couldn't put his finger on what exactly made it so bad. But it was all he had, so he forced down another sip.

At least it was strong. Within minutes, the caffeine hit his bloodstream, waking him up.

"Get ready," Shannon commanded. "We need to get moving. The igloos are a two hour drive, so we'll want an early start."

"We're still going?" Franklin mumbled. "They know we're coming."

"I know," Shannon responded. "We had this exact conversation last night. I'm not having it again."

She sounded tired, exasperated. Again, he wondered how long she'd been awake. He hadn't noticed her leaving, but maybe she'd slipped out during one of the few times he'd briefly dozed off. *Had she even slept?* Her clothes had that rumpled, slept-in look to them, but bags

181

had developed below both eyes and he caught her yawning. She'd admitted to being afraid last night, though he hadn't believed her. But maybe she really was scared…

He shook his head. He was terrified, but didn't want to argue with her. He blinked and swallowed hard, trying to relax the tension in his neck.

"I'm ready," he finally said with a nod and a watery smile that he forced out.

A gray, drizzly morning with the temperature in the mid-fifties greeted them. They drove through the winding roads of the Black Hills for the first hour. The early hours and drizzly weather made for a desolate drive, though they managed to spot a lot of wildlife tucked in and around the evergreen trees, including a massive buffalo that grazed less than twenty feet from the shoulder of the road.

A fog hung ominously over the road as they reached and began to navigate the area known as the Badlands. A collection of bizarrely colorful spires—with stripes of reds and purples and whites—stood in stark contrast to steep ravines and gorges. Miles of desolation in this unique environment, with no almost signs of civilization for miles and a heavy haze, made for an almost extraterrestrial feel as they weaved along the two-lane road. If this were any other day, Franklin would've relished the unique beauty of the area, a mixture of desolation and color not found anywhere else in the world.

The two-hour drive to the igloos was largely in silence, neither one daring to say what was on their minds. If they were caught today, that was it. There would be no second chance. No 'live to see another day.'

No, if they were captured today by Phoenix or her minions, that was it.

They would be killed.

Shannon pulled the car off the road before they arrived at the compound, tucking it out of sight of the main highway.

"We'll walk from here," she answered his unspoken question.

"And if we need a quick getaway?" he asked. "We can't exactly run a mile over rough terrain to the car with armed Russians in pursuit."

"We'll call an Uber," she joked, with a wink.

"I'm serious," he insisted with a groan, rolling his eyes in frustration.

"As you're so persistent at telling me, they already know we're coming," she explained. "We don't need to announce our precise arrival too. Going by foot is our only option."

He nodded, unconvinced. But she was in charge. There was a reason she was a Bureau agent and he'd been a lowly criminal.

"Let's load up." She exited the car and circled around to the back, where she popped the trunk of their rental car. Franklin followed her.

As he rounded the corner of the vehicle, he gasped.

"Where did you get all of this?" He stammered. "*When* did you get all of this?"

He was staring down at a small arsenal tucked into the trunk of their Honda Civic. A half dozen different handguns, multiple clips of ammunition for each, were resting next to a slew of knives of various shapes and sizes. Shannon already had her federally-issued Glock in a shoulder holster, but slid a second gun into her waistband and began taping a long knife to one ankle.

"Pick what you want," she said, not answering either of his questions.

"But what—where—when—?"

"I assume you're getting to 'who' and 'why' and 'how,' but none of that's important. I may be a federal agent, but I still have a couple secrets up my sleeve." She smirked at his confusion, but didn't elaborate. "Now hurry up and grab what you want. I sincerely hope we don't need any of this, but just in case, I want to be prepared."

Franklin tentatively picked a small handgun and what looked like a hunting knife. A very sharp hunting knife. He pricked his finger as he grabbed it and a tiny drop of blood oozed over his bent knuckle and fell to the ground.

He wasn't unfamiliar with weapons; nor was he unfamiliar with carrying them. But today, handling that gun and tucking both it and a knife into an ankle holster felt like a tacit admission they would be needed, that today was going to be a fight. Dangerous, possibly even deadly. And that notion caused bile to rise briefly in his throat before he choked it back.

"Let's go," Shannon's urge broke through his thoughts and his head snapped up. "We have a twenty minute walk ahead of us."

"I'm—I'm ready," he grimaced. Then he shoved the gun into his waistband and followed her off-road.

The ice rink was largely empty, save for a small class of children learning to skate at one end, when Eve slipped in, duffel bag in hand. A young, blonde skating instructor in a black vest patiently propped up a tiny girl struggling to stay upright. Children's laughter echoed through the chilly air, reverberating off the walls and ice. None of them glanced at the new arrival though and Eve didn't wait around to be noticed. The fewer people who could place her here, the better. So she ducked through a side door marked 'Personnel Only' and into the back hallway toward the offices.

The final door on the left opened before she reached it and a tousled mop of hair popped out into the hallway.

"Eve, is that really you?" The scratchy voice of a lifelong smoker rasped. "I thought I recognized you on the security cam, but you haven't showed your face around here in so long, I couldn't be sure."

"I wish you wouldn't use my real name, Whip." Despite her mild rebuke, she smiled. Whiplash Martin's real name was Richard, but he insisted on going by his Internet avatar's nickname. He claimed he never liked his birth name, but Eve knew he secretly wished to be more like the swashbuckling cowboy character he'd created online for one of his role-playing games.

"What does it matter?" he asked. "You're not dark web. You're legit. Work for the feds and everything."

"You'd be surprised who might care."

"Well, alright then," Whiplash grinned. "Come, come in." He beckoned her forward.

Eve followed him through the swinging door, which smacked shut behind them with a satisfying thunk. The noise from the rink ceased.

"So what brings you here?" Whiplash plopped into a monstrous black armchair and took a sip from a large cup. Eve couldn't identify the contents, but she guessed it was some form of high-octane energy drink. Whiplash was the epitome of a stereotypical hacker, the kind depicted in Hollywood. A junk food connoisseur, addicted to all manners of caffeine and sugar, and largely nocturnal. Managing this ice rink was a family business he helped his elderly mother take care of, but night shift suited him just fine. And it helped him maintain a degree of legitimacy too; Whiplash was the go-to guy for all manner of counterfeit documents.

Need a fake passport? Driver's license? Social Security card? Original Blockbuster membership card? Whiplash handled all of that. And it wasn't just hard copies either. He was adept at constructing digital footprints for people as well. That way, in case anyone went looking, the documents would stand up to scrutiny.

"It's Hesko," she said. Whiplash was more active in the online gaming branch of hacktivism than government conspiracies, but he'd surely recognize the name. "He's dead. And his hard drive is missing."

Whiplash blinked twice and took a final sip from his drink before replacing it in the cup holder on the chair. Without saying anything, he stood and dashed over to his computer. A massive set-up, with nine extended screens flickered to life. He tapped on the keyboard and within seconds, Hesko's face popped up on one of the screens, alongside a news article with the words 'South Dakota bar owner slain in gruesome robbery gone wrong' emblazoned across the top.

"Tragic," he finally groaned. "Well…we both know Hesko wouldn't believe their explanation of a robbery gone wrong. But the man was a paranoid nutcase. What makes you think this was any more than that?"

"They stole his hard drive, Whip." She couldn't reveal her connection to Shannon and Franklin. She didn't want

Whip digging too deep into the Nasha Volya either. He couldn't afford to go on the run, not with his mother becoming increasingly feeble. "They didn't go after the money. Not the expensive laptop. Nothing else. And no one else in the bar noticed anything. What does that tell you?"

"Fair enough." He bit his lip as he deliberated. "So who did it? You think he stumbled across a real conspiracy and the government offed him? Or the mob...like JFK?"

"It wasn't the government," Eve mumbled. "Don't push this Whip. I'd tell you if I could."

"But you know? I mean, really know? Not just suspect?"

"I know."

"Huh. So you're going to need papers then? For you? I assume this isn't a social call."

"That's why I'm here. I need everything you can get me."

"What do you plan to do with them?" he inquired, then added, "It will help me know details of how to construct the identity."

"I can't be tracked. Cut all ties from who I am. Make it something airtight."

"What about your old identity?"

She hesitated a minute. But it needed to be done. And the sooner it was, the sooner she could get back to helping the others. Finally, she nodded once and insisted, "Bury me."

Whip blinked twice. Killing an identity surely wasn't a request he got very often. It was difficult and impossible to recover, if minds were changed. But it was within his skill set and he covered his surprise well. "Well, have a seat and I'll see what I can do."

Chapter 25

After a twenty minute walk, Franklin and Shannon finally crested a small ridge and spotted the igloos. Obviously, not real igloos in southwestern South Dakota. But Hesko hadn't been wrong. The buildings did resemble the domed structures normally made of snow and ice blocks.

They weren't white and were largely made of concrete, but the bunkers did have rounded tops and had been built solidly into the ground, covered with earth. Row after row stretched across the barren landscape, solemn observers testifying to an apocalypse that had yet to occur.

Originally a munitions depot for the government, a contractor had—years ago—bought a bunch of them to turn them into doomsday survival bunkers and, if he was being honest, Franklin could appreciate the appeal. If the world came to an end, this would be a great place to wait it out in relative safety.

Far from any major cities that might be targeted with nuclear weapons, built directly into the ground to protect from radiation or natural disaster threats, easy to defend against uprising zombies or robots…if you wanted to survive Armageddon, this was as good a place as any to try.

But Hesko suggested the Volya had bought—or maybe rented—a few of the structures as well. Not as protection against the end of the world, but maybe a headquarters to launch their attacks and kick off the beginning of the end of the world.

"How are we going to get down there without being seen?" Franklin asked. "There's no cover. We'll be sitting ducks."

"No cover for us also means no cover for them," Shannon responded. "We'll see them coming too. Those bunkers may be solid defense against brainless zombies or nuclear fallout, but they aren't exactly equipped for an incoming tactical assault."

"They probably have cameras though," Franklin cautioned.

"Weren't you the one who kept reminding me they already know we're coming?" she scoffed. She crouched low to the ground to minimize possible sightings, but began to slowly edge her way along the ridge toward the buildings.

Franklin didn't answer. The Russians knew of their impending arrival after last night. Being caught on camera was the least of their worries. Besides, he couldn't find evidence of the cameras he'd expected. Maybe these bunkers weren't as technologically advanced as he'd presumed a doomsday bunker would be. Or maybe they never expected anyone to get this far.

"Fine," he finally said. Not loud enough for her to hear as she moved out of immediate earshot, but more for his own sake.

He followed her and it wasn't long before they reached the first bunker.

"How do we know which one belongs to Phoenix? Or the Volya?" Franklin whispered.

"Ones—most likely," Shannon whispered out of the corner of her mouth. She moved among the bunkers, scurrying from one to another, looking for something as Franklin trailed behind.

"What?"

"Plural," she sighed. "Ones. They likely have a few of these."

"That still doesn't answer my question," Franklin pushed. "How do we know which *ones* are theirs?"

"I don't know. Context clues?"

"Context clues. I see. You want to elaborate?" He tugged at his sleeve, then swatted at a fly buzzing nearby.

"Come on, Franklin." Shannon whispered through her teeth. "You aren't an agent, but you're no idiot. I don't know exactly what we're looking for. But I can tell you it's none of these we've passed already. No footprints, no tire tracks, nothing. Yet they've supposedly been here recently, according to Hesko. And they must leave to go into Deadwood, so there should be lots of tracks. Or other signs of life."

"Surely the Volya aren't the only group here though," Franklin added.

"Agreed. We'll have to be careful."

Franklin begrudgingly nodded. And it wasn't long before her theory was confirmed. A few bunkers over, a series of fresh tire tracks came into view. Based on the size of the tread and the spacing, Franklin guessed it was some sort of Jeep, not an uncommon vehicle in the Black Hills.

"There," Shannon pointed. "Maybe that one?" Peering around the corner, he saw no one in sight. No cars either. And no obvious cameras. Just the tracks. "Follow me." She beckoned him and stepped out from the corner.

The two of them scampered over to the door and began to examine it. The lock had fresh scratchings as well, indicating someone had used a key to get inside fairly recently. Shannon grabbed ahold of the handle and gave a cautious pull, but it wouldn't budge. Locked tight.

Franklin reached out and, with a pair of fingertips, gently traced a crude etching in the metal frame that appeared to be a rough scrawl of the letters 'N' and 'V.'

"This is it," he whispered. "Now what?"

"Now we get inside," she answered, deftly removing a long metal pin out of her boot. She slid the thin rod into the locking mechanism and began wiggling it around.

"You can't possibly think it's empty though," he retorted.

"Of course not," she said, choosing not to elaborate.

"Fine, just hurry," he whispered. Not that he had any real frame of reference, but it seemed to be taking too long. Any minute now, that Jeep might return or someone might choose to step outside for a walk in the fresh air. Then again, he had no idea what waited for them on the other side of that door and he wasn't incredibly eager to find out.

"I'm going as fast as I can. Picking a lock isn't as easy as it looks, you know," she snapped back. Then only a second later, "Never mind. I'm in." She turned to him and winked.

Franklin rolled his eyes. *Always the showoff...*

The door swung open without a sound and Franklin breathed a prayer of thanks to no one in particular for that blessing of silence. Slipping inside revealed a dark room, lit by a single, bare bulb sticking out of a rusting metal fixture on the wall. There was no one there to greet them.

Another blessing.

"Shouldn't one of us stay outside?" Franklin whispered. "You know, just in case the car comes back...then we can have a warning."

"Are you scared?" She smirked.

"No," he lied. "I just don't think it's smart to close ourselves in a dark, unknown bunker without knowing what's going on outside."

She looked at him and rolled her eyes, but after a second, she sighed, "Okay, that's fine. You stay out here. But text me if anyone returns."

He nodded.

"And why don't you walk around a few other bunkers too. I'm sure this isn't the only one. Maybe you can learn something about the others. Just be careful."

He pursed his lips into a forced grin at her before the door closed, sealing her inside. He turned back to the surroundings, intent on exploring the other bunkers nearby. It didn't feel right that there weren't any cameras here. *Why wouldn't they want to know who was coming and going?*

His question was soon answered though. A second bunker, not fifty yards from the first, not only had a camera installed above the door—with a blinking red light, indicating it was active—but a young man sat on a lawn chair in front of the entrance.

The man was large—big-boned, as Franklin's middle school bully liked to say—and probably in his late 20s or early 30s. He dressed in casual clothes, but had a conspicuous handgun strapped on his hip. *A security guard*, Franklin mused. Thankfully, the guard was engrossed in something on his mobile phone and not paying much attention to his surroundings, which allowed Franklin enough time to duck back around a corner without being spotted.

He crouched and leaned against an earthen wall at his back. His pulse began to pound as he extracted his own phone from his pocket and tapped out a quick message to Shannon.

Guard and camera at second bunker

He waited a minute, but received no reply, so sent a second.

What should I do? Are you okay?

Still no response. He shook his head and clambered upright. He was going to have to handle this himself.

Not a big deal, he told himself. *He'd handled far worse than a single security guard. Working with Silas had put him in much greater danger than a single overweight guard with a handgun.*

He was right, of course. His years in the Brotherhood had put him in plenty of danger. Deadly danger, on many occasions. But this felt different and he didn't know why.

Maybe because he actually cared about his life this time...

He took a deep breath and poked his head out again to check on the guard.

Gone! The guard had disappeared from his post!

An empty lawn chair sat abandoned by the door to the bunker. And the man who'd occupied it not thirty seconds prior had vanished.

Oh no, oh no, oh no...

Franklin's heart rate spiked and his head spun wildly on a swivel, trying to locate the missing guard.

A soft crunch behind him sent his heart into his throat and he whirled around to find himself face-to-face with the guard. He didn't have time to react before the young man's fist caught him across the jaw, sending him reeling to the side.

Chapter 26

When the kidnappers returned to Sloan, there were two of them and they were bickering. They spoke too fast for Sloan to make out much of their conversation; he hadn't maintained his Italian fluency. But he could read tone. And their voices sounded dangerously tight and stressed, like guitar strings being stretched nearly to their breaking point. Something was wrong.

The two bickered for several minutes, anger building until finally giving way into a sullen bitterness. They fell into a tense silence before the one called Mario turned to him.

"Get up," he snapped. "Stand up."

"You know, I would if I could, but there's the issue of that pesky duct tape…"

The other man stepped forward brandishing a switchblade knife and sliced through Sloan's restraints. "Now stand. And follow us." This second kidnapper appeared to be younger than his partner and clearly more raw. He didn't possess the hardened scars and calluses of a life in the streets. He spoke with a lighter accent as well, likely a mark of higher education or more privileged upbringing.

Sloan rubbed his wrists. They were raw and sore, and covered in sticky tape residue, but it felt good to be able to move them again. He braced himself against the chair and slowly pushed himself to his feet. He nearly toppled over, but caught and steadied himself. His legs felt weak and stiff. He was grateful it was stiffness and nothing worse.

"So if you're Mario, does that make your friend here Luigi?" he quipped and gestured for them to lead the way.

"Luca," the other man grunted as he opened and held the door. Sloan followed Mario through. Now he had one man in front and one behind, solid prisoner transfer technique, and it made him uneasy.

"Too bad," Sloan shrugged. "So where are we going?"

"You're not being swapped."

"I told you they wouldn't negotiate for me," Sloan smirked. "Americans don't—"

"It wasn't that. Your precious Americans were desperate to pay up. A little too desperate, we noticed. We ran your name up the chain of command and our boss had a better idea for you."

"Oh yeah? What's that?"

"You'll find out soon enough."

"Who's your boss? That Phoenix woman?"

"Phoenix? The Russian nut? Hardly," Luca scoffed. "We're answering to someone else. The man with the ring." Mario turned and glared at his partner, seemingly angry to hear him badmouth their leaders.

"So it's Hyde then. He's the European capo of this little cabal, right?"

Mario grunted, "Nope."

"Then who? It wouldn't be Mara or Shango. They wouldn't have any power here in Italy." Their intelligence had been thorough on those two. They were regionally powerful, but easily overshadowed by the others on the global stage.

Neither man answered. They turned a corner, directed Sloan through a series of doors, an industrial laundry room that confirmed his theory of an office building, and finally an exterior door leading to an alley.

There, they nudged him toward the backseat of a waiting sedan. Sloan hesitated, noting they took care to hide their guns in pockets now that they might have witnesses outside. The area was seedy and grungy, but it was far from a ghetto. The building they'd just exited was old, but otherwise appeared to be a working series of offices. They stood behind the building in a cramped alleyway, but Mario's choice of a "quiet" gun now made sense.

He quickly calculated the risk of trying an escape, but dismissed the possibility as Mario jabbed the barrel of the Welrod into his spine. His hands were free, but his legs still felt weak beneath him and his wrists ached. Even if he was able to knock out one of them, he'd need to make it twenty yards to the main street before the driver of the vehicle stopped him.

So after a moment of hesitation, he decided to wait for a better opportunity. He slid into the backseat as Luca clambered in beside him, careful to keep his gun directed at Sloan's midsection, and Mario climbed into the passenger seat. A third man sat behind the wheel. No one said a word as they pulled away from the building.

"If it's not any of the four..." Sloan trailed off before taking a shot in the dark. "It's not—it's not the fifth... is it?"

Luca's head snapped toward him. "You know about the Warhawk?"

"Idiot," Mario growled from the front seat. He turned to scowl at his partner. "He didn't know until you just confirmed it."

"Who is it?" Sloan asked. His mind whirled. His suspicion was correct. Phoenix and the other three weren't alone. A fifth, he existed. *The Warhawk.* He'd never come across that name before. Not that 'Warhawk' was a name. More of a title, a pseudonym like the others. But names are chosen for a reason.

Phoenix, Mara, Shango, Hyde...and now Warhawk. Why Warhawk? What did that mean? Who could it be?

Luca fidgeted silently, knowing he screwed up, but even he wasn't dumb enough to answer that question.

"Ok, fine. You can't tell me who. But I'm going to find out eventually, right? He's the one who wants me. So can you at least tell me where he is? Where he's from? Is he even a 'he'?"

"He's American!" Luca blurted indignantly, as though that was a slur, but he drew a sharp look from Mario before falling silent again.

"American?" He'd never considered an American might be behind attacks on fellow Americans. Not that it was impossible, or even unprecedented. But this was different. And Luca's comment about Warhawk having more power than Phoenix didn't make sense. What terrorist in America would have more power than Phoenix? Everyone knew she ran the Nasha Volya there.

Unless...unless he didn't mean power within their group. Unless he meant political power. Could Warhawk be someone in government? A politician? A lobbyist? Maybe someone in Congress? The White House? He didn't have a good retort this time and the three of them fell quiet as the car pulled onto the interstate.

Sloan stared out the window as the Italian countryside flew past, his gears churning. They were leaving the city, heading north in the direction of the rural mountainous region outside Milan. He didn't know much about the area, but there was a private airport this direction. It served a dual purpose, acting as a military airport, but also a civilian one for private tourists.

If he was going to meet an American, like Luca said, that likely meant they were leaving the country. A private airport would be their best option for smuggling a prisoner out of the country. But it was risky with the military on site as well.

An airport wouldn't give him many options for escape, unless he could somehow alert any military personnel. If they were even using the airport today. He closed his eyes and tried to walk through the process in his mind. They'd likely drive right into the hangar for the plane and march him straight up the steps at gunpoint. No real options there unless he got a head start out of the car.

But his heft and age—not to mention his bad knee— made it unlikely he'd be able to outrun two fit Italian men in their late 20s or early 30s. Once on the plane, he was trapped too. Nowhere to run once those doors closed. He might be able to take the plane down over the ocean, but that seemed extreme. And there would be no survivors. Himself included.

That sacrifice wasn't worth it to take out two low-level thugs; he wasn't suicidal.

The more he pondered it, the more he believed his best bet for escape might be upon landing, especially if he used the flight time to his advantage. And it would be nice to get a free ride back to the States, if that's where they were indeed headed. But there were still too many unknowns. He'd have to play it by ear.

Finally, he broke the silence to ask, "Where's Mostafa?"

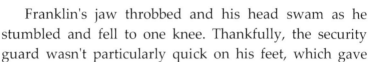

Franklin's jaw throbbed and his head swam as he stumbled and fell to one knee. Thankfully, the security guard wasn't particularly quick on his feet, which gave Franklin a few crucial seconds to recover before the second punch arrived. By the time it did, he managed to duck and the fist whistled harmlessly above his head.

With his attacker off balance from the missed swing, Franklin balled his fist and slammed it into the guard's side, just below the ribcage. The guard grunted as he lurched sideways, but this time when he turned back, he held a Walther pistol in his hand.

Franklin drove the edge of his hand down onto the guard's wrist with a karate chop and the gun dropped to the soil below. They both reached for the weapon, but Franklin managed to wrestle the Walther away first and swung its butt upward toward the guard's face. The guard raised a beefy arm, deflecting the blow. Franklin charged forward and drove him against the wall of the building with a heavy thud. But the guard was too big, too strong, and he countered.

The man's fist drilled Franklin hard on the right biceps and his arm went numb. Unable to maintain his grip, Franklin's hand released and the gun once again fell to the ground, this time bouncing and skittering several feet away, out of reach.

The guard, seeking to build on his advantage as Franklin's arm dangled limply, drove his fist toward

Franklin's solar plexus. Franklin barely deflected the blow and stumbled backward, buying himself time to regain feeling in his right arm.

But it wasn't enough. The guard drilled Franklin with a flying tackle and the two men hit the ground with a heavy thud and a couple of grunts. Franklin's gun fell, jostled loose in the scuffle. They grappled for position, but the guard was much too large for Franklin to gain the upper hand, not in a wrestling match. After a few seconds of scuffling, the guard twisted Franklin onto his back and pinned his shoulders to the ground with one beefy arm. The other arm repeatedly pummeled Franklin across the cheekbone until he felt a crack.

Franklin yelped in pain.

He tried to grab for the knife he'd tucked into an ankle sheath earlier, but he couldn't reach it at this angle. Frantic, he grabbed a handful of dirt with one of his spare hands and threw it into the guard's face. Dust filled his mouth and eyes. Caught off guard, the man coughed and drew back, giving Franklin time to land a forearm in his chest and throw him off balance. It wasn't much, but it was enough. He launched two quick jabs, both of which connected, then planted his foot into the man's chest. The guard tumbled backward and fell onto the soil, still coughing.

Scooping up his gun from where it had fallen earlier, Franklin levied it at the guard. It was over.

"Freeze! Or I'll shoot."

Franklin froze. That was what he wanted to say, had planned to say, but those words hadn't come from his mouth.

He slowly turned his head and, through sweat and some blood, he realized they weren't alone. He groaned.

Two more security guards stood about ten feet away, weapons drawn. There was no way he'd be able to fire fast enough to drop all three of them.

"Lower the gun and get on your knees," one of the men commanded.

Franklin sighed, then tossed the gun to the side, wistfully watching it tumble into the dirt. Then, raising his arms above his head—an excruciating proposition—he knelt. The man he'd just defeated clambered to his feet, his face red with anger and exertion.

Franklin watched as the guard sauntered over to him, chin held high, and snarled. He raised a fist and swung it toward Franklin, a prize fighter finishing off his foe with a hay-maker.

There was a flash of pain. Then it all went black.

Chapter 27

Having the barrel of a gun in your mouth makes it difficult to answer questions. Nearly impossible, in fact. Franklin had never known just how important your lips are for talking. Pronouncing consonants simply isn't achievable without them.

That wasn't a revelation he'd hoped to learn at any point in his life, much less so soon, but his captors hadn't gotten the memo.

After hauling him into a space that resembled a small living quarters in one of the on-site buildings, they'd bound his wrists and knocked him into a chair. His jaw had been pried open—excruciatingly, given his cheekbone fracture from the fight outside in the dirt—and the barrel of an MSS Vul pistol shoved into his mouth. Not gently. The metal scraped against his teeth, creating an unpleasant reverberation throughout his skull that made him cringe. Franklin could taste the gunpowder of past firings. It was sharp and metallic, with a bitter peppery aftertaste. It wasn't particularly tasty.

As a high schooler, he read a story about how Napoleon's forces used gunpowder to season horse meat in emergency situations. He couldn't explain why his mind chose to remember this now, and he couldn't explain why they believed gunpowder to be an appropriate flavor for their meat, but it was suddenly all he could think about.

His captors kept demanding things of him. Half in Russian, half in broken English. He only understood a fraction. Mostly, they seemed to want to know how he'd found them. But he couldn't explain. Not that he would, even if he was able—that might endanger Shannon—but in this case, he literally couldn't explain. He managed a few grunts and weird vowel utterances, but that didn't satisfy them. They only became more and more angry.

There were two goons. The main one, the one who kept the gun barrel wedged between Franklin's cheeks, was large and hairy, with shoulders of an ox and the gut of a potbelly pig. He reminded Franklin of a greasy, overfed, unkempt bear. The other loomed large as well, but leaner and more muscular, a physique honed in a gym and not at a buffet. He sported a large tattoo on his wrist of a clock face, no hands. He was the one who kept yelling questions at Franklin in his dual-language effort to terrify his prisoner. And the effort was working.

Franklin had technically been in the Russian Brotherhood for years, but he'd never been on this end of things. In fact, he'd never been on their end either. He'd served as a getaway driver and a part-time con artist mostly. He'd been used to procure some items—the feds would call it theft—and to shuttle members from one location to another. He'd certainly never shoved a gun in anyone's face before, nor had one shoved in his.

But Franklin was determined not to give in to their demands—even if he could have. He had other people to think of. He couldn't be a coward his entire life. So he cried inwardly, but refused to permit even a single tear to escape his ducts.

He winced as he watched one of the bruisers—the hairy one—rear back, his beefy hand clenching into a fist.

He knew what came next, so he closed his eyes. Somehow, watching it happen made it even worse than not knowing. But nothing came.

"That...will be enough," a silky, feminine voice knifed through the air. It ended his torment—temporarily, at least—but the words sent an icy chill down his spine.

He slowly opened his eyes and turned toward the origin of the voice.

Phoenix. He'd found her.

Her once-auburn hair had been cut to her shoulders and dyed a darker shade of russet-brown. And she wore bulkier clothes to hide her thin frame, making it unlikely she'd be recognized from a distance, but there was no mistaking those eyes. A wild blue, like the color of unadulterated ice, pure, straight from an iceberg. Her eyes both enchanted and unsettled, as they bored holes into his skull. A strange energy reverberated around her, like a ring of fire, that made him even more uneasy.

"I think he's had enough," she remarked. "Isn't that right, Franklin?"

Franklin didn't say anything, but found himself subconsciously nodding.

"Leave us," she commanded her goons. "Give me five minutes with him. And don't let anyone in."

The two Russian brutes grumbled, but obeyed and stepped out into the hallway.

"Let's talk, Franklin," she crooned, her voice like smoke. "I'm told you speak a little Russian, but I realize you may not have understood my assistants' questions. Their accent is a bit...blue collar, at times, I know."

"I have nothing to say," Franklin sputtered, spittle flying with every syllable. The sputtering wasn't out of fear—though he was plenty scared. His cheek and jaw had already begun to swell and he found it increasingly difficult to get the words out cleanly.

"Oh no...well, I sincerely hope that's not the case." She frowned and circled the chair until standing behind Franklin, walking with such minimal effort that it almost appeared like she was gliding. "Because if you have nothing to say, you're of no use to me, are you? And I believe your friend Silas told you what I do to people who are of no use anymore, didn't he?" She placed her hands on his shoulders and squeezed. What might have been reassuring in any other circumstances was terrifying now. Her bony fingers dug into him and he flinched.

Franklin swallowed hard. Silas had been killed six months ago by one of Phoenix's henchmen, but before he did, he'd related the story of how she'd murdered a bodyguard for failing to frisk a visitor. She'd done it casually, the decision to end a man's life no more affecting than if she'd been deciding lunch plans.

"Here, maybe you're just uncomfortable," she whispered as she bent down. He could feel her fiddling with his hands and a couple seconds later, his wrists fell apart. She'd untied him.

Grateful but wary, he slowly twisted his arms around to the front and rubbed his sore wrists, but he stayed seated for the moment. He'd have to wait for an opportunity. Stealing a glance at his feet, he noticed his ankle knife had been removed while he was unconscious. That was expected, but he'd hoped it might've been overlooked.

Phoenix eased around in front of him with the silky grace of a feline predator and gazed down.

"How's that?" she asked. "Any better?"

"Your thugs didn't have to cuff me in the first place," he snapped.

"Yes well, they get anxious at times. Overzealous, I suppose," she mused. "Not the best trait for an underling, but it's better than the alternative."

He didn't respond.

"Here." She offered a small flask to him. He hadn't noticed where it had come from, so hesitated.

"It's just a splash of vodka. It'll help with the pain of your swelling. I know that has to hurt by now."

She was right. His cheekbone throbbed. So he reluctantly accepted the flask and took a swig. She wasn't lying; it was pure vodka. It was strong and he cringed as it burned. But after a second, he took another swig, then handed it back to her.

"So," she began, capping the flask and slipping it inside the pocket in her jacket, "let's get to it. Where is your partner? The woman, I believe…Agent Faye?"

They hadn't caught Shannon! A twinkle of hope burned. It wasn't much, but it was more than he had a minute ago. He chose to say nothing, but couldn't keep a slight smile from peeking out of his lips.

"Interesting. That grin…you realized we haven't caught her yet? Because I assure you, we will. Soon."

Franklin still said nothing, but his fingers gripped the arm of the chair as though he wanted to throttle it.

"Are you willing to die for this Agent Faye, Franklin?" Phoenix cocked her head to one side to stare at him. "Because that's what we're talking about here. This isn't just a friendly question and answer session. Your life is on the line right now."

"You're going to kill me whether I tell you or not," Franklin muttered in defiance, breaking his vow of silence.

"Fine, fair point," Phoenix murmured in a monotone that gave Franklin chills. "I am curious though. How exactly did you find me?"

"I used to play a lot of 'Where's Waldo?' as a kid," he mumbled through puffy lips.

"You have jokes," she chuckled.

He glared at her.

"But now we have a problem. For while they didn't beat your sense of humor out of you, they did apparently destroy your common sense. Because cracking jokes is a stupid move right now, Franklin. A very stupid move. You've chosen to make your final moments on Earth...very...painful..." She crouched in front of him, bending down until they were eye-to-eye.

This was it. His opportunity.

He lunged forward from his chair, arms outstretched, aiming to hit her right across the shoulders and drive her to the ground.

She was too quick. Quicker than he'd anticipated. Or maybe he was too slow. Either way, he found himself suddenly sprawling across the floor. Alone.

And then the pain started. A steady bolt of lightning coursed and sizzled through his body.

A taser!

Franklin tried to scream, but it came out like a rasping wheeze instead. He tried to curse, but it came out like a whimper. His body twitched and contorted violently, like a bug flipped over on its back unable to right itself. Hundreds of volts robbed him of any motor control.

Flashes of pain pulsed throughout his body, every nerve on fire. His hands spasmed, clenching and opening repeatedly, uncontrollably. His limbs flailed every which way, his back arched. His whole body convulsed, racking his muscles until it seemed his bones would break under the pressure.

And then it was over. Franklin lay there on his back, his muscles still twitching, but slowly returning to his control. He gasped for air as his lungs burned.

"That's exactly what I hoped you'd do, Mr. Holt."

Through the electricity-induced double-vision, he could just barely make out her face.

She was smiling.

Then everything faded away. Again.

Chapter 28

Franklin flipped on the headlights of his beat-up pickup truck, the beams fighting to cut through the billowing dust his tires were kicking up on this back country road. The truck bounced over the rutted dirt, as trees flew past on either side.

He didn't know where he was, nor where he was going. But as long as his path was lit as far as his headlights shone, he trusted he'd get there eventually.

The radio only sputtered static as he flipped stations. Wherever he was, he was well outside the range of any stations.

"I'm hungry, Unca Frank."

Franklin nearly jumped out of his skin. He thought he was alone. But as he turned his head, he noticed his little nephew, KJ, sitting in the passenger seat.

"Kayj, what are you doing here?"

"Can you feed me?" the boy asked.

"I—I don't have anything..." Franklin stuttered. He patted his pockets in hopes of discovering some snack tucked away, but found them all empty.

"But I'm hungry." KJ folded his arms across his chest in defiance.

"I know, kiddo. I know. But I can't help you."

"Help me do what?" Without warning, the boy's voice deepened. Franklin glanced over, but found himself staring at his brother's concerned gaze.

"Jeremiah?"

"Do you honestly think this is wise?" his brother asked in that annoying tone only an older sibling can achieve. *"You've barely escaped death several times now. And for what? A little revenge?"*

"It's not revenge, Jay. It's vengeance. There's a difference."

"You're angry."

"Of course I'm angry! They killed Joanna. They tried to kill you. And kidnapped KJ!"

"Anger doesn't produce the righteousness that God desires."

"What?"

"That's the book of James. The Word is clear. We shouldn't act out of anger. Haven't you been reading the Bible I gave you?"

"What are you talking about?" Franklin glowered. *"Someone needs to pay. Nathan Hook needs to pay. Phoenix needs to pay."*

"We're supposed to refrain from anger. It leads only to evil. Psalm 37…"

"But what am I supposed to do?" Franklin blurted, throwing his hands in the air.

"Your brother's right, you know…" The voice changed again and Franklin glanced over to recognize Silas's twisted grin staring back.

"You—agree with Jeremiah?"

"Of course. Anger is a useless emotion. It's a bloody mist over your mind, a fog that clouds the way you look at the world."

"Okay…"

"What you need to do is channel it. Anger is fog. But wrath! Wrath is clarity."

"Wr-wrath?" Franklin stuttered.

"That Bible your brother loves so dearly says a lot about wrath. It's what God pours out on the world. It's good. Righteous even, Jeremiah might say."

"What's the difference?"

"Anger necessitates malice. But a man of wrath? A man of wrath has no malice. He hungers only for justice. It's a pure motive. As pure as it gets. Your God—your brother's God—is a righteous judge, a God who displays His wrath every single day."

"Aren't you dead?" Franklin interjected, shaking his head. "You're supposed to be dead."

"Hey, this is your dream. Dead...alive...I'm just a figment of your imagination. Your subconscious, you might say."

"My brother says anger leads to evil. Wouldn't wrath lead to the same?"

"Evil, evil, evil...what is evil, anyway? Wouldn't you say Phoenix is evil? Nathan Hook?"

"Well, yes..."

"And if wrath ends their terror, it ends evil, right?"

"I guess... What if I can't do it? If I can't kill them?"

Silas laughed. "You've killed before. You can again."

"That was self-defense. Not the same thing. Killing in cold blood, even in revenge, is different. That's—that's—"

"That's the dark side," Silas broke out in a loud guffaw. "Right? Star Wars...light, dark, two opposing sides. That's not how the universe was built. It's all gray. We all have a dark side. If we're pushed hard enough, we're all—every one of us— is capable of doing things that might seem unthinkable otherwise. You can be spineless at times, sure, but I have no doubt, you'll rise to the occasion when it presents itself."

Franklin scowled. Silas's bluntness was honest to the point of cruelty. But perhaps he wasn't wrong. "And if I can't do it? If I can't kill them?"

"Kill who?" Silas's voice faded, then replaced by a much more familiar one. A voice Franklin had known his entire life.

"Dad?"

"Who are you killing?"

"We're going after the people who killed Joanna, Dad. The ones who took KJ. And shot you!"

"Communist pricks," his father grumped.

"They aren't communists. They're anarchists."

"Same difference," he grunted.

"Actually, they're opposites, Dad. Communists are big government, anarchists want no government..."

"I know you've picked up some big words from your brother, but it doesn't matter. They're all the same. Fools with no concept of democracy. They'd rather watch the world burn and collapse together than work to give it hope for a future."

Franklin didn't want to argue with his father. His grasp of political ideologies around the world was minimal, but he was the only one in the family with any real-world experience overseas. He'd served multiple tours abroad and that gave him invaluable practical international relations knowledge.

"Still," his father continued. "I'd rather you didn't keep putting yourself in harm's way. These people are dangerous."

Franklin nodded, trying to formulate his rebuttal. His father was the one member of his family who probably understood better than any the need for justice, for fighting evil. He needed to appeal to that sense of absolute truth, good versus evil, and doing what's right.

"But Dad," he began.

"Don't argue with your father!" A female voice interrupted his argument mid-stream. His mother.

"Mom? Is that really you?"

"Don't be a fool, Frankie. Of course it's me," she tutted. "And your father only wants to protect you."

"I know that, but this is something I really need to do. To protect people. The people I care about."

His mother smiled. "I know, sweetie. I know."

"You—agree with me?"

"Of course I do. For the first time in your life, you're taking responsibility. You're being the protector."

His pride stung a little at the words, 'first time,' but then it dawned on him that his mother was approving. Of him. Pride swelled within his chest, bringing a tear to his eye.

"I'm so, so proud of you, Frankie. You're doing the right thing," she said. "But there's still one more person you need to talk to."

"Wait, mom—"

"Hi Franklin." The voice again shifted and he twisted in his seat to see his ex-wife. Joanna.

"J-Jo—" Franklin stammered and the tears began to flow like a waterfall. He couldn't see the road anymore through the blurred vision. "I'm—I'm so sorry...I couldn't save you."

"Franklin, Frankie." She reached out and touched him on the cheek. Her fingers felt warm, electric against his skin. "Don't do that to yourself. Don't say that. I made my choice."

"Do you—" he stammered. "Do you want me to avenge your death?"

"I want you to do the right thing."

"What does that mean?"

"It means I trust you. I have faith you'll make the right call."

And suddenly, she was gone. He sat all alone in the car again.

It had begun to snow outside; he hadn't even noticed with the steady stream of visitors. It wasn't enough to cover the ground, but it was beginning to leave patches here and there.

He couldn't feel the cold flakes on his skin, but he shivered anyway as the icy chill penetrated to his soul.

Franklin jolted awake as cold water drenched his face. He was back in the wooden chair, this time held down in the seat by a pair of abnormally strong paws. The two men who'd stepped out into the hallway had returned.

"There you are!" Phoenix's voice pierced through his groggy haze. "I worried we'd lost you there for a second."

"How long was I out?" he muttered. Shannon had to be looking for him by now. Maybe he could stall. If he held out long enough, she'd find him.

"Only a minute or two," she replied with a sickly, twisted smile. "But I'm glad you're awake. I wasn't going to, but Boris here convinced me to give you one more chance. He's a bit of a softy."

Franklin stared blankly, unsure what she meant.

"So let's try this one final time. How did you find me? Find us?"

Oh, he thought. *This again.*

"I—have—nothing to say," he sputtered.

"You see, Boris?" She turned toward the taller goon, who stood off to one side. "I told you. He's too stubborn. Or ignorant. I'm not sure which. But he's useless to us."

Franklin's head slumped to one side for a second before he straightened it. He still fought the loss of motor control from the taser bolts.

The room fell silent for a minute as Phoenix sauntered over to a dresser he hadn't noticed before and opened a drawer. She fiddled with something inside—Franklin could hear the rustling of paper—and then closed it again.

As she turned, he noticed she grasped something tightly in one fist. Something small.

"You must think I'm a brutal woman, don't you?"

"Evidence would suggest that, yes," he responded.

"That may be true," she nodded. Her voice took on a sing-song quality, almost hypnotic as she talked. "We have—all of us, all of my people—we have all been brutalized. Brutalized with loss. Loss of family or friends. Our homes and livelihoods. Our safety. For many of us, our very identity. Stolen, ripped from us...sometimes still alive and beating, sometimes already dead. So am I brutal? I suppose so. But life...it has made me so. It has made all of us so."

Franklin didn't know what to say. His wounds throbbed and a million tiny, painful spasms twitched in his muscles, as he was pinned to the chair by the two men. So he said nothing.

"This life, the one we chose...nay, the one we were forced into. The life we seek? It's not for the weak. Not for the kind," she smirked. "But we do what is necessary. We sacrifice so that others do not have to. We are, truly, the noble martyrs of a great cause. So brutal? Yes. But heroes, nonetheless."

"You're no hero. You're depraved. A monster," Franklin snarled as best he could.

"Heh," she chuckled. "A monster, you say? Yes. Yes, I suppose I am." At that, she straightened and spun on her heel to face the hairy goon. She held out the item in her hand and he took it. "Now kill him. And make it look good."

With one final glance at Franklin, she cocked her head as if to analyze his final expression, then swiftly exited the room, the door shutting behind her with an ominous thunk.

Franklin felt his skin tighten as he swallowed hard and gawked at the hairy Russian before him. The muscles in his neck tensed.

The Russian opened his palm to reveal what Phoenix had handed over. A pill bottle, the prescription kind you get from a pharmacy. He uncapped it and tossed the lid to the side, then tipped it over. A single, large, white pill fell out.

Franklin's eyes widened as the man moved toward him. The burly biceps of the man she called Boris clamped down on him from behind, and a hand grabbed him by the jaw. Franklin tried to fight it, but he wasn't strong enough anymore. The man pressed one finger along his right cheek and his thumb along the left, positioning them directly behind the last tooth on each side. With a little pressure and a lot of pain, Franklin felt his upper and lower jaws separate, forcing his mouth open. He tried to shake his head, but felt powerless. The hairy Russian stepped closer, then clamped his hand with the pill over Franklin's mouth, forcing the white capsule inside.

The other man forced Franklin's head to tilt back, while the hairy one kept his hand firmly over his mouth.

"Swallow!" one of them demanded. "Glotat'!"

Franklin tried to fight it, but there was no use. He was overmatched, in agony, and the alcohol wasn't helping. Reluctantly, he swallowed.

The Russians released him as the pill went down and he gagged for a second, bending over in the chair.

"What was in that pill?" Franklin demanded. "Was it poison?"

"Poison? No, no. Just something to relax you," one responded in his heavy accent. "Take a deep breath."

The other man handed him a bottle. More vodka, it smelled like. "Now drink."

"I'd rather not," Franklin protested.

"Drink! Or we make you drink. Same way we did with the pill."

Franklin stared back and forth between the two men, each looming over him. He was out of options.

He grabbed the bottle and took another swig, this time cursing aloud at the burn.

Chapter 29

The process for Whiplash to create entirely new documents for Eve was a lengthy one. He could've mocked up something simple to get her into a nightclub or past airport security in an hour, but she needed more than that. She needed something airtight and those took time.

As she waited, Eve took Whip's advice and walked out to the rink to relax and clear her head. She kept a baseball cap—identifying her as a Washington Nationals fan—pulled low over her brow, just in case anyone important happened in. But no one did. The rink was still empty except for that toddlers skate class at the far end. She watched as the blonde instructor—a college student, perhaps—patiently coached the little ones in circles. Few of the children managed to stay upright longer than a few seconds at a time, but they were cute to watch. And they were resilient. Adults who fell that many times wouldn't keep getting back up, but the kids kept at it. There was probably a lesson in there about staying the course and not letting life wear you down, but Eve was too tired to truly process it.

She eventually drifted away from the rink and found a couch in one of the offices to rest. She hadn't slept in who knows how many hours. And she needed to. She fell asleep in seconds.

The horse beneath Eve was an Arabian. Powerful. Beautiful. Hers. Technically, the horse was owned by her father, but it belonged to her. She's the one who took care of it, who groomed it, who rode it nearly every day. Oakley—named for her favorite outlaw, Annie Oakley—had been a gift on her 16th birthday. She didn't know how her father had managed to afford to purchase a horse, not on his modest salary, but she didn't question it. Computers were how she planned to pay her own bills someday and she possessed a real gift with them, but horses? That was her passion.

Sunset fast approached and she was still miles from home. This field belonged to Uncle Mark. He wasn't a real uncle, just one of her father's childhood friends, but he and his wife were around constantly when Eve was a child, so the moniker stuck. When his wife—Aunt Pearl—passed away, Eve and several other teenagers from the community pitched in with the chores to keep the farm running. It was essentially a part-time job to keep the high schoolers of the town busy, but they loved it. Still, Eve was always Uncle Mark's favorite and she was the only one allowed in the stables without a chaperone nearby.

As she watched the sun begin to dip below the horizon and a subtle orange streak across the sky, she smiled. Out here, it was peaceful. It was quiet. And it gave her time to think. But not today, because as the disappearing rays of sunlight pushed through the clouds, a warm, drizzling rain set it. The land needed the water; it cleansed the arid countryside, baptizing it anew. But it made for a less than enjoyable trail ride, so Eve tugged on the reins and directed her horse toward home.

Oakley broke into a trot for a few paces before sliding smoothly into a canter and finally launching into a dead run, his galloping long legs covering the ground with a powerful grace Eve wished she had, but it was a grace she could only manage virtually with her computers. She could feel pure joy rippling through the horse's powerful muscles beneath her; this is what Oakley had been created to do.

The two arrived at the barn mere seconds before the sky opened up, turning the drizzle into a downpour. Eve stroked the horse's muscular neck and dismounted. The horse shook its body, spraying water in all directions.

A pronged lightning blast flared across the sky and a stinging rain pummeled the metal roof as Eve began to unsaddle Oakley and hang her gear on the wall, creating a deafening cacophony. But it was a welcome percussion because in a strange way, the noise acted as one final insulation. With it, she couldn't hear a thing outside the barn, forcing her focus and her attention into the immediate task at hand. It also gave her an excuse to work slowly, to delay heading back to the house, as she waited for the torrent to abate.

As she finished untacking Oakley, the rain began to slow, but she still wasn't ready to go home. She reached into her pocket and pulled out a butterscotch candy, the same brand her grandmother always used to buy. Unwrapping the crinkly paper, Eve popped it in her mouth and then closed her eyes. As she listening to the raindrops drumming off the metal roof, she allowed the familiar flavor of a buttery brown sugar wash over her taste buds.

And then all of a sudden, the rain stopped.

Eve's eyes shot open. She was still in the office of the ice rink, still on the lumpy sofa. And Whip stood over her, saying her name.

"Wake up, wake up!" His eyes were wide and round, and he fidgeted, shifting his weight from one foot to the other, and back again.

"I'm awake, Whip." She stifled a yawn, then narrowed her stare. Whip had always been a little wired, but this time seemed different. "What is it?"

"You need to go."

"Are my papers done?"

"Yes, yes...here." He shoved a folder into her hands. "Now go!"

"What's the rush? I know I said I was in a hurry, but..."

He waved her off before blurting, "They know you're here."

Any cobwebs of sleep vanished and she bolted upright. "Who? Who knows I'm here, Whip?"

"Nasha Volya. They're coming."

"How—? How did they find me? I was so careful..."

Whip didn't answer, but his swaying became faster and sharper. Almost twitchy.

"Did—did you tell them?" she stammered.

"They threatened us, Eve. Anyone with information on you was supposed to report in at first contact. It's all over the dark web..."

"I can't believe—" Overcome with frustration, she slapped him. Hard. Right across the face.

"...and if they found out we'd hidden you," he sputtered, "they threatened to kill us and our families...but I had to warn you!"

"And I appreciate that. I do. But c'mon, man! There's a code..." She shook her head and darted across the hall to grab her go-bag. "How long do I have?" she called over her shoulder as he followed her.

"You'll have maybe a half hour's head start. At most. Probably less."

A concern suddenly hit her. "Do they know my new identity? The one you just created?"

"No!" He shook his head vehemently. "I didn't tell them. I'm trying to help!"

"Alright. That does help. A little." She slung her bag over her shoulder and headed for the exit.

"Wait…there's one more thing…"

She paused in the doorway and glanced back. "What is it, Whip? I don't have time for this…"

"The one who put out the wanted poster for you, who threatened us…he goes by the alias, Mercury."

"And…?"

"Well, I did some looking into him. There's a lot of chatter online. I couldn't track down an actual identity, but…" he gulped. "He—Mercury sounds dangerous. Be careful."

She didn't respond at first, but finally nodded. "Take care of yourself, Whip. These guys are deadly." She didn't wait for his response, but disappeared into the blackness of the night.

"Why are you doing this?" Franklin slurred. The alcohol had fully kicked in. He'd built up a fairly strong immunity over the years, but this was much stronger stuff than he'd gotten used to. Russia was infamous for their elevated rates of alcoholism and this had to be why.

"We make it look like suicide," one of the Russians grunted in broken English. "Then dump you in hotel. No one will question."

"But Shannon—"

"Maybe. But no one believe you. Everyone knows you're depressed. About your ex-wife."

Franklin's mind still functioned, but only just enough to be cognizant of his surroundings, not enough to actually do anything about it. The men might be right. Shannon would know better, of course, but was it really that much of a stretch? His depression was common knowledge. Everyone from his brother to Director Sloan had tried to cheer him up. Suicide would be an easy answer. Few, if any, would question it.

His body felt weird, as though being controlled by someone else. He could observe his arms moving and his hands opening and closing, but he was confident he wasn't doing it. He couldn't feel his hands, his arms, his legs. He couldn't feel the throbbing in his face anymore. He felt no pain at all anymore. In fact, he could barely even remember being in pain.

Worst of all, his sense of urgency had disappeared. His sense of the danger was lost. He felt groggy, yet somehow content. Well, not content, per se, but nihilistic. His depression had peaked and he was just lost in the moment. He'd lost track of time, how long he'd been captive in this chair, in this room, but he didn't care anymore. In that moment, nothing seemed to matter.

"On p'yan," the hairy Russian growled to his partner. "He's wasted. You have the gun?"

The other man nodded and produced a small, snub-nosed pistol from his waistband. The two approached Franklin, who tried to stand. But he couldn't get his balance and slumped into the seat.

"Relax. Rasslab'tes'," the thug with the gun insisted. "It's almost over."

The hirsute one placed his beefy paws on Franklin's shoulders, more to hold him steady rather than to pin him down, but it accomplished both. The other grabbed Franklin's hand and slid the gun into his palm.

Franklin didn't bother trying to resist anymore. He wasn't sure he could if he tried.

The man manipulated Franklin's fingers until he placed his right forefinger on the trigger.

A ghost of a smile crossed Franklin's lips. The Russian buffalo was right. It *was* almost over. He was going to see Joanna again.

"Stay still," the hairy one commanded. But Franklin didn't have any control over that anymore. "Don't worry, this won't hurt a bit."

Franklin watched as his arm, and the hand holding the gun, were lifted. He watched as his elbow was bent, his hand turning the barrel toward his own head. He felt none of it, but he could watch it happening. His life, playing on a silent movie screen.

The two men held Franklin's head and hand steady, positioning the pistol against his right temple. He closed his eyes.

"Gotovy?"

"Da. Strelyay."

BANG!

Chapter 30

*B*ANG!

Franklin flinched, but notably, he didn't die. His eyes snapped open just in time to witness one of the men—the hairy one, not the tall one—collapse in a heap at his feet. His head lolled to one side and unseeing eyes stared at Franklin, through Franklin. The man was dead before his body hit the floor.

BANG!

BANG!

BANG!

More gunshots rang out as the tall Russian drew his weapon and returned fire at the unknown attacker at the doorway. Using one of his massive paws, he grabbed Franklin by the shoulder and lifted him out of his chair effortlessly in an attempt to create a human shield. But Franklin was dead weight, so after a second, the man tossed him to the side like a rag doll. Franklin tumbled over, unable to break his fall because the drug slowed his reaction time, dulled his senses. His knees hit first, then his head smacked hard into the floor and stars danced before his eyes. But he was alive.

The fall left him dazed and he struggled to follow what was happening. He'd fallen facing the wrong way, but his body wouldn't cooperate to roll over. More blasts from various gun barrels echoed through the room, but after what seemed like an eternity, the second Russian toppled, his body hitting the ground with a loud thud that shook the floor. Then the gunfire ceased and the room fell quiet.

The pill they'd forced down his throat had screwed with all of his senses. His vision was dim and splotchy, at best. His ears rung like they were inside a cathedral bell tower at high noon. He couldn't even smell the putrid mixture of gunpowder and blood that coated him. And he felt cold. Surprisingly so. It was late August, he reasoned; even in South Dakota, it shouldn't feel this cold.

He felt, rather than saw, Shannon fall to her knees at his side. Her mouth was moving, as though talking to him. But it was gibberish; she seemed to be speaking in a language he couldn't understand. It might as well be Icelandic.

Why was she speaking Icelandic?

Then the lights began to fade and he didn't hear her at all.

The transition from SUV to plane had gone about as Sloan expected. He'd been driven straight into a private hangar and marched onto the plane at gunpoint. No chance to alert any security personnel, much less the Italian military. He didn't even see another soul until the pilot poked his head out of the cockpit.

The pilot was older than the other two, maybe in his early-50s, but Sloan had trouble pinpointing. He'd clearly had plastic surgery done—his skin stretched tautly and unnaturally over his pronounced cheekbones—and a bad spray tan gave him an orange hue. Dark black hair, as though dyed with shoe polish, had been slicked backward, highlighting a receding hairline. He spoke a few words to Mario—too quickly and softly for Sloan to make out—and then disappeared into the cockpit again, closing the door behind him.

The aircraft was an old cargo plane, the type where the back opened into a ramp for loading and unloading heavy boxes and other items, even vehicles, if that was needed. Mario and Luca had brought him into a separate section, nearer to the front and insulated from the rear door. Up here, it was much more suitable for passengers and had the feel of a private plane with comfortable seating, carpet, and a drink cart.

Sloan's hands had been bound to the arm of the chair with a heavy rope, giving him enough leeway to scratch his nose, but not tie his shoes, while Mario and Luca lounged on the plush bench seats of the jet. Less than ten minutes later, they were in the air, bound for who knows where.

For the first hour, Mario and Luca prattled in Italian while Sloan stared out the window. He spoke Italian, but their version was fast, accented, and laden with slang. And to top it off, they kept throwing in words Sloan recognized as Sicilian—often seen as an Italian dialect, but different enough that many argued it was its own language. The conversation between the two men sounded like a blend of the two—an intriguing observation that meant they likely grew up on the island of Sicily, but it made following their conversation impossible and Sloan stopped trying after a few minutes.

Out the window, he could track their flight based on sun position to recognize they were flying west, but heavy cloud cover meant any orientation by landmass below would be impossible.

His bonds were tight on his wrist, but wrapped loosely around the metal arm of the airplane seat. The rope was too thick to break or rip, but a rope this size had disadvantages. A larger diameter also means a larger knot, with more grip. And large ropes are just a collection of smaller ropes. If he could fray a few of those, the tensile strength of the entire cable would plummet exponentially. Feeling around the underside of the metal revealed a rusty patch, but nothing sharp enough to use. It was likely to be a long flight though; he'd find a way to improvise.

There's little point in breaking free mid-flight, he rationalized. There was nowhere to go. Even if he overpowered Mario and Luca, he'd still need the pilot to land, where he'd undoubtedly be met by more men with guns. *Unless...*his eyes scanned the interior of the plane. Three backpacks were tucked onto a high shelf. To an untrained eye, they were unremarkable, but Sloan recognized the trademark signs of parachute sacks. If he managed to overpower the men, he could steal a chute and jump out...

...right over the Atlantic Ocean. Except for maybe the final couple hours of their trip, when they'd be traversing south along the eastern seaboard of North America, he'd have no way to get to shore. Barring a miracle, that was as good as a death sentence. And he'd always hated oceans too. He could certainly swim, but as a child, he'd witnessed a shark attack a surfer during a family vacation and he'd never quite been able to rid his mind of the screams. He didn't know if the young man had survived or died, but it didn't matter now. The ocean hid way too many dangers beneath its tranquil surface. He hadn't gone further than knee-deep in its waters since. Even now, it made him shudder to think about landing in its vast expanse, unable to see land in any direction, not knowing what moved beneath, just waiting...waiting for death...

And of course, that was if he managed to even open the door, which was unlikely. Doors in pressurized planes weren't meant to be opened mid-flight. Most had an override lock controlled by the pilot in the cockpit, but the differences in air pressure inside and outside created thousands of pounds of pressure keeping that door sealed shut.

"Hey! Walter Mitty!"

Sloan's head snapped up to see both Mario and Luca staring at him.

"Can you settle a debate for us?" Mario asked, a mischievous grin on his face. "You see, there's all sorts of myths and legends about the great Jacob Sloan and the Midnighters. Did you really break *into* a Soviet gulag and then back *out*?"

Sloan shrugged. "It wasn't hard."

Luca chuckled. "How did you manage that?"

"I bribed a guard."

"That's it?" His eyebrows arched and eyes widened.

"That's it," Sloan shrugged. "Look, here's the thing you need to know about the Soviets." The two Italians leaned forward, eager grins on their faces. "There's no such thing as a true believer in socialism."

Mario frowned. "What do you mean? Of course there is..."

"I mean," Sloan smirked, "I gave the guard my shiny new Rolex and he looked the other way. And he wasn't an exception. All socialists become capitalist pigs when backs are turned and cameras are off."

Mario and Luca fell back into their seats, laughing. Sloan smiled. Maybe he'd found his way out. The two men loved a good wartime story, especially one at the expense of the Russians. Despite the long history of friendship between Italy and Russia, there still existed a wariness among the Italian civilian population about the Russian superpower and telling stories that cut the global giant down to size were beloved. And he had plenty of those to tell.

If he engendered a little bit of goodwill—a friendly camaraderie, that might relax them enough to let down their guard.

And so Sloan regaled Mario and Luca with wild tales of his Midnighter exploits. Most were true, some embellished for a more compelling story, and a few were just outright fabricated, but his captors hung on every word.

The story-telling lasted for hours, but when the conversation finally died, you could almost feel the cabin take a deep breath and relax. A few too many drinks and an exciting, edge-of-your-seat conversation and both of his captors were soon napping.

And that was exactly what Sloan needed.

Chapter 31

As Franklin came to, he gradually became aware of his new surroundings. Whitewashed walls on all four sides, a faint beeping…he was in a hospital. The room was sizable enough, but the overhead light had a soft flicker every five or six seconds that made him feel uncomfortable.

A knit blanket had been pulled up to his chin. His skin itched beneath it and after a few uncomfortable seconds, he discarded it on the floor with a painful grunt. In fact, every movement he made was agonizing.

After a short coughing fit, he took stock of his injuries. He flexed and wiggled his fingers; they worked. Same with his toes. He turned his head left and right. His neck protested the movement, but it, too, was functional. His cheek and temples throbbed, his side ached, and his entire body felt like it'd barely survived the worst workout of his life. But he was alive and all body parts were still functioning.

"Well, well…awake now, are we?" A rasp resounded from the doorway as a portly nurse bumbled into the room and grabbed the clipboard hanging from the base of his bed. The woman looked to be in her late-forties, a fact her obviously-bleached hair and thick makeup failed to hide. She wore a set of scrubs two sizes too small and the fabric stretched at her chest. Franklin assumed she did it on purpose. Another way to make herself look younger than she was.

Franklin tried to mumble something, but his voice caught in his throat and he coughed.

"Easy now," she cautioned.

"I—I—I'm awake," Franklin finally managed to whisper.

"What happened to you?" She poked her head up from the clipboard and sidled around the bed to talk to him. "Not often we get someone in here as beat up as you. You look terrible."

Franklin shook his head, half because he didn't want to tell her and half because it hurt to talk.

"It says here..." She glanced over her notes. "A broken rib, fractured cheekbone, cracked tooth, borderline alcohol poisoning, chafing on your wrists indicative of being bound, hundreds of small muscular tears you usually find in electrocution cases, bruises all over...and that doesn't count the nasty gash you have there." She pointed to her own temple. "Probably got a concussion from that."

Franklin still didn't respond, but with each affliction she listed, he found himself wincing as though the mere announcement of his injuries made them hurt worse.

"Let me guess..." She smiled. "You had a few too many of these..." She mimed taking a shot. "Maybe more than a few too many. And managed to get yourself into a bar fight with a guy a lot bigger than you."

Franklin grunted. "Something like that," he mumbled.

"Figured as much. We've all been there. Oh boy, when I was your age..." She paused, as though she'd revealed too much about her own age. "You know, I can't tell that story. That would be wildly inappropriate. I'm a nurse and this is a hospital." She cackled at her own joke, lost in some timeworn memory, but she was the only one who laughed.

Franklin attempted to swallow, but his mouth was too dry and it ended as a painful cough.

"Oh hon, here…" She handed him a small plastic cup of water that seemingly materialized out of nowhere. "Drink this. It'll help."

Franklin eagerly lapped up the water, the liquid sloshing over his cheeks and dripping onto his gown.

"Good, good," the nurse murmured. After he finished, she refilled the cup at the sink and handed it back. "The doctor will be in to see you soon." She picked up a remote control from a small table at his bedside and, with the press of a button, the screen on a mounted television on the far wall crackled to life.

She handed the remote to Franklin and left. After watching her disappear around the nurses' station, he flipped through the channels for a minute before settling on an old episode of *M*A*S*H*, one of his father's favorites. He remembered this episode too; a concert pianist had damaged the nerves in his hand, never to play again, and Major Winchester—not the most sympathetic character—was tasked with consoling him. It was oddly moving and displayed a softer side of an oft-snobby surgeon.

"More than anything in my life, I wanted to play, but I do not have the gift. I can play the notes," Major Winchester explained to the injured soldier. *"But I cannot make the music!"* The agony was etched across his face as he implored the young man to understand, *"The true gift is in your head…and in your heart…and in your soul."*

A small tear squeezed its way out of Franklin's eye and traversed over his cheek, along his jawline, and dropped to the bed sheet. It wasn't the speech itself that brought out the emotion—though it was certainly affecting, and a strong acting performance by David Ogden Stiers—but rather it reminded him of his own childhood.

The many evenings spent as a child, sitting on his father's lap, watching *M*A*S*H* on a classic shows television channel. His father was a soldier, waiting to be deployed in those early years, and something about that show resonated with the Holt family. And even after Irving Holt had been deployed overseas, Franklin and his brother, Jeremiah, would still watch re-runs of the medical comedy/drama whenever it came on. It was their own childish way of feeling close to their father, despite being on opposite sides of the world.

He closed his eyes and, without meaning to, found himself whispering a short prayer. Not to anyone or any god in particular, but he asked for protection over his father and brother. Over his whole family. Somehow, he knew his brother would be proud of him for that.

"Mr. Holt!"

Franklin's eyes left the screen and quickly found the source of the voice.

A young doctor in a long, flowing white lab coat had entered the room. He was dressed sharply, in a collared shirt and tie, and wore his hair in a perfectly-coifed look that suggested his bathroom cabinet was full of mousse products. His face was oval and clean-shaven and he appeared to be in impeccable physical shape. He paraded in holding a clipboard and never looked up from it as he spoke.

"Mr. Holt, Mr. Holt...can I call you Franklin? Frank?" The doctor talked fast and didn't wait for a response before forging ahead. "I'm Dr. Chandler Craig. You can call me Dr. Craig."

"I—uh," Franklin stammered.

"We're gonna keep you here another day or two for recovery and observation. Your injuries are numerous, but largely superficial and should heal, albeit with possible scarring. But we're a little concerned about possible internal bleeding. We'll run tests in the morning, but otherwise, you just need to take it easy and recuperate. I'm going to have a nurse up your meds a touch so you can sleep. Capiche?"

"Umm, yes...?"

"Excellent. I'll be by again later." Dr. Craig tapped the clipboard twice with his pen, creating a sharp staccato that echoed in the sterile room. He glanced up and his eyes met Franklin's for the first time. Then, he turned on his heel and sauntered out.

"You what?!" Marcus Hartwell erupted. "How?" He grabbed the nearest thing on his desk, a stone paperweight given to him by a group of seventh graders from his district on their field trip to DC, and chucked it across the room. It smashed against the far wall, leaving a sizable dent in the plaster.

At the commotion, his assistant Lydia burst into the room. He growled and grabbed a stapler to hurl at her head. He missed by several feet, but she yelped and darted out, the door slamming closed behind her. The stapler snapped in two, but otherwise fell harmlessly to the carpet.

"How did he escape?" he snarled into the phone. "You promised me you had this under control. You swore he'd be dead. Today. Yesterday!"

He fell silent as he listened to the sniveling excuses. There was not one competent person he could count on. The only other person he knew would get things done was Phoenix, but she didn't listen to him. In fact, she considered it a point of pride that he didn't scare her.

"Do you know where he went?" he barked. He could hear the blood rushing through his head, pulse pounding in his ears. "Well if you know that, then why are you talking to me? Go find him. And this time don't screw this all to hell. Because if you do, you're gonna find yourself in the market for a new head. And those are hard to find."

He hung up the phone without waiting for the response and gently placed the device in the pocket of his jacket, which he'd draped over the back of his office chair.

Then, in one fluid motion driven by a rage-filled scream, he swept everything off his desk.

Pens went flying. His lamp shattered. Papers tore, crumpled, and tumbled to the floor.

He didn't trust his men to find Franklin. They were fools. Imbeciles. And Franklin apparently had a guardian angel. First, his damn ex-wife saves his life, then he escapes the shooting at the DC motel, and now he managed to slip out from beneath the noses of two professional killers.

Maybe there was another way...

Franklin was protected, it seemed. Almost supernaturally so... But that wasn't the only way to hurt a man. And he'd suffered loss before. His ex-wife, his mother. That was it. His weakness.

He might have a guardian angel keeping him alive, but the people around him didn't.

An evil smile crept across his face and he retrieved the cell phone from his jacket, still hanging loosely on the chair.

There was one call he could make. To end this.

It was time to bring Typhos back into the fold.

Chapter 32

Franklin spent the next few hours drifting in and out of consciousness, thanks to the increase in dosage from his IV drip. At one point, he felt sure Phoenix had snuck into the hospital disguised as a nurse, only to be escorted out by a security guard. Another time, he was confident he was being cared for by an alien life form from Melmac.

Both felt extremely real.

When he awakened from the haze, the sun was peaking over the treetops outside his window and his pillow was damp with sweat. Or tears. He wasn't sure which. Maybe both.

The morning dragged and by noon, Franklin was stir-crazy and ready to get out of the hospital. He was a sitting duck, trapped in a prison of white-washed walls and beeping monitors. But his injuries had been deemed too serious by his nurse.

He could just check himself out, he reasoned. But he honestly wasn't sure he'd be any better off. He was injured, with a target on his back. And hospitals had security.

Then again, Silas was killed in a hospital, wasn't he? Security hadn't helped him much.

Franklin couldn't stay here forever.

Shannon had visited him that morning, bringing news from the Badlands igloos. There'd been three casualties, none of them Phoenix or Hook. A guard and the two goons who'd tried to kill Franklin. But Phoenix had slipped away again. Shannon hadn't even seen her.

She'd also updated him on the others. Sloan was missing in Europe. His body wasn't recovered in the bombing in Prague, which meant he'd almost certainly survived. But he never checked in. They hadn't heard from him since and Franklin could tell that made her nervous. She kept pacing and rubbing the back of her neck when she thought he wasn't looking, but her constantly furrowed brow was unmistakable.

After Shannon left around ten that morning, however, he hadn't had any visitors for hours. That was expected. No one even knew he was in the hospital. He'd made sure they didn't call his father. Or his brother. No need to worry them...or put them in danger.

Still, as the hours dragged on, he found himself needing to hear a familiar voice. Something, someone to remind himself why he was doing this. But how could he, without revealing his condition or his location?

He'd never be able to fool his father. Both of his parents were able to read through his tone, ever since the boys were young. They'd never gotten away with a lie in their lives. But he might—just might—be able to fool his brother. The two of them had spent most of their childhood playing pranks on each other. He might be able to pull one over on him again. For a couple minutes at least, if he was lucky.

His phone had been recovered from the igloo— Shannon told him it'd been discarded on a table—so he took a deep breath, coughed to shake out the rasp in his voice, and dialed the number.

After a few rings, he heard the telltale sounds of the receiver being picked up.

"Hello?"

Tara Holt's dulcet tones echoed through the phone's speaker. His brother's wife was one of Franklin's favorite people in the world. Always ready to protect her loved ones, she'd accepted Franklin as family from Day 1, without question. In many ways, she reminded him of his mother: sweet, loving, but tough as nails when she needed to be. Tara was the backbone of Jay's little family and, in many ways, had stepped into that role for their entire family since Franklin's mother had passed.

"Hi Tara," Franklin said. He spoke softly, barely above a whisper, in hopes of hiding the rasp in his voice.

"Franklin!" she exclaimed. She sounded genuinely excited to hear from him. He couldn't help but crack a smile, which he immediately regretted as his bruised cheekbones protested the movement. "How are you?" she bubbled. "I haven't seen you in forever! When are you coming by the house again?"

"Soon, I hope," he answered. And he meant it.

"Your brother says you're off doing secret work for the government? Is that true?"

Franklin smiled again. Leave it to Jay to leave out a few details.

"Something like that," he said through a forced chuckle. He supposed it was true, in a way. He was working *with* government agents, anyway.

"Are you staying safe?"

Ah, there it is. The first lie.

"Of course, Tara. Of course." He gritted his teeth, hoping those words sounded truthful coming from a hospital bed where he was too injured to be discharged.

He'd been in a fight for his life now twice in the past few days. Three times if you count the casino, which he didn't. He wasn't in mortal danger there. At least not in the immediate sense.

"I'm so glad. Jay will be too. He's worried about you, ya know," she insisted. "More than anyone, I think."

He knew more than anyone too, Franklin mused. *The worry was appropriate.*

"Jay actually isn't here right now. He's on campus."

That's right. He teaches today.

"That's okay. Just tell him I called."

"Do you want to speak to KJ? I know he'd love to say hello." She didn't wait for his answer and he could hear her call out for her son to come to the phone.

Franklin considered hanging up, but he froze. He hadn't seen KJ in a long time, hadn't heard the child's voice in months. He wasn't sure he was ready.

Finally, though, he heard a soft voice say "Unca Frank?"

Franklin exhaled sharply and took a deep breath. "Hey buddy."

"Unca Frank! Where are you?"

"Somewhere boring, little man," he chuckled.

"Oh okay."

Kids are so easily satisfied. Jay wouldn't have let it go that easy. Then again, he doubted KJ knew what South Dakota was, much less where it was.

"How's school?" Franklin asked, eager to turn the subject away from himself. At six, KJ was barely old enough for school, but he'd been excited to start first grade this Fall.

"It's okay. Wanna hear me count to one hundred?" KJ joyfully started before Franklin had a chance to respond.

He really is his mother's son, Franklin chuckled. "One, two, three, four, five, six, eight, ten, seven eleven…"

"Good job, honey," Franklin heard Tara say before taking the phone back. "Sorry about that," she apologized. "He just learned that this week and, as you can tell, it could use some work."

"He'll get there," Franklin responded. "He's a smart boy. With you and Jay as parents, it's only a matter of time before he's top of the class."

"KJ's just too busy to learn, or to pay attention. He's constantly moving. Not like he has attention-deficit or anything…he can focus just fine on the things he wants to. He just has places to be and things to do that he thinks are more important than counting to one hundred."

"If I remember right, Jay was the exact same way as a kid. And he turned out alright."

"Eh, he's okay," Tara laughed and Franklin smiled again. *Ouch…*

"Can you just tell Jay I called?" he requested.

"Of course," she said sweetly. "Just take care of yourself, Franklin."

"I am," he insisted.

"Oh, I know the sound of a hospital room when I hear it, even through a phone. I'll add your lies to my list of prayers. You just be safe."

Franklin didn't answer right away. *She knew. Just like Mom would have.* "I will," he finally whispered. "But don't tell Jay that part. Please?"

"Of course not, hon. He's worried enough, as it is. You just make it home safely, in one piece, and you can tell the whole story then. Deal?"

"Deal."

Franklin hung up the phone and laid the device on the bedside table. He should've known better than to try to fool Tara. But in a way, he was glad she knew. It wasn't just his secret anymore. He had a confidante, one that wasn't a government operative. A family member, even. And one he could trust not to divulge his secret like the town gossip.

He leaned his head back into the hospital-provided pillow and closed his eyes, more assured now of what—of who—he was doing this for. For his brother and his wife. For their son. For his father. For his mother and his own wife, already gone. His agony began to fade, as his consciousness drifted and soon, he was sound asleep again.

———⌇———

As soon as he confirmed both Mario and Luca were asleep, Jacob Sloan set to work. He'd had time during his storytelling to figure out a plan. He'd actually pulled off something similar during one of his missions in the '90s in Bosnia, though not on a plane.

Of course, that time he had a partner backing him up and he was nearly thirty years younger, but there were fewer men this time. At least he hoped so. There was no way of knowing who waited on the receiving end when the plane landed.

Not yet.

First step was to get out of his rope bonds though. He quickly loosened his watch and slid it over his wrist until it hung loosely around the rope and between his hands. The watch had been a gift from his son and he paused for a second to consider any other option, but it was his only choice. He gripped it tightly, muting the sound with a beefy palm, and pressed downward with a grimace. With a little leverage from his other hand, he felt the glass face crack and finally break. A glance at his captors confirmed they still snored, sound asleep, dead to the world in drunken stupors.

Perfect.

Carefully, he extracted the largest shard of glass and, after testing its edge, he twisted his wrist around and sawed at the knot. Within mere seconds, the cords began to fray and in less than two minutes, he'd compromised the threads enough to unravel them completely with brute force.

He flexed his wrists. A dull ache carried into his forearms and the skin had been rubbed raw.

Pushing himself to his feet as silently as possible, he stretched, relieving the stiffness that had built up in hours of sitting. He didn't recover as quickly as he used to and he would need to be agile.

He edged over to Mario and Luca, both still passed out cold. This part wasn't going to be hard. Even at his age, he could handle two drunk idiots. Still, doing this with as little noise as possible was important. If he managed to incapacitate and gag them without the pilot having any inkling there was something wrong, that would be ideal. Cockpits are fortified, so anything he could do to keep the man flying and acting normally— and not radioing ahead for backup—would benefit him once they landed.

After looking around for a few moments, Sloan's eyes settled on the seatbelts. They'd make nice gags to keep the men silent when they awoke. Using the same glass shard he'd used to free himself, he quickly cut two pieces of the material. He ripped off his own shirt sleeves to serve as the ball to shove in their mouths.

He started with Mario, who seemed infinitely more competent than his partner. On the off chance the second man woke up before he finished with the first, he'd rather it be Luca, who would be easier to control in a panic than the better trained man.

He hesitated for a second to examine the scars that covered the man's face. He counted at least three burn marks, but the most prominent was a jagged scar running along his jawline, ear to chin. It was old, but he could tell it had been deep. He shuddered to think what might've caused that.

Shaking away that image, Sloan moved quickly, deftly removing the firearm from Mario's waistband, his phone from his pocket, and binding his limp arms together and to the arm rests. He even managed to get the gag inserted into Mario's mouth and nearly bound before the man began to stir. By then, all Mario could manage were a few angry groans of confusion.

Luca was even easier, as he stayed passed out the entire time despite Mario's increasingly frantic kicking and grunting.

The whole process took maybe half an hour to get both secured and silent. As soon as he finished, he began a search of the cabin, starting with a row of cabinets near the cockpit. He wasn't sure what he was looking for, but you never know what might come in handy.

A couple parachute backpacks caught his eye first, tucked behind the door on the far right, but a mid-flight jump from this plane would be impossible. Another cabinet revealed several expensive bottles of Italian wine tucked away. He was surprised the two passed-out winos hadn't already emptied them. Those might have been useful in a different scenario, but a broken bottle wasn't the most practical option given that he already had a couple pistols to work with.

The final cabinet, however, proved fruitful. A tool kit was stashed in the back. He unzipped the bag to find all kinds of handy items. He dumped the contents into one of the airplane seats and began to sort through it.

Working quickly, he found a foldable knife, a screwdriver, and a coil of wire. All three had seen better days as the knife, in particular, was quite dull, but he stuffed them into his pockets all the same. *You never know...*

When Luca eventually emerged from his drunken coma, Sloan addressed them.

"As long as neither of you cause any trouble, no one here will die," he began. "You're both good men just following orders and I respect that. I truly do. But I can't have you interfering with my plans or alerting the pilot, so your...restraints...seemed necessary."

Mario's eyes narrowed and his brow furrowed as fury raged from his glare.

"That said, I need to know something, so I'm prepared to negotiate. Whichever of you tells me how many people I can expect to find in the welcoming party when this plane lands...that person will leave here with their kneecaps still intact."

Both men's eyes widened and Luca snorted through the gag.

"You both were so curious to hear stories of my years spent in black ops. Now you get to experience it firsthand." Sloan flashed a slight grin, then frowned, his eyes narrowing into slits. "I'll give you ten minutes to think it over and decide who's going to cave first."

He reached over and patted both men on their knees, then stood and returned to his seat.

Time to wait...

Chapter 33

The next time Franklin awoke in his hospital bed was different. His body still ached, but the medications that dulled his senses were wearing off. The alcohol poisoning had been finally cleared from his system, which made a huge difference in how he felt. His injuries—while still serious—didn't seem as restricting as they had before. His side was tender—the nurse had diagnosed him with a broken rib, hadn't she?

His whole head felt swollen and a dull soreness engulfed his entire body. Every muscle ached. But he was conscious, thinking clearly, and largely mobile—albeit slowly. It could've been worse.

Maybe it was the paranoia brought on by dreams of Phoenix disguising herself as a nurse to finish him off, but he felt uneasy lying there, especially as the drugs continued to wear off. He remembered how easily they'd gotten to Silas, killed him, and that had been in a prestigious DC hospital. He'd received good care here in South Dakota, but he couldn't imagine their security was at the same level as a facility that routinely housed famous politicians and other members of the political glitterati.

Thankfully, Shannon surprised him with a change of clothes and a discharge order from the doctor. He didn't ask, but he suspected she'd pulled her identification to secure his release.

He waited until he'd eased himself into the car before asking, "Where are we going?"

"The airport in Rapid City," she answered. "I'm sorry that lunch in your mom's hometown will have to wait, but we're heading straight back to D.C. I think we've learned all we can from here. Phoenix is long gone."

"What about the igloos though?"

"I called that in to local authorities, who are currently combing through the buildings, but I doubt they'll find much. I also left a message for Eve, but haven't heard back." She pulled the car out of the parking lot and onto a highway. A sign announced the airport was six miles away. "We came here to find Phoenix and we did that... temporarily. But I think I know where she's heading."

"D.C. again? Why?"

"Because of my other news," she turned her head a couple inches toward Franklin and smiled. "Graham O'Brian is talking. Again."

"O'Brian??" Franklin's surprise mixed with a surge of anger. This was a man who'd betrayed Joanna and tried to kill her. While he hadn't succeeded initially, it was his actions that ultimately led to her death and now he wanted a new plea deal. "What's he saying? I thought he already told us all he knew."

"That he wants to talk to me."

"And that means Phoenix will...what? Why would that bring her to DC?"

"She's not going to want him to talk. I imagine she'll make a move to take him out."

"I'm okay with that," he muttered. "But isn't he in protective custody already?"

"He's in isolation, if that's what you mean. No other prisoners will get to him."

"You're worried about a guard," he breathed out in a sigh.

"If the Volya can infiltrate Congress, they can surely get a guard on the inside." She nodded. "I've ordered no one to enter his cell until I arrive. Hopefully, that will keep him alive."

"Do we want to keep him alive?"

Shannon reached out and laid her hand on Franklin's arm. "I know. But that's not how we do things. Society—heck, civilization itself—rests on the foundational ethic that we treat our criminals better than they treated their victims. He'll get justice, I assure you—maybe even death, when the trials all finish—but he'll get it through the system. Besides, we need him alive long enough to squeeze every last bit of information out of him. If he's talking again, we might learn something useful to help us destroy the entire organization."

After a few seconds, Franklin grunted his approval. The rest of the ride to the airport was in silence.

He didn't like it, but she was right. He wanted the man to suffer, but there was a bigger story at play here. This wasn't just a personal vendetta; there was a country at stake, a global system being threatened. And as much as he might want personal revenge, he needed to let this play out. He needed to wait.

Eve wasn't an expert, but even she recognized a tail when she spotted one. A black Chevrolet moved into her lane, two cars behind her. She'd seen the same black Chevrolet before, several times, always two to four cars behind. She'd lost sight of it a few times, but it always reappeared, even as she made several seemingly-random turns.

The windows were tinted and the glare made it impossible to get a good look at the driver, but she could make out a profile of a long-haired woman wearing glasses. Always the same person, always the same car.

She turned a corner and stepped on the accelerator. The car lurched and engine whined as its gears struggled to shift faster than its old transmission could handle.

Why didn't she have a nicer car? One capable of handling simple acceleration?

She knew the answer to that. All of her money went into her work, her systems, her security components. The same systems she'd been forced to scuttle and abandon in her loft. Then again, she never expected to be in a car chase either, of any kind. This wasn't her world. She operated in cyberspace, not real world spycraft. But here she was, and she would have to make do with what she had. It was just a shame that what she had was a piece of junk.

Her initial attempts at evasion didn't work. The Chevy made the same turn and kept pace. She'd never be able to lose the tail through speed or agility. It would have to be something else. Which gave her an idea. If she couldn't outrun the Chevy, maybe she could lose it in traffic. She swung the wheel and pulled onto an expressway ramp leading into the District. The Chevy made the same decision, always staying two to three cars behind. Within minutes, she was crossing the bridge and re-entering DC. It was nighttime, so any traffic had disappeared and gone home, unfortunately. The District is a heavy commuter city. When things shut down, almost everyone leaves. But there were exceptions if you knew where to look.

The way she saw it, she had two viable options. Northwest of downtown was an area known as Adams Morgan, known for its Victorian-style rowhouses, murals, and diverse establishments. One of the few areas in DC with a truly vibrant nightlife, she hoped she might be able to blend into the crowds out for a night on the town. But it wasn't a large area.

The other option she considered lay further south, along the river, near the colleges. Most people know the District of Columbia for its political sphere, but it was home to several prominent universities as well. Two of them lay in the eastern part of DC: George Washington and Georgetown, and George Mason was just across the river. A mess of students going to the bars or clubs, having a late dinner out with friends, or simply loitering and exploring the streets of the city would provide excellent cover.

Or was it still too early for students? Classes didn't start until next week, but this was the weekend they all moved in. That meant this would be the first weekend they were able to go out…and the only weekend before classes—and thus, homework—began. She decided it was worth the risk.

Taking the ramp into Georgetown, she sighed in relief as, almost immediately, she saw people lining the sidewalks and cars lining the streets. She'd made the right decision.

With the car "chase" slowed to a crawl through stoplights, stop signs, and dodging pedestrians, she managed to put extra distance between herself and the tail within only a couple blocks. When she finally felt comfortable, she swung her car onto a side street that dipped down by the river and ran underneath the busy highway above. She pulled into a parking garage and parked, waiting.

After a minute, the black Chevrolet inched along the same road, but after a tense moment, it drove past and Eve whispered a silent prayer of thanks for the shadows shrouding her vehicle. She grabbed her bag and a baseball cap from her backseat, pulling the brim low over her eyes, then exited the vehicle.

For all its flaws, DC had a robust public transportation system. It was finicky, never on time, and expensive, but it was intricate and covered nearly the entire city, even extending out into the broader metropolitan areas in Virginia and Maryland. Which was good, because she'd be relying on that system of metro trains and buses from here on out.

As she descended into the Georgetown metro station, she couldn't help but wonder what her next move should be. She'd landed on the radar of someone. Whip told her it was the Nasha Volya, but she hadn't been able to identify the person in the car. She couldn't go home, couldn't go to any of her immediate family. She had to assume her normal routes and stops had been compromised, just in case.

She could always go straight to the NSA. The National Security Agency had security and, despite butting heads over the years, they respected her. They respected her work. They'd even used it a few times. But could she trust them? The Volya had infiltrated government agencies before. They'd killed Joanna, hadn't they? And the FBI was an intelligence agency every bit as secure as the NSA. Powerful people had been uncovered and there was no guarantee they hadn't gotten to the NSA too.

Maybe it was time to vanish, to lay low for a while. She wouldn't be able to help the others, but she wasn't any good to them on the run either. She needed to get off grid. Temporarily.

But she could help in other ways. And she knew the right place to go.

Chapter 34

It took Mario and Luca less than two minutes to both cave and reveal that only two men would be waiting for them on the ground. They clearly valued keeping their kneecaps and he didn't blame them. He didn't admit it aloud, but he was glad they did. While that was certainly a move he would've pulled off in his younger days in the field, that wasn't him anymore. He was a different man now, one more measured and less reactionary, less violent.

They also quite willingly gave him details on their destination—a private airstrip in Baltimore County—and where the men would likely be standing as they waited for the plane to taxi into a closed hangar. It was amazing what you can accomplish through fear.

The best information comes out of fear of pain, not actual pain. In fact, once you cross the line into exacting pain—physical torture—any details gleaned must be treated as suspect and requiring outside verification. At that point, the person is willing to say or do anything to make the torment stop and will spill what they think you want to hear, not the actual truth.

It wasn't that physical pain was useless; it often proved handy when playing captives off each other or proving you aren't bluffing. But it was hardly efficient and often produced bad information. Another reason Sloan was glad he didn't have to go that route.

When the plane did land, it followed the exact plan the two men had explained and within a few minutes, they'd taxied inside a private airplane hangar and the gigantic hangar door closed behind them.

Satisfied everything was in place and ready to go, Sloan took a moment to close his eyes and shut out the world. He fought to steady his breathing. He'd done a lot of crazy things over the years—most on behalf of his government, even if they'd never admit it—but he'd never needed to fight his way off an airplane, through a hangar held by terrorists, and escape a private airport. A clear head would make that much easier.

Showtime.

Sloan pressed his body against the wall just around the corner from the cockpit. As the pilot emerged, Sloan wrapped a beefy arm around his neck and squeezed, flexing his biceps. It was a trick he learned in boot camp. If you position the person's windpipe in the crook of your elbow, your muscles squeeze the carotid arteries on either side, cutting off oxygen to the brain. It knocked someone out much faster than suppressing their oxygen intake into their lungs. A person can still remain conscious without breathing for a while…just try holding your breath. But cut off flow directly to the brain and they'd be out cold in a fraction of the time. And if you use your other hand to add pressure to the back of their head, you push their neck into your arm. It hastened the process. Within seconds, the pilot's arms stopped flailing and he slumped over, unconscious.

He'd removed Mario's and Luca's weapons, but neither carried any extra magazines of ammunition— *amateur move*, Sloan grumped. That only gave him about twelve rounds total and one of those guns was that infernal Welrod. It was a handy weapon when you needed quiet, but it was most effective at close range, pressed up against the person execution-style. Sloan considered himself to be extraordinarily well-trained in firearms, but even he wasn't used to such an old, unusual weapon.

The other gun was a more standard Glock, something he was extremely familiar with. He'd lean hard on those rounds and he couldn't squander them. He was grateful there were only two men waiting for him. Wait...were there only two? Mario and Luca had sworn it, but he'd almost forgotten to verify.

He peeked out one of the windows to see two men—they were telling the truth—waiting at the end of a concrete walkway. Both looked trim and in shape, with the thin, but muscular physique you might find in a wrestler, and were dressed nicely in dark suits. One was bald, but with a thick goatee that dominated his face. The other was clean-shaven, but kept his hair slicked back in a manner one could only achieve with excessive amounts of hair gel.

Sloan tucked one of the guns into his waistband to free a hand and, with a little effort, hefted open the door of the plane. It swung outward and downward to create a staircase to the ground. He stayed out of sight as it settled into position.

At the sudden mechanical noise, Goatee and Hair Gel straightened and descended a short set of steps to the hangar floor to greet their new arrivals. They strode six feet apart from one another—a military tactical move to make aiming harder for any enemies—and they moved light on their feet, indicating an agility their appearances belied. But neither suspected a thing; in fact, they laughed as they ambled toward the plane, their hands free and open, nowhere near a gun or hidden holster. At this angle, though, he'd need them to get much closer before he could take them out. He might be able to drop one pretty quickly, but unless his aim with an unfamiliar weapon was miraculously impeccable, he'd never take out both of them before one managed to return fire. It would be a one-in-a-million double shot.

As they got within about thirty feet of the base of the staircase, though, they paused as though waiting for something. He couldn't read their lips from this distance, but he watched their eyes scan the aircraft. Both of their hands disappeared under their jackets, extracting guns from waistband holsters. The two men fanned out, putting distance between each other and turning that one-in-a-million shot into a completely impossible task. Sloan swore under his breath. *What had spooked them?* He knew they couldn't spot him from his vantage point. *Was there a sign Mario and Luca had failed to tell him about? Something he'd been supposed to do to tell the waiting party all was okay?*

He turned around and ducked into the main cabin.

Are you kidding me?

Luca had managed to sit up straight from where Sloan had carefully laid him across the seats. It was pretty obvious that he was now visible through the cabin's windows to Goatee and Hair Gel outside. They had spotted him bound and gagged, notably not the prisoner they were expecting to find.

This escape just got much harder. But not impossible.

He just needed to improvise.

Keeping low to avoid giving the two men outside any clean shot through a window, he rolled up his sleeves and stomped over to Luca. He quickly grabbed the man by the arm and yanked him to his feet.

"Come on," he growled, his lip curling upward, nostrils flaring. "Your little stunt just earned yourself the opportunity to be a hostage."

The guard who met Shannon and Franklin at the front gate to the prison was a pudgy man with an immense head, round face, and doughy hands. Not a person you'd think could handle an unruly prisoner, though his weight surely packed a punch if he was forced to use it. He introduced himself as Officer Scofield and offered a chubby, sweaty hand. He kept his other hand with a death grip on his belt.

"Welcome to Edgewood Correctional Institute, Agent Faye. Mr. Holt."

After shaking hands, he removed his badge and held it to a scanner on the concrete wall. After a second, a beep echoed and the locking mechanism popped open with a loud pneumatic hiss, followed by an echoing clack. The gate swung silently, with the ease of a freshly-oiled hinge that stood out in contrast to the rusted bars. He waved the two forward.

Edgewood was a maximum security prison almost an hour outside of DC, housing primarily those accused of crimes against the state. Traitors, anyone charged with treason, and a handful of federal crimes. A handful of mass murderers, as well, but those were rare.

Officer Scofield pulled the door shut and held it there for a moment, waiting for the automatic lock to re-engage. Then, he led the way down the hallway. He reminded

Shannon of a penguin as he walked, his weight shifting back and forth in a heavy waddle.

"You know, I met your Director a while ago. Sloan, was it?"

"Yes, that's him," Shannon confirmed.

"He was a quiet chap. Didn't say much. But I guess that's not uncommon in your line of work, is it?" He didn't wait for an answer and just kept rambling. "Can't be all chatty with all those secrets you keep tucked away, rattling around in your head." He seemed unfazed that they never responded. "Sad to hear about Nathan Hook. Of course, that wasn't our fault. That prison transport bus he escaped from belonged to the other facility."

They began passing barred cages as they continued. Shannon tried not to stare, but many of the cells were occupied and the prisoners eyeballed them as they passed. She avoided eye contact, but felt their glares burning. A few whistled and made catcalling remarks about her appearance, but she ignored them.

"Sorry about this," Scofield apologized. "We don't get many ladies in here, so it's a big deal for them, I guess. This here is D block. We've got an interrogation room at the end of the hallway. Your man's waiting for you in there. We cuffed him—arms to the table, legs to the chair—for your safety, but I can go in with you, if you want."

"We'll be fine," Shannon insisted.

"That's what your Director said too," he chortled. "Guess you federal folks aren't scared easily by prisoners. Sometimes, we get fresh-faced lawyers shaking in their fancy Italian loafers and need a guard with them."

"I'm sure that's amusing," Shannon deadpanned.

"And when you're done, your second interrogation is in the adjoining room."

"Second interrogation?" Shannon probed. She put a hand on Scofield's arm to stop him. "We're only here for Graham O'Brian."

"Are you sure?" the guard asked. "Your office said you'd be handling the guy they just brought in."

"My...office?" *Who did they mean?* Sloan was still missing and her partner, Dominic, was still on leave to take care of his father. Their office had other agents, obviously, but none she was close to. Or who knew she was here. "Who is the prisoner?"

"Oh, he's not a prisoner here. I think he's simply a person of interest. They only brought him here for interrogation."

"Is that legal? To interrogate someone without charges at a federal prison?" Franklin inquired.

"Beats me. I didn't go to law school. I only know what I'm told."

"Ok, can you get me the dossier on this guy too?"

"Sure thing. I'll bring it by when you're finished with Mr. O'Brian." They continued down the hallway until finally stopping in front of a door. It was solid and metallic, with kind of a dull sheen. "Well, this is it. You're welcome to head on in. The door will lock behind you when you go in...it's a safety feature. But when you're ready to leave, just press the button on the wall and it'll alert us to open it for you."

Shannon waited for a minute for the guard to leave, then placed a hand on the door's cold handle and pushed. It swung open without resistance, much like the front gate. She waved Franklin in, as well—she'd made him promise to keep his temper in check, but agreed he needed to be able to face O'Brian himself—and the two of them entered.

"Wow, I get both of you? I must be special." O'Brian sat in the typical orange, prison jump suit, with his arms chained to the table. Two chairs sat opposite him, so Shannon and Franklin took their seats. She was taken aback by how different the man looked now. He was pale...and gaunt. He had to have lost at least 25 pounds in six months, maybe more. His eyes were dark, empty.

"I wasn't expecting you, Franklin. Didn't think you'd be able to pass the clearance to be here." He smirked.

To his credit, Franklin ignored the barb, instead leading with, "We hear you're ready to talk. Again."

"So much like your new boss, Jacob. No chitchat, no banter," he shook his head. "Well, straight to it, I guess. I hear you found Phoenix."

"You—what?" Shannon gasped. It wasn't like her to break her veneer of professionalism, but that was a surprise. They'd only just found her the day before and hadn't told a soul. He had to have gotten the news from the Volya. Somehow. *Maybe another prisoner? A guest? A guard? Maybe Officer Scofield?* "How did you hear that?"

"What? You think a guy in prison doesn't still have a few connections?"

"Well, it doesn't matter. She slipped us."

"Yeah, that's what I understand." He turned toward Franklin. "You got put through the ringer, didn't you? I haven't seen a person who looked worse since...that mobster turned up dead in the river. What was his name?" He turned back toward Shannon.

"Viktor Polzin," Franklin interjected.

"Polzin! That's right. Now I remember."

"You should. Your group had him killed. His sister-in-law too, Kseniya," Shannon added with a scowl.

"I'm surprised you care, detective. Polzin was a monster."

Shannon didn't appreciate the direction this conversation was heading and tried to steer it back around. "So...Phoenix. What more do you know? You said you wanted to talk. Or did we travel all this way for nothing?"

"How bad do you want to know?"

"You know, Graham...you don't look so good yourself," Franklin interjected. "You're pale as a ghost. Thin too. And is that a black eye? Did something happen?"

O'Brian glared daggers. "I need out of here. And I can give you information if you make that happen."

"Forget it." Shannon shook her head. She shoved her chair back and stood. "He has nothing more than he gave us months ago. He's just miserable and trying to score more posh digs or better food."

"No, no. Please. I-I swear." O'Brian's eyes widened and his face seemed to pale. He tried to stand, but his cuffs wouldn't allow him.

"Where would Phoenix go after leaving the Igloos? Where is she?"

"I—I don't know that. But I can tell you where she's going to be."

Shannon paused, then sat back down. "I'm listening."

"She has a place in Maryland. The Volya does, I mean. In Silver Spring. I've never been there, but she had a name for it. The Lighthouse."

"The Lighthouse? Is it an actual—?"

"I don't know. Like I said, I've never seen it."

Shannon sat quietly for a minute. "Not good enough." She stood. "He's playing with us. Let's go, Franklin." They were going to have to play this differently, but she had an idea. Franklin stared at her for a second, then stood, as O'Brian began protesting from his seat. Begging, almost.

The two agents approached the door.

"Wait, what's going on, Shannon?" Franklin asked, grabbing her by the shoulder.

"That's not real intel. He's wasting our time." Shannon spoke softly, as though to mask the conversation, but intentionally kept it loud enough for O'Brian to overhear. "The Lighthouse? That's a codename. One he doesn't know the meaning of. For a place, he claims, but he doesn't know where it is. And that's assuming he's not just making the whole thing up."

"You think he doesn't know anything?"

"Oh, I think he knows something, but he's not going to talk."

"Then why get us to come all this way?"

"To waste our time. Our resources. Maybe to find out what we know. What we learned in South Dakota." She shook her head, then glanced over at the stunned O'Brian, who had stopped protesting, but was listening intently.

"What do you mean?" Franklin asked.

"I mean, he's a lackey. Low-level grunt. That's probably why they had no extraction plan in place for him. He was on his own."

"Hey now—" O'Brian started to interject, but Shannon pretended she didn't hear him.

"I see this all the time in groups like his. On suicide missions, they always send the one person they can most afford to lose. The one no one will ever miss. I mean, no wonder he failed. No wonder he got caught."

"Wait—" O'Brian spoke again. "I—we did *not* fail."

"Oh right, your bombs at the Lincoln Memorial were a rousing success..." Shannon rolled her eyes. "Killed all of...how many now? Zero?"

"We didn't," O'Brian spat defiantly. "That was just Stage One. We knew it only had a small chance of success. Just you wait..."

"Wait? For what? You're in prison. The members of your group still living are scattered, on the run, in hiding."

"This is so much bigger than you seem to believe. We have people in places higher than you'd think, people you can't touch. Just wait until November when we—" He suddenly stopped talking, as if realizing he'd said too much.

"November? What's happening in November? Is that when Stage Two happens?" Shannon barked.

O'Brian pursed his lips, but said nothing.

"Well, I guess it doesn't matter to you." She shrugged. "You'll still be rotting in here. And that's if you're lucky. I'd wager you're looking at the electric chair eventually."

O'Brian didn't respond at first, but finally he smirked, "I can't wait to enjoy something other than four concrete walls. It may be sooner than you think."

Shannon heard Franklin start to growl and reached out to place a hand on his shoulder to calm him.

"We're done here," she said and punched the button on the wall. "Let's go."

Chapter 35

"Weapons down!" Sloan yelled. "I have hostages!" His voice rumbled, echoing throughout the largely empty hangar.

He shoved Luca forward, inch-by-inch, until the Italian was visible in the doorway from the hangar floor. Sloan kept one hand on the Glock he'd wedged into the man's spine, urging him to comply, and the other hand with a firm grip on his wrist. By twisting the wrist just so—backward and up—he generated enough discomfort to give him maximum control over Luca, keeping him from trying to run while not causing any permanent damage. He kept himself hidden from view, so the men below couldn't get a clean shot. He doubted they were particularly skilled marksmen, but didn't want to take that chance when he didn't have to.

"Here's what's going to happen," he shouted. He paused every few words to let them echo. "You're going to allow me and my friend here...you're going to let us exit the plane and leave the hangar intact. No gunfire, no one needs to get hurt."

The men didn't respond, so he kept going.

"Then I will get into a car and leave. If everyone agrees, I'll release Luca once we're off the premises."

"What makes you think we won't shoot you anyway?" He couldn't tell which one finally responded, but the man's voice was strong and notably American. Maybe even a hint of a Southern drawl.

"Then I'll use this man as a human shield while I fire from behind his body," Sloan yelled. "I assume you know who I am. My reputation. And what I'm capable of. You wanna bet that you'll be able to take me down before I kill you both from behind my shield?"

Neither responded. They'd moved out of eyesight too.

"Do we have a deal?" he shouted, his eyes flicking back and forth trying to locate them.

"Fine," one of them yelled after a few seconds, his voice resonated from off to Sloan's right. "It's a deal."

Sloan nudged Luca forward with the barrel of his gun until they stood at the top of the steps. From here, he could finally see the two men. They were poised about thirty feet on either side of the base of the staircase. Both had lowered their guns, but neither had placed them on the ground.

"I said, guns down," he barked, twisting Luca's wrist upward a half-inch more, eliciting a yelp that reverberated through the hangar. "On the ground. And kick them over to the stairs."

The man on his left—Hair Gel—unhesitatingly obeyed, sending his gun skittering across the concrete until it collided with the metal stairs with a resounding clang. The other man—Goatee—waited a couple seconds, but ultimately followed suit.

"Both of you, against the wall." He removed his gun from Luca's spine long enough to wave it in the direction of the far wall behind Hair Gel. Goatee slowly edged over to join his partner and both retreated until their backs touched the metal siding.

Satisfied, Sloan nudged Luca down the stairs one step at a time, careful to keep himself as hidden as possible. His size—combined with needing to be close to his captive to maintain the shield—made it difficult, but he kept a wary eye on the two men in case either made any sudden move.

When their shoes hit the concrete floor, he bent over and picked up the discarded handguns—both Glocks— and, after making sure their safety switches were on, stuffed them into his waistband.

It took a minute to cross the hangar and reach the far door, but soon, he found himself with only a metal emergency door between himself and the outside.

"Thank you, gentlemen, for not doing anything stupid!" he called out, his words echoing again in the large room. Hair Gel and Goatee hadn't moved from their spots against the wall. "You probably just saved all of your lives!"

BANG!

A bullet went wide and ripped through the metal door frame a foot above his head. Everyone jumped.

BANG!

Another plowed into the plastic emergency exit sign hanging over the door, sending shards of red and white plastic raining down around him.

Where was that coming from? Who was shooting?

His head spun toward the plane, but he barely had time to notice Mario silhouetted in the doorway before Luca abruptly snapped his head backward, slamming the crown of his skull into Sloan's nose.

Something cracked from the blow, sending a shockwave rippling throughout his entire face. His vision blurred as the pain overwhelmed his senses. Instinctively, he released his grip on Luca's wrist and put it to his nose. Blood poured over his face and lips, and through his fingers, creating large splotches on the floor. In all the years Sloan had served in the military, in black ops, in intelligence...he'd suffered many injuries. Some serious. Concussions, broken ribs, a dislocated arm, burns, bullet wounds. He couldn't list them all. But he'd never—not once—broken his nose. The sudden gush of blood and the sensation of a hundred bees swarming up his nostrils was not what he expected.

As he reeled, a shoulder drilled him in the stomach, knocking him backward and driving him into the wall.

Luca!

His once captive—now assailant—flew into him hard, taking care to force his shoulder as deeply into Sloan's midsection as possible.

Sloan had to act fast; Hair Gel and Goatee were surely on their way to join the fight in some way. Still holding onto the Glock, he swung the butt of the gun down with as much force as he could muster, hearing a satisfying crack as it collided with Luca's head. Luca staggered backward, then slumped to the ground, unconscious and bloody. A gash in his forehead looked deep; he'd need medical assistance or else he wouldn't survive.

Confident his immediate assailant was comatose, he tried to locate the others. The throbbing pain in his face made it difficult to see—and more difficult to focus, but he raised his gun and fired in the general direction of the plane, hoping to force Mario's retreat, if only for a moment. He swore loudly—his epithet sputtering through the blood that oozed over his lips—as another bullet crashed into the door behind him.

The door!

He fired another shot toward the plane—unsure where Mario was now—and two in the general direction of where Hair Gel and Luca had been, then spun and shoved the emergency exit bar. The door swung open and a shrill alarm wailed.

Turning left, he began to run, but he needed another plan fast. He was in decent shape for his age and weight, but he wouldn't be able to outrace his pursuer.

Thankfully, he spotted a dark sedan only fifty feet away, likely the vehicle Hair Gel and Goatee had arrived in. It was old and worn out, not a car anyone would give a second glance to if they passed it on the street. Which made it perfect for that line of work. To his surprise, the door had been left unlocked, and he leapt into the front seat. Right as he did, the door to the hangar banged open again. He spun and, seeing the two men emerging, fired for cover.

Goatee yelped and fell on the spot, while Hair Gel quickly ducked back inside. Sloan slammed and locked the door, then turned to look at the console in front of him.

Despite what is shown on television shows, the average vehicle car door offered little protection. Police vehicles were often armored with special metal or solid doors without a hollow cavity inside, but unless a civilian reinforced their vehicle themselves, any ammunition of sufficient caliber would tear through the thin metal with ease. It might cut enough speed to turn a fatal wound into an almost-fatal one, or it might deflect one enough to make accuracy a challenge. But that was it. And it meant he had very little time before those two managed to get an accurate shot. They'd be cautious, knowing what he could do with a gun, but that would only slow them a little.

But here he found his second stroke of fortune. The vehicle was pre-90s—he guessed an '88 or '89—and most cars from that era could be fooled into starting by inserting something vaguely resembling a key into the ignition and damaging the locking pins. Something just like that screwdriver he'd fortuitously grabbed from the plane.

He dug it out of his pocket and jammed it into the ignition. A little force and the pins cracked easily.

The engine fired up and he punched the gas right as the rear windshield exploded in gunfire. The car was hemmed in by other buildings in this direction, so as he hit the gas, he spun the wheel to the right, throwing dirt and gravel as the car fishtailed and whirled around 180 degrees.

Now facing the hangar again, he spotted Goatee's body lying motionless by the door. Mario and Hair Gel stood in his way, weapons drawn.

Mario started to yell something, but Sloan didn't wait to find out their plan or demands. He stomped his foot on the gas pedal and the car lurched forward, barreling straight at the men.

Both immediately began to unload their weapons and his windshield cracked and splintered. At least three bullets penetrated the pane, but none hit him and the glass laminate held its integrity. He briefly ducked below the steering column to avoid the barrage.

Another volley of bullets tore through the windshield and dashboard and a searing pain scorched across his right temple as one projectile grazed him before embedding itself into the leather seat with a thud.

He grunted, but poked his head up again, just in time to notice Hair Gel step to one side for a better shot as he sped past. Sloan made a quick decision and yanked the wheel to the right and a half-second later, he was rewarded with a thud as the front corner of his bumper collided with Hair Gel, sending the man tumbling to the side.

And then, the car left them in the dust. He peeked at his side mirror and saw Hair Gel writhing on the ground. Whether out of ammunition or choosing not to waste any more bullets, Mario had dropped his aim.

Sloan kept a lead foot on the gas as he peeled away and within a couple seconds, he was too far away for it to matter.

Shannon took a minute to compose herself in the hallway after talking to O'Brian. He hadn't given them much, but they did have a time frame now. November. That was the next phase.

She had completely forgotten about that second interrogation with the mystery man until Officer Scofield arrived with a manila folder containing a pretty thin dossier on him. She insisted Franklin wait outside for this one.

She entered the new interrogation room to find Chester Page, a balding man in his mid-40s wearing a leather jacket, his hands resting lightly on the table, and a sharp, well-dressed female standing beside him. The man was tall, but thick, with an even thicker midsection.

"Agent, agent, finally," the woman snapped, drawing Shannon's attention away from the suspect. Clearly this was his legal representation. "Can we please get my client released and on his way? We've been waiting for an hour."

"Your client?" Shannon extended a hand, but it was ignored. "I wasn't told he had a lawyer here."

"So you admit you planned to interrogate him without a lawyer present?" The lawyer leaned forward and raised a finger to point in Shannon's face.

"Talk to, not interrogate, Miss...?"

"Alex Jacobi. Now about those cuffs."

"Sure thing, Ms. Jacobi." Shannon nodded to the guard who'd followed her into the room. "My understanding is that he's not been charged with anything. Not yet."

"Then why is he here? This is a prison, not a police precinct."

"This is a federal case, Alex."

"Ms. Jacobi," the lawyer interrupted. "You may call me Ms. Jacobi."

"Fine. Ms. Jacobi. This is a federal case and we need to interrogate him. Normally, we wouldn't bring someone to a prison for interrogation, but this is a time-sensitive issue and my bosses felt this was the best place to have a quick conversation since he was picked up not far from here. Not to worry, though. If he's innocent, he'll be free of Edgewood soon enough."

"He better be. This goes against my client's Constitutional rights. You can't hold him here without charges." The lawyer leaned over, pointing a bony finger in Shannon's face. "We will sue. You, this prison, the federal government."

"We have reasonable cause, Ms. Jacobi. He's a person of interest. A suspect, even."

"Of what, exactly?" she scoffed.

"Terrorism," Shannon divulged. She was beginning to not like this lawyer very much. It was her job, but she seemed too aggressive, too pushy, too big of a chip on her shoulder. "Which, incidentally, means we can hold him here for quite a while. That's a federal offense. We found dozens of photographs of high-profile individuals in your client's residence."

"That's your justification for holding him here for terrorism?" Jacobi threw her hands in the air before pointing a bony finger in Shannon's face again. "My client is a photographer by trade. It's his job to have photographs."

"These were surveillance photographs, taken without consent and from a distance. And of strategic locations."

"Taken in public. Without complaint. Paparazzi photos, if you will. He sells candid shots to magazines and newspapers around the country. It's a little squirrelly, if you ask me," the lawyer shrugged, "but not exactly a capital offense. It's a legitimate way to earn a living."

"Relax, Alex." The client spoke for the first time and leaned back in his chair, tipping it onto two legs. "I appreciate the spirited defense, but I didn't kill anyone. Save your rabid guard dog routine for when I do. I have nothing to hide here."

"So you'll answer a few questions?" Shannon asked.

"Of course," he smirked in a smug way that caused Shannon to cringe. "As I said, I'm an open book."

"Good," she studied the dossier the agent had handed her in the hallway. "So you're a paparazzi?"

"Paparazzo. That's the singular form," he explained with an exaggerated roll of his eyes.

"Interesting. How much money do you make from that?"

"Enough," he shrugged.

"Is that your only job?"

"It is not." Chester cocked his head to the side as he stared at her, unblinking.

"What else do you do? For a living, I mean."

"I'm a part owner in a nightclub in downtown DC."

"Which nightclub?"

"Blue Ice." He cocked his head again and smiled. "Maybe you've heard of us."

"That's...more strip club than nightclub," she spat. Blue Ice had a tawdry reputation, gaudy and loud, low class.

"So you're familiar with us?" he leered, his gaze traversed her body in a provocative way that made her crave a shower to wash off the slime. "You know, we're always looking for new talent. You're...older...than our typical employee, but I think you'd be surprisingly popular."

Shannon gritted her teeth and fought to ignore him. She forged ahead. "Where were you on the day of the Lincoln Memorial bombing?"

"I was out."

"Out? What does that mean?" She pulled a pen from her pocket and began to take notes.

"I was...occupied," he smirked as one corner of his mouth turned up.

"With friends, you mean? Family? Or work?"

"No, not exactly."

She glanced up. "Well, then who were you with? Who can verify your whereabouts?"

"I honestly don't know."

"How can you not know?"

"We didn't exactly exchange names, if you know what I mean," he winked.

"You didn't..."

"She was tall and blonde though, if that helps. Though most of them are, if I'm being honest. I have a bit of a type."

"I see," Shannon muttered and rolled her eyes. "Can anyone corroborate that? Did anyone notice you?"

"When I go out at night, everyone sees me, doll."

The cheesy pet name dripped off his tongue like syrup and Shannon hated everything about it. The guy was a creep and a misogynist. But that wasn't illegal. She needed to steer the conversation back to the photos. To the evidence. "You had a whole host of photos in the collection at your apartment of the Congressman who died in the Rayburn attack."

"Is that a crime?" he asked, raising an eyebrow.

"Not directly. But it's not a good look."

"You're going to need to do better than that, agent," he mockingly chastised her.

Shannon knew he was right. *She had nothing here. Nothing concrete. He was suspicious. A creep. There were too many coincidences here to be random. But it was all circumstantial. And what use was a paparazzi—paparazzo— strip club owner to an anarchist terrorist organization?* The dossier on Page was slim and there was a lot of missing information.

"You have no idea what you're into here, do you, Agent?"

"Chester, quiet!" his lawyer admonished, but he waved her off.

"Do you have any clue? These people you're after—and I'm not saying I'm one of them—these people will kill you. You know that, right? They won't even bat an eye."

"We all know they're killers, Mr. Page."

"That's where you're wrong. They aren't killers." He paused and stared off into the distance as if reconsidering his answer, then shrugged. "I mean, they are. But that isn't their end goal. They will kill you, but only if they have to."

"Who are we talking about here, Mr. Page? The Nasha Volya and their quest for anarchy? Just so I'm clear…"

"You don't get it, do you?" He shook his head and leaned forward in his chair, resting his arms on the table. He cocked his head to the left as he spoke, like a curious puppy. "Do you even know about Warhawk?"

"What's a Warhawk?" That was a new term and it piqued her interest. *A program? A place? A name?*

"I didn't think so," he crowed with a chuckle.

"Mr. Page, I firmly recommend you stop talking," his lawyer interrupted again.

"Don't worry, Alex," he said, rolling his eyes. "She's clueless."

Shannon sat still for a moment, watching a silent argument fly back-and-forth between lawyer and client, each glaring daggers. After a long stare, Page blinked and bowed his head, and Ms. Jacobi smirked in victory. Shannon wasn't going to get anything more out of him. "Thank you for your time, Mr. Page. You're free to go."

Shannon stood and turned to walk out of the room, but paused in the doorway to glance back.

"I wouldn't leave town, if I were you."

Chapter 36

"Well...do you think he did it?"

"Hmm?" Shannon looked up from her phone.

"The creepy photographer. Do you think he did it?" Franklin repeated the question. "I was listening in on the interrogation from the next room."

The two of them waited for a prison guard—not Scofield this time—as he fumbled for his key card to open the gate and usher them back into the visitor's area and lobby of the facility.

"He definitely isn't innocent," she answered with a heavy sigh. "But I'm not sure he's any more than a creepy photographer. Maybe he ran recon. We'll hold him as long as we can legally, but it won't do us much good to hang onto him."

"So he'll walk?" Franklin groused. That didn't seem right.

"We can still charge him, but it'll be tough to get much to stick without his confession. Or without some witness testimony. He'll probably plead down to something minor and be out in six months. Tops."

The gate swung open with a push and, at the beckoning of the guard, the three of them slipped through. The metal bars clanged shut behind them.

They began to retrieve their various personal items—surrendered upon entry—when an eerie feeling crept over Franklin. He knew it was cliché, but it felt like the hairs on his neck stood up. Glancing around, his attention fixated on two guards behind the counter, who had suddenly started whispering and muttering into their radios. They stood on the other side of a thick pane of bulletproof glass that also acted as soundproofing, so he couldn't make out what they were saying, but their eyes had narrowed and posture tightened.

Something was wrong.

He glanced at Shannon to direct her attention to them, but she was already watching the interaction carefully as well.

"What's go—?" she began to ask, but her question was interrupted by the answer.

KABOOM!

A loud explosion resounded through the concrete halls, shaking the walls, and freeing a layer of dust from all surfaces, which hung in the air like a mist.

"What was that?" Franklin blurted, but he wasn't sure Shannon could hear him. An alarm blared, merged with the shouting of guards to create a din which drowned out all possible sounds. The cacophony deafened and disoriented him as the sound waves doubled over each other, seemingly getting louder with each shrill echo of the siren. His head still ached from his injuries and the roaring commotion sent shocks of pain throughout his skull, so intense his vision blurred.

Shannon grabbed him by the elbow to get his attention. She held up one hand in the universal "Stay here" sign, and then approached the gate. She tried to yell through the bars at a guard, but he either was choosing to ignore her, or more likely, he couldn't hear a word she was saying.

After a few seconds of trying to get his attention, Shannon spun around. She pointed to the front door, which led out to the parking lot, and the two of them stumbled out into the crisp air and sunlight. The alarm still boomed outside, but it wasn't deafening now that it wasn't echoing all around them as well.

"What was that?" Franklin shouted.

"It's O'Brian," she asserted. Her head spun in both directions, searching for something. But she didn't have to look far. A billow of smoke already rose over the eastern side of the prison. "We need to get to him before he escapes. If he makes it out of here, we'll never find him."

"O'Brian? How do you know it's him?" Franklin asked.

"He told me! Remember? I told him he'd be lucky to avoid the death penalty, but he smirked and said he couldn't wait to enjoy something other than four concrete walls. I thought he was being metaphorical. I thought he was just being his smug self. But he meant he was actually getting out of here."

"But why ask for us to visit—?"

"Because he needed us." She closed her eyes and groaned. "We were his ticket out. Interrogation rooms are less secure than his cell."

"So how do we stop him?"

"The only way in or out of this area is by car. And that blast had to come from the outside. He has an accomplice. Let's find that vehicle." She took a step toward the smoke, but Franklin grabbed her arm.

"Is—is that—it?" Franklin moaned.

He pointed to a dark sedan tearing out of an access road that ran around the prison. It took the final corner way too fast for a normal vehicle, nearly hopping up onto two wheels before it screeched down the long drive to the front gate.

Shannon swore, but ordered, "Follow me, get to the car. We're going after him."

———❧———

Sloan knew he'd have to change cars sooner rather than later, so after fifteen minutes or so, he pulled into the parking lot of a strip mall and parked in the back, away from the prying eyes of anyone on the road and along the trees lining the property.

The strip mall was old and decrepit, but in an up-and-coming neighborhood, so several newer-looking businesses had moved in. One of those hipster indoor cycling studios was positioned on the end, followed by a juice bar, a dry cleaner, a pizza place, and a small veterinary clinic.

Finally stationary and safe—for the moment—he decided to take stock of his condition and stared down at himself. Blood still dripped from his hands, a mixture of both his and Luca's. *That can't be sanitary,* he mused, *though I've seen worse.*

Then he caught a glimpse of himself in the rear-view mirror.

Maybe not…

The entire lower half of his face was stained red with blood that still oozed from his nose. Thankfully, it was already beginning to clot, so the flow had slowed dramatically. But his nose was definitely broken. It sat crooked and slightly off-center on his face. He looked like a monster, a carnivorous beast who'd recently devoured a bloody feast.

He glanced around the car. One of the men had left a light fleece jacket in the back window and he grabbed it to clean himself. He wiped his hands on the fabric and did his best to remove as much of the gore as possible from his face. The nose had swollen, so every time he put even a little pressure near it, a jolt of pain shocked him. He didn't think he'd be able to re-set it here, but he managed to remove enough of the sticky red liquid to make himself passable...at a distance, anyway. At the very least, no one who glimpsed him would immediately think to call 9-1-1 until they got closer.

He was fairly confident no one at the hangar had radioed out for reinforcements in time to track him, so he was totally alone. Safe, even. He closed his eyes and took a deep breath, forcing out images of raised fists, firearms, and dead assailants.

And for one moment...a brief, fleeting moment...he felt his body relax.

Moments like that were rare in the field and learning to savor them was a skill. They were the moments of clarity that allowed for reflection, but also for recovery. Not that the human body could heal that quickly, but mental recovery was every bit as important as physical and even fleeting seconds of relaxation allowed his mind to recharge.

Quiet, peaceful, alone...

For a few seconds, he managed to force the ache of his fractured nose out of his mind. He found his mind drifting to his fractured family and especially his two kids.

His daughter Tracy had recently started her first semester at the University of Pennsylvania as a member of the school's volleyball team. His son Ben was still in high school, but already showing a strong mechanical aptitude, with dreams of managing a car dealership. He was proud of them both, even if he didn't see them as often as he'd prefer.

As his thoughts dwelt on his kids, he extracted the cell phone he'd taken from Mario out of his pocket. He'd swiped it while restraining the men on the plane and disabled the GPS tracking, so they wouldn't be able to follow him off its signal. Almost without thinking, he found himself dialing the number for his son. He had it memorized.

He hadn't spoken to either of his kids since leaving for Budapest. He desperately wanted to hear their voices again. But personal phone calls in the middle of a mission were dangerous, compromising even. It played havoc on your emotions and wasn't recommended except in emergencies.

But what if he didn't make it? He almost hadn't. When would he speak to them again?

He stared at the ten digits on the screen, his finger itching to hit 'Call.' But after a minute, he deleted the number and tossed the phone in the backseat.

No distractions. Time to get to work. I'll call after this is all over, he promised himself.

He exited the car and closed the door. He'd need a new vehicle, one they wouldn't be looking for. But as he caught another glimpse of his reflection in the tinted windows of the car, he knew he needed to make a stop first.

The rear side of strip malls all have rear exits for each business, typically used for deliveries, taking out the garbage, or smoke breaks. And the veterinary clinic was no different. He managed to pick the lock pretty easily and slipped into a back room.

He found himself in a delivery entryway and then a sort of closet, with supplies lining metal shelves on both sides. Beyond that was an open door, through which he could overhear voices.

"Linda, can you set up Mrs. Fonseca and Rajah with that medicine we talked about?" A female voice rang out clearly and authoritatively. She must be the primary veterinarian at the practice.

"Of course. Anything else?" A gentler, saccharine voice responded, more submissively. *A receptionist, maybe? Or veterinary assistant?*

"I'd like to see Rajah again in two weeks, so please schedule that visit. But that'll be all. You're free to take off after that. I'll close up."

"No problem, thank you." Then a little softer, as though walking away, "This way, Mrs. Fonseca."

Sloan listened as the woman identified as Linda disappeared into the front of the practice, through what sounded like a swinging door, followed by Mrs. Fonseca and her dog. But the doctor stayed behind in the medical area. Her shoes clacked loudly on the tile floor as she walked. He waited until he couldn't hear the assistant anymore.

He wished he still had his credentials from SISA. But those had been lost in all the chaos. He hadn't seen his badge since the Budapest bombing, now that he thought about it. It was probably buried under rubble and layer after layer of dirt and dust.

Poking his head around the corner, Sloan spotted the vet about twenty feet away, standing at a counter. Her back was turned as she typed at a computer. Sloan's hand moved instinctively to the handle of the Glock he'd kept tucked into his waistband, but he stopped himself. A gun was his last resort.

No need to threaten violence. Yet.

Slowly, quietly, he stepped out from his hiding spot in the closet and edged closer.

"Excuse me," he whispered, then coughed softly. "Excuse me, could you help me?"

The doctor whirled and gave out a soft "Eek!"

"Shh shh," Sloan insisted. "I'm not here to hurt anyone. I just need help." He gestured to his deformed face, still speckled with the dried, caked blood he couldn't get off. "I can't prove it to you now, but I'm a federal agent. I work for the government."

"Who—who are you?" she demanded, her voice cracking like a teenage boy in puberty. But she immediately softened her tone slightly as her gaze took in his appearance. "What happened?"

"My nose is broken," he explained, deliberating ignoring her first question. Nothing he claimed about his identity could be verified at the moment, so it would do nothing to alleviate her anxiety. "I need someone with medical expertise to set it and then I'll be on my way."

"I'm a veterinarian, not a physician," she shook her head.

"Close enough. It's all bones," he insisted. "And if you want, I can talk you through it. I just need a second pair of hands. And maybe a stronger painkiller than something over the counter." He attempted a smile.

"I'm sorry, Mr…" she trailed off for a second, but Sloan again didn't offer his name. "I'm just not comfortable doing this, not like this. I have to ask you to leave."

"Please, Doctor. It'll just take a minute."

"I'm sorry, sir. But I'm going to have to call the police, if you don't leave."

"Great," Sloan grunted, then sighed. This is what he wanted to avoid. "I apologize, but you're giving me no choice." He reached behind him and revealed the gun. "Please, don't scream. I didn't want to do it this way, but you've given me no other option."

Chapter 37

With Shannon behind the wheel and heavy pressure on the gas pedal, they made up ground quickly on O'Brian and his getaway vehicle. They blew through the guard gate which had been smashed to bits by the sedan seconds earlier.

Wood shavings floated in the air, buffeted by the wind as they sped past a stunned security guard frantically bellowing for help into his handheld radio.

The car they chased was a small, charcoal-colored Honda Civic sedan. Not a car designed for a high-speed chase. It was a car of practicality, not going to raise any eyebrows and would blend in nicely in traffic. But it wasn't exactly incapable of hitting top speeds either, if you gave it enough time.

She pressed the gas pedal to the floor as she raced to catch up, and it wasn't long before they were nearly bumper to bumper. The road was only two lanes and ran alongside one of the many Virginia lakes. This one was a man-made reservoir that sat at the bottom of a steep drop-off on the right side of the road. A metal guard rail ran along the shoulder to prevent vehicles from running off the road toward the water.

With a quick glance to make sure no cars were coming the other direction, she swung into the oncoming lane to edge next to the Civic. Best case scenario, she'd be able to force the car off the road and pin it on the shoulder, but as they pulled close to even, Shannon noticed the driver's side window of the vehicle retract into the door and yelled for Franklin to take cover.

She reached over and shoved his head into his own lap and bent low as gunshots shattered the passenger window. She eased off the gas slightly to drift a few feet behind, but the two cars still flew along the two-lane road side-by-side.

The vehicles shook dangerously back and forth as their sides scraped.

A burst of semi-automatic gunfire exploded from the backseat of the other car, ripping off their side view mirror and shattering another window.

"Did you see her?" She yelled, breathless.

"Who?" Franklin mumbled, his voice muffled.

"Phoenix," Shannon insisted. "It's her."

"Are you sure?"

"Brace yourself," she ordered, nodding. "I have an idea."

With one hand on the wheel and the other keeping Franklin's head pushed into his own knees for safety, she deftly maneuvered the car until her front bumper lined up with the rear tires of the other. It was a police tactic used in car chases, one she'd learned from an old boyfriend she'd dated as he attended the police academy. It was one of the few positives she remembered from that brief relationship, one she didn't even see as a positive until this precise moment.

Then, after a quick glance at the other car, she gave the steering wheel a quick, short pull to the right. Her bumper collided with the rear third of the other car with a solid thunk. Called the PIT maneuver, or tactical ramming, it caused the pursued car to turn sideways abruptly, which forced a sudden stop.

But as soon as she did it, she realized why her ex-boyfriend had explained it should only be used at lower speeds.

The two cars were hurtling down the road at nearly sixty miles per hour, so the sudden lurch sideways caused the car ahead of them to flip, and launch into the air.

Shannon slammed on her own brakes and the two of them gaped in horror as the other car did several rotations in mid-air before crashing to the asphalt with a violent, horrendous crunch.

It landed square on a guardrail, half over the road and half over a narrow, grassy shoulder. The car skidded dozens of feet along the metal railing with a spine-tingling screech before its weight and trajectory tipped too far and it tumbled down the hill and out of sight toward the reservoir's surface.

"Holy—" Franklin exclaimed, his words cut off by a loud crash from below, followed by a massive splash.

Shannon quickly flicked on her hazard lights and brought their car to a stop near where the other had gone over the edge.

They both leapt out and rushed to the edge to try to spot the car, but the path of destruction it had caused was largely obscured by the bushes, trees, and brush it had torn through. They could just barely see the tops of spinning, off-kilter tires before they sank and disappeared from view.

"Hurry," Shannon insisted. "We have to get down there."

"Do you think they're—?" Franklin trailed off before uttering the final word, but he knew they were both thinking it.

"I—I don't know," Shannon faltered, a grim smile on her face. "I don't know."

"Thank you, Doctor." Sloan studied himself in the mirror at the veterinary clinic. The vet had done an admirable job on his nose. It was swollen—that was expected—but otherwise, it appeared fairly normal, he imagined. Or at least, situated where it was supposed to be. It wouldn't draw any immediate stares from passers-by on the street. She'd also provided stitches on his busted lip. "I'm sorry I had to get forceful with the gun. I promise, that wasn't how I wanted to do this. It may not look like it, but I'm one of the good guys. If I had my badge, I'd show you."

She didn't answer, but only glared at him. She was mad, understandably so. Probably scared too, though she hadn't acted afraid. He had no proof of his identity or federal affiliation, and he'd already brandished a weapon. But to her credit, she'd reacted professionally and competently.

"I'll make sure you're compensated for your time and your expertise," he nodded. "I promise."

She turned and began to wash her hands in a small sink in the room.

"Is it okay if I exit out the front door?" he attempted a smile.

She didn't say anything, but nodded.

Sloan slowly exited the room and headed for the waiting room and entrance lobby. The receptionist had already left for the evening, but the television in the waiting area was still on. A news anchor was speaking about an upcoming memorial celebration for the terrorist bombings six months ago. In the chaos of the last few days, and the bloodbath he'd survived in Budapest, he'd completely forgotten the six-month anniversary had already arrived.

He paused to watch the broadcast as they showed a replay of the attacks from someone's phone camera. It wasn't the best quality, but it certainly captured the chaos and screams from that day. As the footage ended, they shifted to showing the list of speakers at the event. The Vice-President topped the speaking list, followed by a handful of members of Congress—Lawson, Hartwell, Little, Richardson, D'Alessio—and two other names Sloan recognized from among the President's cabinet, Trent and Allen, alongside a live video of the speakers gathering.

The camera slowly panned from person to person as a talking head spoke over them about the importance of this day in remembering the thwarted attack, but also to those who lost their lives—both in DC and in the other cities around the world.

As the image moved through the congressmen, something caught Sloan's attention. One Congressman scratched his face and as the sunlight hit his hands, a sudden glint created a lens flare in the camera, like a J.J. Abrams science-fiction movie. The camera shifted and the flare diminished enough to reveal what caused the refraction, a large golden ring. It looked heavy...and old. Something...ancient, almost.

And as he watched, Luca's words about Warhawk echoed in his head...*The man with the ring...*

Luca had implied the Warhawk was someone with a lot of power, more power than Phoenix. And O'Brian had implied there were others in government, others who hadn't been discovered yet.

What if—? What if that Congressman—? Could he actually be the Warhawk? Is it possible the Warhawk is a member of the United States Congress?

His mind whirled and he tried to identify which politician was wearing the ring, but his hand obscured his face. And then the camera had moved on.

"Ahem!"

Sloan whirled around to see the veterinarian watching him from the doorway.

"You're still here," she snapped.

"I—yes, I'm sorry. I was just distracted..." he stammered, pointing at the television, and quickly moved to the front door to exit. He paused for a second to ask, "Did you happen to notice who that one Congressman was? The one with the ring that caught the light?"

"Hartwell," she replied. "From New Jersey, I think."

"What do you know about him?" Sloan breathed. He tried to remember everything he could about the man. They'd never formally met, but had been the same room for security briefings before. He served on the House Intelligence Committee.

A little brash and quick to speak, Sloan had always felt, *but still quite intelligent.* A second—maybe third-term—Congressman; he couldn't remember. He'd also been one of the suspected targets in the bombing at the Rayburn Congressional Office Building.

What if he was never a target, after all? Maybe he was...the one in charge? The mastermind? That would also explain his presence at the scene...

"I don't know much," the veterinarian shrugged, crossing her arms. "But rumor is, he's on the short list to announce he's running for the election next year."

"Which election?" Sloan demanded, his voice deepening as he stared at the screen.

"The President," she said, "of the United States."

Sloan slowly turned to face her.

"Can I use your phone?"

Chapter 38

It took Franklin and Shannon a couple minutes to work their way down the steep, rocky incline to the reservoir's surface and they approached the crash site with an abundance of care. The last thing they wanted to do was disturb anything that might be evidence. Shannon arrived first, leading the way with her gun extended. Franklin limped behind as fast as his injuries would allow. But this was no trick as they watched the final hints of the car disappear beneath the water.

It had hit the lake upside-down, with all the windows smashed out, doors hanging crooked on broken hinges. One lone taillight floated loosely above the sinking hull. Flaming metal chunks of Japanese engineering—probably assembled at the Honda plant in Ohio—burned around them on the shore.

His broken rib and other injuries made Franklin unsteady and he tripped over a disconnected side mirror and nearly fell, but caught himself against a tree by the water.

"Careful!" Shannon cautioned. "Take it easy."

He glanced back with a sharp glare, but didn't say anything.

"Phoenix, O'Brian…it's over!" she called out. It seemed unlikely they'd escaped before the car hit the water, but Phoenix, especially, seemed to have nine lives.

No response.

"Hello?" The two neared the water's edge, looking for any signs of life. But there were none.

Shannon reached down to examine a plastic shard, one razored edge now coated in a red, viscous liquid.

"I've got blood," she announced, standing back up. "A lot of it."

"Should we, I dunno, jump in after them?" Franklin asked.

"It's too dangerous with the cloudy water, too deep. And too late," she said. "Anyone in that car has been below water for minutes now and badly injured. They're gone."

"Any chance they were thrown from the car?" Franklin wondered aloud.

The two glanced around. Bits of metal and plastic littered a fifty by fifty foot area, but no bodies. No trails of blood. No people anywhere. Just hunks of metal and plastic that had ripped from the car's frame during its tumble down the hill.

"If they weren't wearing seatbelts, getting tossed is a possibility. But this isn't a huge area. We'd be able to see them."

"Over here," Franklin's voice rang out. "I've got more blood!" She quickly joined him and found him staring at a broken pane of glass. It appeared to be the front windshield, popped out during the crash. Two, jagged splotches of blood smeared from corner to corner.

"What do you think?" he asked.

"That's a lot of blood," she repeated with a sigh, but was cut off by the distant sound of sirens. Emergency services were almost there, but as they stared at the scene, they realized it would be futile. There was nothing about this crash that suggested it had been remotely survivable.

Franklin limped over to the edge of the reservoir and stared down into the water. The car had vanished, too deep to see, its hull masked by plant life and murky water, stirred up by the sudden disturbance. But as he stared, the ripples and waves caused by the crash were already lessening, calming. And eventually, it stilled.

It's over, he whispered to himself. *It's over.* He wasn't sure how he was supposed to feel, but numb wasn't what he expected. It didn't feel right. He hadn't gotten his cathartic final confrontation with Phoenix, hadn't gotten to accuse O'Brian of betraying Joanna, of attempting to murder her. He'd wanted revenge, but fate had stolen it from him.

Any chance of vengeance had vanished in the span of a heartbeat, just out of reach. And he felt nothing. No sense of happiness, no joy at seeing them gone. Certainly no sadness at their demise. But he didn't even feel angry at losing that opportunity. It was just...nothing.

A few bubbles drifted up from the water below, popping on the surface, followed by an amorphous dark shape that gently rose upward. Too small to be a person, but too big to be a fish. He rolled up his pant legs and waded out a few feet to retrieve it.

It was a black jacket, the kind Phoenix had been wearing. It was ripped and bloody, but it was empty. He pulled it from the water, depositing it on the rocky shoreline.

"Are you okay?" Shannon asked, still watching from several feet further up the incline.

"I—I don't know," he stammered as he knelt next to the jacket. "I don't know." He patted down and reached into the pockets, but found nothing of value. A few scraps of paper ruined by the water, but that was it.

"It's weird," she said. "This isn't how I thought this would end."

"I thought I'd feel...different," he muttered back, though it was more for his own sense of closure than in response to her. "I thought her death would be...more meaningful."

"Revenge doesn't bring someone back," Shannon said, her voice soft and kind, but as one with authority on the topic. "It never brings the release we want."

He looked up at her and noticed an ambulance slow and come to a stop along the shoulder of the road up above. Before the medics were able to exit the vehicle and clamber down to the water, however, their conversation was broken up by the sudden ringing of a cell phone.

It rang twice before Shannon asked, "Are you going to get that?"

"It's not mine," Franklin responded, patting his pockets to be sure.

"Well mine's always on vibrate," Shannon retorted. "It must be—wait..." She patted her pockets, then frowned. She reached into an exterior pocket on her jacket and extracted a small cell phone. "What? This...this isn't mine." It continued to ring, displaying an unknown number on its lighted display. She slowly tapped the screen to answer it.

"Hello?"

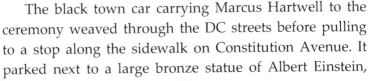

The black town car carrying Marcus Hartwell to the ceremony weaved through the DC streets before pulling to a stop along the sidewalk on Constitution Avenue. It parked next to a large bronze statue of Albert Einstein, one of the lesser known DC monuments. Hartwell always felt it was a poor likeness, but it remained a curious statue, seemingly out of place among the political monument glitterati in Washington honoring Presidents, military war victims, and Reverend King, a civil rights leader.

But here, tucked in a small grove of elm and holly trees outside the National Academy of Sciences, across the street from the Vietnam Veterans Memorial, was a twelve-foot bronze statue of the physicist genius, slightly disheveled, holding a stack of manuscripts in hand.

As Hartwell stepped out of the vehicle and rebuttoned his suit jacket, he watched several schoolchildren climb onto the lap of the man, laughing and giggling, and he found himself—for one brief second—hating them. Not because of anything they did, but because of what they had.

Something he never did as a child.

Happiness. That pure, unfettered, ignorant, taken-for-granted happiness. They were privileged and didn't even realize it. He'd been forced to struggle for everything in life, fighting tooth-and-nail through the death of his parents, being raised by an emotionally-abusive grandparent, the foster system, the slums...and he'd never once had what these children had been simply handed on a silver platter. The world had dealt him a bad hand and he'd never forgiven it.

There was a brief spell, a year or two dalliance of youthful idealism early in his academic career, when he'd seen things differently. He'd believed himself to be the epitome of the American dream, the hope for every child born into poverty to rise above, to make something out of a life of nothing. But a course on political ideologies he took his junior year of college set him on a new path, one of enlightenment.

His professor, an eccentric personality, had revealed a deeper truth about humanity, the oligarchical power structure that ran the world. No matter what your political leanings, whether democratic or authoritarian, capitalist or socialist, Republican or Democrat, every system had one thing that lay at its core. Power.

All ideologies were simply disagreements about how best to conquer and consolidate power at the top. Europe was dominated by the Victorian family tree, with World War One fought between cousins. The royal families of the UK, Germany, Norway, Romania, Russia, Greece, Sweden, and Spain were all related through the early part of the 20th century.

Even long-standing, famous democracies like the United States always seemed to have the same families near the top. It was an elite system run by the Kennedys, the Bushes, the Clintons, and a dozen or more cronies. They all knew each other, inbred with one another. He'd never been much of a conspiracy theorist, but the more this professor unearthed for his students, the more Hartwell came to believe some measure of truth existed behind the theories of international elite societies.

Call them the Freemasons, the shadowy Bilderbergs, the Rothschilds, or the Illuminati...they were all the same. Elites using the globe as a giant chessboard, exploiting and manipulating societal structure for their own benefit... money, power, control.

It was corrupt. It was nefarious.

It needed to be destroyed.

And in a few short minutes, he would be the one to start that process.

Before he traversed the grassy mall over to the memorial ceremony, he pulled out a nondescript flip phone. There was only one number saved in that phone: Typhos.

Quickly, he tapped out a message.

All set?

He received one word back.

Yes.

Satisfied, he tucked the phone into his jacket pocket and smiled. His moment neared and he was finally ready to take that next step.

He waited until the car pulled away from the curb and disappeared into traffic before he turned to face the Lincoln Memorial. He straightened his jacket and tugged on the sleeves of his shirt, looking over the crowd that had gathered. A bevy of black balloons flanked both sides of the stage as a memorial and the front of the stage had been lined with roses, one for each American who had died in the attacks six months ago.

None had been killed in the detonations in DC, though that one agent had been shot while in pursuit of Nathan Hook. But Washington hadn't been the only city the Volya targeted and other attacks saw varying degrees of success.

The Memorial itself had suffered minor damage to the marble steps and buttresses. The trademark white stone had cracked and been darkened slightly by the explosion and the pristine repair stood out against the dirtier, old marble. But the ceremony served as the official reopening for tourists and visitors as well.

As Hartwell approached the stage, accompanied by two security members, he observed several of his colleagues already in attendance. He took a deep breath, then smiled and waved, putting a bounce in his step and donning his 'politician' face, the one that came out at fundraisers and rallies. It was a mask, but one he didn't mind.

That was his role. An important role. Perhaps *the* most important role in the global chess match the Volya was playing against worldwide intelligence agencies.

So it was a role he was happy to play.

And now it was time to take that next step, to stop playing around with pawns and get one of the most powerful pieces involved.

Chapter 39

"Hello, Detective." Nathan Hook's distinctive drawl took on a weird mechanical tone through the cell phone's speaker. It crackled, like a bad connection.

"Hook? Is that you? Where are you?" Shannon peppered him with questions.

"Miss Faye, is it not?" Hook crowed. "No small talk, I see."

Franklin echoed, "Where are you?"

"Is that Franklin?" Hook sneered with a chuckle. "Put him on."

"How did you put this phone in my pocket?" Shannon demanded.

"Franklin, are you there?" Hook ignored her.

"I'm here, Hook," Franklin finally said with a sigh. "We're going to find you. And then we're going to stop your plans."

"Stop us? You can't stop us now," Hook responded.

"We just stopped your boss. O'Brian is dead, Nathan. And Phoenix too. Their car just went face first into a lake."

Hook was silent for several seconds, but finally said, "Well, even so...it's too late. The wheels are already in motion. And soon—very soon—we'll have the power we need."

"What do you mean?" Shannon asked.

"You've lost, Agent Faye...Franklin. You've already lost."

Shannon gawked at Franklin, unsure how to respond. "It's never too late," she grunted.

"You know, there's no shame in losing. You did well, but you came up against a stronger opponent. It happens. The only shame here is in your vanity, your hubris that made you think this would end any other way." Hook spoke slowly, enunciating each syllable. "I commend you for trying, I really do. Most would have given up after...having...lost so much. But your arrogance will only end in more death. More destruction. More loved ones hurt."

"Where are you, Hook?"

He answered in his staccato enunciation. "There's an abandoned mall in Alexandria, near the Van Dorn metro stop. Are you familiar with it?"

Franklin was. That mall had been a popular hangout spot for many of his friends in high school. Even in his youth, it was decaying, a hot spot for a seedier clientele. More than once, cops had busted drug dealing rings in that parking lot. Ultimately, the mall slowly crumbled and faded over the years as stores moved out and none moved in.

"I am," he finally murmured.

"I'm glad, Franklin. Because that's where you'll find me." He paused for a second before adding, "And your father."

"My—my father?" Franklin stifled a gasp.

"Yes, your father. I believe he attended young KJ's soccer game today, did he not? Along with the rest of your family?"

"Don't you dare...don't you dare touch my nephew!" Franklin sputtered.

"Don't worry," Hook cautioned. "Unlike my boss, I'd never hurt a child. I have a bit of a soft spot for kids."

"Well aren't you a regular Mr. Rogers..." Shannon snapped.

"To be perfectly honest, I'm not interested in hurting your father either. But you see, my boss wants you. You have caused way too much trouble and she's ready to take you off the board. Your father is the way to do it."

"What do you want?"

"I want you to come, to trade your life for his. And I want you to do so alone. Agent Faye isn't welcome and neither are any of your other fed friends."

Franklin didn't answer, but stared at Shannon with pleading eyes. She vehemently shook her head, but he ignored her.

"Ok, I'll come. But don't hurt him." Franklin begged. "This has nothing to do with him."

"Good," Hook quipped, taunting him. "And if I were you, I'd hurry."

And the line went dead.

"You can't go," Shannon grabbed his arm as soon as the call ended. "It's too dangerous."

"It's my father," Franklin insisted. "I have to."

"It's a suicide mission. You have to realize that."

"Maybe. But if anyone is going to die, it should be me," Franklin explained softly. "The life I've led...I deserve it. But I'm willing to, because he doesn't deserve it."

"You think he's going to just let your father go? Does Nathan Hook seem like that kind of man to you?"

"It's not likely, but if I don't, then my father is definitely dead. At least this way, there's a chance."

Shannon just stared at him, but finally she nodded. "I don't like it..."

"Neither do I," he interjected.

"I don't like it," she repeated, "but I understand. Please be careful. And whether you like it or not, I'll be praying for you."

"I would appreciate that," he whispered. And he meant it. Whether a little prayer would help or not, he couldn't say. But it certainly wouldn't hurt to know there was someone out there thinking about him, sending good vibes. And on the off chance that it put him on the same side as an omnipotent God, it was worth trying.

Shannon gave him a quick hug and handed him the keys to the car. "I'll find another way back," she said. "Just make sure you end this."

"I will," Franklin said through a grim smile. "One way or another, this ends today."

Just hopefully not in my death...

Shannon watched Franklin speed off, the tires squealing as he took the first turn way too fast before disappearing from view. She closed her eyes and whispered a simple prayer for him. She knew he wasn't particularly religious, despite his family's influence, but he was going to need all the help he could get, even if it came in the form of supernatural intercession.

She turned back to the scene, to ask the emergency crew if there was anything she could do to help, but it seemed futile. No one on the scene moved with any sense of urgency...just a steady acceptance of what they'd find. Upon approaching the scene and recognizing the dangers of an underwater retrieval, the medics had elected to wait for the dive team, which pulled up a few minutes later, but as their vehicle came to a stop, Shannon's phone began to ring. The caller ID revealed an unknown number, but carried a local area code. Hesitantly, she took a few steps to the side, out of earshot of the others, and tapped the green 'Answer' button.

"He-hello?"

"Shannon?" The familiar gruff rumble of Jacob Sloan boomed through the phone's speaker.

"Director? Is—is that you?" Shannon sputtered. "What happened to you? Where have you been?" The questions tumbled out of her mouth before she could stop herself.

"Listen, Shannon." He used his boss voice—deep, authoritative, intimidating—the kind he used in the office to boss the agents around. "I don't have much time...we don't have much time."

"Where are you calling from?" she asked.

"A veterinarian's office in a strip mall," he quipped in his trademark deadpan. "Long story."

"Wha—?" *A vet's office? Why?*

"No, just listen," he cut her off. "I can explain everything later. But I need you to meet me at the Lincoln Memorial."

"A—again? I'm like...45 minutes away."

"Yes, again. It's the six-month remembrance ceremony today. Should be starting there any moment now."

"What—what's happening?" She'd forgotten about the ceremony.

"You know that fifth Volya leader I believed existed, but could never find?"

"You found him?" she exclaimed, then paused. "Wait…is…he going to be at the ceremony? Is there going to be another attack?"

"No. Instead, he's speaking at it. Apparently, he's a United States Congressman…"

"What…?" *Was that even possible? A sitting Congressman is one of the highest-ranking members of a global terrorist organization?* It seemed unthinkable.

"Congressman Hartwell, from New Jersey. I'm about 90% sure. I'll explain later, but he's got the ring. It all makes so much more sense now."

"The—ring? What ring?" *Maybe the Director was hit on the head in the Budapest explosion,* she mused. He'd never mentioned anything about a ring before.

"And he goes by a name too, like the others," he continued. "Warhawk."

Shannon's head snapped up at that reference. That was the name Chester Page had mentioned in her interrogation. He mocked her, asking if she knew about the 'Warhawk.' She didn't know what he meant at the time, but if Sloan had stumbled across a man who went by that same name, that wasn't a coincidence.

"Again, I'll explain later," he added. "Meet me at the Lincoln Memorial."

"Ok," she responded. "I'll need to find some transportation, but I'm on my way."

Chapter 40

Shannon arrived quickly downtown after calling for a ride-share vehicle and was standing off to one side of the Lincoln Memorial when she spotted him. The Director hobbled with a noticeable limp and kept a hat pulled low over his brow to conceal his identity, but it was clearly him.

The ceremony was already starting, with a whole slate of individual speakers lined up. At the moment, a celebrity emcee—a former Marine turned actor—was introducing a first-term Congressman from Utah.

"Director!" she exclaimed as he got close. "You're alright...I...think...?" She pointed to his face.

"I'm tough to kill," he grunted. "Did you find him?"

"Yes, that's him there," she pointed to a cluster of men standing at attention at the right of the stage. Sloan recognized several members of the government. The Vice-President wasn't among them—though he'd certainly emerge at the last minute from a Secret Service limousine, but other faces stood out.

There was Howard Lawson, one of the survivors of the attack on the Rayburn. Senators Victor Martin and Reuben D'Alessio, both members of the Senate Select Committee on Intelligence, stood in line waiting their turn. Grant Allen, the White House Chief of Staff attended as well, alongside several others. It was an impressive lineup.

And at the far end of the line was the face they wanted to meet. Congressman Marcus Hartwell. He stood erect, shoulders pushed back, his gaze drifting over the crowd with a smirk on his face. Like the others, he was dressed professionally in a dark suit, light-colored shirt beneath, no tie, and with an American flag pin—currently askew and hanging vertically—stuck on his lapel.

"What's our plan?" Shannon asked. "Do we need to call the FBI?"

"We can't. As they've proven time and again, the FBI can't be trusted in matters of national security. Hook and O'Brian worked there for years without getting caught. They failed Agent Talbott."

"Ok, so we do this alone," she responded. "But how? We can't just accost him right as he's about to go on stage."

Sloan considered the situation for a minute, his eyes scanning the area. "No, you're right. And we don't have enough proof to publicly arrest a sitting Congressman, in front of a thousand news cameras and cell phones."

"So we wait?" she complained. She didn't like that plan. "Maybe we talk to him first. Before he speaks. Get him to talk, maybe squeeze a confession out of him."

"A confession?" Sloan snorted. "If he is the Warhawk, he's too smart for that."

"What other choice do we have?"

"Okay, okay. Let's pull him aside to talk to him. And then after…"

"Afterward, we bring him in." Shannon nodded. "For questioning. Without cameras." She turned and began to walk toward the line of speakers, but Sloan grabbed her by the arm.

"Wait…" he whispered. "Who's that man?" He nodded in the direction of Hartwell, who'd turned away from the stage and was talking to an unknown person.

This mystery man was about average height, brown skin, clean-shaven, and dressed in a leather jacket over jeans. He was a little gangly with a mop of thick, gray curls on his head. A pair of dark, wrap-around sunglasses sat on a hooked nose.

"No earpiece," she noted. "So not security."

"No," Sloan whispered. "But doesn't he look familiar?"

"Another Senator?" she suggested.

"Dressed so casually at a formal ceremony? Unlikely."

"CIA?"

"I know every official at the CIA."

"A lobbyist, perhaps?"

"Hrmm," he muttered. "Perhaps."

As they watched, the man stopped talking and left, walking across the blocked-off roadway, and finally got into the backseat of a dark SUV waiting for him. As soon as the door closed, it sped off, disappearing around the corner.

Shannon stared at Sloan. His brow furrowed, eyes narrowed, deep in thought. "What is it?" she asked.

"I…I don't know," he answered softly. "But something about that man…" he trailed off.

After another minute, he turned to face her and Shannon took the opportunity to break the silence.

"Look. Before we go confront Hartwell, there's something you need to know about Phoenix," Shannon interjected, but Sloan waved her off and turned to walk away.

"Later!" he called out over his shoulder. "This is more important." He took one final glance after the SUV, now long gone, then led the way over to the Congressman.

———◆———

"I'm here, Nathan. Let him go." Franklin stammered. It hadn't taken him long to speed across town, not with his foot plastered to the floor of the car. He'd left Shannon to deal with the aftermath at the crash site. The parking lot had been empty when he arrived—a common sight even before the mall had formally closed its doors—so he screeched to a halt outside the front entrance near what used to be a department store. He was met at the sliding doors and roughly ushered into the building, led up a broken escalator and inside one of the abandoned shop fronts, once a shoe store.

He was shoved from behind by one of the Volya burly goons and he stumbled forward, nearly falling at Hook's feet before he caught his balance. His eyes flicked around the store, hoping for any sign of his father. But the room was bare, no sign of him anywhere. Nathan Hook leaned against a sales counter holding a gun casually in his hand. Some sort of revolver. The weapon dangled loosely from his fingers as he sauntered forward toward Franklin. His other hand was open, rolling a coin across his knuckles back-and-forth like Doc Holliday in that western movie. It was difficult to tell from this angle, but it appeared to be a Rosomakha coin again.

"You don't want him, Nathan," Franklin insisted. "You want me."

Hook paused and smirked at him.

For a flash, Franklin swore there was something different in his face. Something demonic hidden beneath, wearing a Nathan Hook mask. A crooked grin that somehow conveyed the impression it was too wide for his face. Eyes that almost glowed. Pulsing temples.

And then it was gone. Just like that. And it was Nathan Hook again.

"Leave us," Hook snapped.

"What?" Franklin stuttered. "I don't—"

"Not you, you imbecile," Hook groaned, then raised his head to glare at his burly henchman. "You, King Kong. Get out of here. Leave us alone. Why do you go to the memorial ceremony? I'm sure they could use some help."

"Uhh...boss?" The man mumbled, his hands nervously clasped in front of him. A man of his size shouldn't be afraid of a twig like Hook, but power doesn't always follow strength. "But what if—?"

"I can handle it, you buffoon." Hook rolled his eyes and groaned. "His hands are bound and I have a gun. What exactly do you expect to happen here?"

"Sir," the goon assented with a nod. He turned and left the room, the door swinging closed with a loud, echoing click.

Now it was just the two of them.

"Kneel," Hook ordered, waggling the barrel of his gun toward the ground.

"What?"

"I said kneel!" he snapped, the gun's motions becoming sharper and more pronounced as he waved it around. "Or this will be over before it even starts!"

Franklin hated ceding his stance to the man, but he wasn't the one with the gun. So carefully, Franklin winced as he lowered himself to both knees.

"There now," Hook snarled. "Isn't that better? It's the natural state of mankind, men like you...you crave oppression, submission."

"I thought you were anarchists. No man above another."

"Americans..." Hook shook his head. "You think this fight is all about freedom, don't you? A quest for individual identity, for individual power. Control, really. But in your tussle for power, you always finish in the same place. On your knees. And in the end, you will always kneel before the true power. Those—like me— who bring down the system. Who instill something better."

"You're mad," Franklin countered. "Anarchists are just authoritarians without any power. Yet."

Hook smiled, then almost laughed. More of a chortle. "You're hardly the first to kneel before me and you surely won't be the last. Soon this will all be in ruins. And everyone currently in power...politicians, CEOs, titans of industry...they will all bow before the Nasha Volya."

"Did Phoenix know about this?" Franklin asked. "Anarchy is about total freedom, no one in control, not even the Volya."

"That's a lie. Anarchy isn't lack of control. It's being out from under *their* control. The elites, the...State."

"You've gone mad." Franklin responded. "You've not only lost sight of the freedoms and liberties America stands for, but you've lost sight of what you're fighting for."

"You know—I didn't actually expect you to come," Hook sneered.

"To save my own father? Of course I was—" Franklin suddenly stopped talking. He felt a cloud fall over the room as it hit him. Something was wrong. If Hook didn't expect him, why would he bother keeping his father alive? For that matter, even if he did expect it, what good did it do to keep a polished military veteran alive. He'd be more trouble than it was worth. "He's dead already, isn't he?"

"Who?" Hook leaned down, a devilish smile plastered on his face.

"My father. My father's already dead," Franklin's face flushed and bile rose in his throat. This man had killed Joanna in cold blood. He'd probably killed his father now as well. Franklin knew he was supposed to be sad, but right now all he felt was anger. "He was dead before I walked in here."

"What—?" Hook feigned a surprised denial with an exaggerated slap of his hand over his mouth, but it wasn't convincing. He rose up and paced away.

"He is, right?" Franklin growled. His hands worked furiously behind his back, tugging at the knot. He could feel it loosening. "You didn't need him."

Hook froze, as though thinking, then dropped his guard. He snarled, "Your father isn't even here." He strolled over to one wall and grabbed a wooden chair, dragging it to the middle of the room, where he spun it around and plopped down in it.

"You—lied—?" Franklin sputtered as a roaring filled his ears. He felt the knot finally give way. His hands were free. And Hook seemed too proud of himself to notice.

"Don't worry. We plan to kill him. Just…not yet. But I have no doubt, he will beg for his life when we do—"

"Aaaarrrrgghhh!" Franklin cut him off with a scream. With a single motion, he propelled himself upward toward Hook.

He flew across the room, colliding with Nathan Hook shoulder-first, catching him off guard. His shoulder drove into the man's torso, shattering the chair into a hundred splinters, as they both went down in a heap. He felt— rather than heard—a dull crack as the duo smashed into the ground and Hook gasped. At least one rib was broken.

Hook still had a grip on the gun though and raised it. He fired once, but Franklin swung an elbow just in time to connect with Hook's wrist at the moment of trigger-pull. The bullet missed by millimeters, the heat burning Franklin's arm.

Climbing to his knees, Franklin pummeled Hook with his fists. Left. Right. Left. Right.

All of the rage and anger that had been building inside him for months was being unleashed in that moment and for a minute, his body didn't care that he'd been hospitalized recently. He felt no physical pain as all of his emotional anguish and suffering coursed out of him and through his fists. Any second now, that bodyguard would come rushing into the room to stop him.

Finally, he stopped and his shoulders fell forward. Glancing around, he spotted the fallen gun and crawled over to it. He wrapped a bloody palm around its grip and staggered upright.

Slowly turning toward Hook, Franklin let out a primal growl. It was a guttural snarl, like a lion drawing in on its prey.

Hook had rolled to his side and propped himself upright on one arm, wincing in pain. His face was battered and coated in blood, but through the cuts and cracked lips, he managed a twisted smile.

Franklin limped a few paces until he stood over Hook, glaring downward. He leveled the gun barrel until the sight aimed right between the man's eyes.

Then he paused.

"Just do it already," Hook spat, blood spraying outward in a fine mist with every word. "Pull the trigger. Stop hesitating."

"I'm not hesitating," Franklin growled. "I'm savoring the moment." In that moment, he could feel the power of what he was about to do. The man lying below him had killed Joanna. He'd threatened his father. He'd tried to kill Franklin repeatedly.

This...this was what revenge felt like.

Pure, unadulterated revenge.

His thumb pulled back on the gun's hammer, feeling the mechanism lock into place with a satisfying clack.

"Just end it already. It's what Joanna would want you to do. What your Dad would want too. We both know that."

"Don't—don't say her name." Franklin stammered.

Joanna probably wouldn't want this, if he was being honest. Killing an unarmed man while he's still lying on the ground? That's not right, he could almost hear her chiding him. *And his military father? He definitely wouldn't approve of executing a prisoner who's already been beaten.*

"Jo...ann...a." Hook sneered, her name rolling around in his mouth like he was tasting it before releasing. His tongue snaked out from between his lips and licked at the blood. "What a beautiful woman. Shame I had to—"

"Shut. Up!" Franklin snapped at him and his hand began to quiver.

"But she was very by-the-book, wasn't she? A rule follower?"

Franklin didn't answer. *Why hadn't he pulled the trigger yet? He couldn't let Hook's words get to him! It didn't matter what Joanna would want. Or what his father would want. They weren't here anymore. They weren't here anymore because of this man. He had killed them and justice needed to be served.*

"Do you really think this is justice?"

How did he know that's what I was thinking? Franklin's mind whirled in chaos. He didn't know what to do. His thoughts wrestled each other, each trying to out-yell the other.

"Stop! Quiet!" Franklin yelled and closed his eyes, hoping to shut out the voices, if only for a second. "Please stop," he begged them.

It took precisely two seconds to realize he'd made a mistake. And that was about one second too late. He snapped his eyes open just in time to see Hook whip a broken chair leg around. The thick, wooden club impacted the side of his knee and it buckled beneath him. Something tore with a painful 'pop.'

He instinctively pulled the trigger, but he was off balance and the shot went wide. The bullet crashed into the floorboard with a thud.

Franklin tried to re-aim, but a second swing of the club struck his wrist and he lost control of the gun. It fell and skittered out of reach. *How was he still so strong?*

A swift kick caught him on the chin like a professional boxer's uppercut and everything went blurry, then gray, as he dropped to his knees. Like he was watching a black-and-white movie on a channel with terrible reception. Something hit him in the chest and he tumbled backward, hitting the ground with a thump.

Chapter 41

"Congressman, Congressman Hartwell?" Shannon flashed her badge as they approached. "I'm Agent Faye, this is Agent Sloan. We're with SISA. Can we talk to you for a moment?"

The Congressman's gaze flickered over Shannon without betraying emotion, passively eyeing her, but when his gaze landed on Sloan, his eyes widened and nostrils flared.

And did his cheeks turn a slight red?

Shannon couldn't tell in the sunlight, but he definitely recognized the Director.

"Congressman?" she prompted again. "A word?"

"Yes, yes. Of course," Marcus Hartwell grunted. "This way." He extended an arm to direct them to step off to the side. Shannon led the way and Sloan brought up the rear, effectively sandwiching Hartwell between them, a fact that seemed to make the man uncomfortable. He kept glancing over his shoulder at Sloan, as though uneasy about the Director's presence. *Maybe he suspected they were onto him?*

"There a problem, agents?" Hartwell crooned, finally out of earshot of the other congressmen.

"Maybe," Sloan grumbled. "I'm not sure yet."

"What do you mean?"

"I'll get to the point, Congressman." Sloan took the lead. "How familiar are you with the Nasha Volya?"

Hartwell took a breath before answering. "About as familiar as any of us. Maybe a little more since I was near the Rayburn bombing."

"I see. And do you think you were a target?" Shannon asked.

"Isn't that your job to tell me, agents?" he quipped, a half-smile appearing on his lips. "How do I know?"

"Are you connected in any way to the Volya?"

"You mean, other than the Rayburn bombing?" He snorted. "Don't be ridiculous." He stared at the agents, alternating his gaze between the two for several seconds. No one spoke. "Well, if that's all…"

"That's quite the nice ring you have there, Congressman." Sloan interrupted, pointing at his hand.

"I—yes, yes. Thank you." Hartwell stammered slightly, thrown off by the change in questions. "It was my…grandfather's. He brought it home from Europe after the war."

"World War Two, you mean? May I see it?" Sloan stretched out an open palm.

"Yes, the second world war." Hartwell held up his hand, but didn't remove the ring. "It's extremely old, Agent Sloan. Surely, you'll understand if I don't just hand it over to every fanboy who appreciates German relics."

"Those engravings on the top don't look German to me," Sloan countered. "It's worn, but isn't that Cyrillic writing?"

"Well, I'm no expert," Hartwell spoke quickly and dropped his hand, shoving it into his pocket—concealing the ring. "If you say it's Cyrillic, maybe it is. My grandfather never told me."

"I see," Sloan muttered and shot a glance at Shannon. They'd hit a nerve about the ring, but that wasn't enough.

"Ok, well I really need to get back..." Hartwell shot Sloan one final look, then turned to leave. "My speech is about to start."

"One more question, Marcus," Sloan added. "Are you familiar with the Warhawk?"

Hartwell froze mid-step, then pivoted back to them.

His entire countenance had changed. His eyes were dark and had narrowed to slits, his brow marked with deep lines, a snarl etched on his lips.

"What did you say?" he hissed, his voice falling an entire octave lower. "Where did you hear that name?"

"The Warhawk," Sloan repeated. "I see you recognize it though. Because I never told you it was a name."

Hartwell didn't respond for a moment, then took a couple steps closer to stare directly into Sloan's eyes. The two men stood mere centimeters apart, neither giving ground.

"If I were you, Agent," Hartwell enunciated slowly, nostrils flaring, "I would forget you ever heard the word Warhawk."

"Did you know you'd betray our country when you were first elected, Congressman?" Sloan spat the words out through gritted teeth. "Or did that part come later?"

"Any youthful idealism...any belief I once had in this country's greatness was burned away, melted as if in a crucible, long before I came to Washington." Hartwell muttered softly. Shannon strained to hear what he was saying. "I possessed no purpose as a young man. But eventually, I became something new, something different. Most people lose their identity when they put on a mask, but I found mine."

"When you joined the Volya. You're under arrest, Congressman," Sloan snapped, his jaw clenched tight. "Turn around, hands behind—"

"Or what, Agent? Who do you think they'll believe? Besides, the Volya?? Those were your words, not mine."

Shannon knew he was right and could tell Sloan did as well.

Hartwell had been careful with his response, avoiding any admission of guilt, or even association with the Volya. Heavy implication, but nothing concrete. And without a camera or tape of the conversation, he'd deny it anyway.

"You'll pay for this, Marcus," Sloan swore. "We're going to find a way and we're going to take you out."

"I'm sure you think you will," Hartwell retorted, his words an angry hiss. "Now, if you'll excuse me, I have a raucous crowd—nay, an entire country—to win over and an announcement to make. Why don't you stick around? I think you're going to enjoy this one."

Hartwell threw his shoulders back and shook his head, allowing his public mask to fall into place. It was like staring into the face of an entirely different man. He marched off and returned to his place by the stage, right as the emcee announced his name, introducing his speech.

Hartwell glanced backward over his shoulder at Shannon and Sloan for a second and winked, then ascended the stairs with the confidence and poise of Fred Astaire or Gene Kelly, bouncing lightly on the balls of his feet with each step, as though music played in his head.

Sparks danced in front of Franklin's eyes and everything felt fuzzy. His head ached and his breath felt like steam burning his lungs. All of those pains from the last couple days—the physical ones—came rushing back, overwhelming his senses. He attempted to clamber to his feet, but his equilibrium seemed off.

The world swam in shades of gray around him and he toppled over. He threw his hands out and caught himself, stopping the fall only long enough to be drilled with a flying tackle by Nathan Hook.

Franklin shoved Hook off and tried to rise to one knee, but Hook kicked his leg out from under him and Franklin tumbled onto his side again. Hook rose to his feet and aimed a kick at Franklin's face, but Franklin threw his hands up and caught the foot before it made impact. He wrenched it as hard as he could to the left.

Hook grunted as something snapped in his ankle. He hit the ground and rolled, grabbing Franklin's arm. He twisted and pinned Franklin to the ground. Each movement elicited its own grunt or roar of pain from Hook, but he still hadn't lost much in the way of strength and Franklin felt paralyzed.

Hook pounded Franklin with a flurry of blows to the side of the head, his ribs, his stomach. He was helpless. One fist connected with his ear and a dull ring overwhelmed him. He couldn't hear anything but a low roar, punctuated by the frantic throbbing of his heartbeat.

He reached out and managed to grab Hook's fractured ankle and squeezed hard. Hook screamed and reeled backward.

The pummeling paused for a moment and Franklin tried to roll out from underneath.

But it wasn't enough. Hook retaliated with another punch, and then planted his forearm across Franklin's throat. He pressed downward. Franklin fought the pressure, knowing that soon enough, Hook's weight would crush his trachea and that would be it.

Black flecks crept in at the corners of his vision; he was losing blood, losing consciousness, losing hope. He was running out of time.

He couldn't feel anything anymore and he was about to lose consciousness, so began to thrash. He flailed his arms, hoping to fend off the agent as long as possible, but the pressure on his throat continued, pressing further into his flesh. He could feel his throat constricting, his oxygen diminishing.

In the bloody haze and shrinking black tunnel of his vision, a sudden glint caught his attention to his right.

Something shiny, something metal.

Out of instinct, no plan or strategy, he reached for it and as the metal hit his palm, Franklin closed his fingers around the object.

He couldn't tell what it was, but it was sharp. He clenched it so hard that it sliced into his flesh.

And just before the tunnel of darkness closed, Franklin swung the metal shard around. It struck Hook in the chest and sank in. Franklin thrust in deeper, driving it into the Russian's heart.

Hook's mouth opened wide and he froze mid-punch. His eyes gawked at Franklin—through Franklin—with shock and incomprehension. Then, they rolled up in his head and he sank to the ground, his torso hitting the dirt beside Franklin with a thud.

Franklin's legs were stiff, his whole body in agony, barely responding to commands from his brain. He felt cold and unfocused. His thoughts were as jumbled and foggy as his vision. His head throbbed with the force of ocean waves pounding a rocky shoreline. He pushed

Hook's body off his legs and tried to get to his knees. He gasped and fought to catch his breath, but couldn't and fell back over.

All around him, it felt like fires burned too close for comfort. The dark tunnel vision slowly collapsed and a darkness swept over him, only to be replaced by a sea of red, pulsing to his racing heartbeat.

The red fog was interspersed by bursts of light, supernovas that broke through like fireflies that exploded for a second, then disappeared.

After what seemed like an eternity, his heart rate slowed and his whole body relaxed.

It was over.

Joanna's killer was dead.

Phoenix was dead.

O'Brian was dead too.

And everyone was safe.

In the moment, that was enough.

Chapter 42

Franklin lay still on the worn-out carpet inside a former shoe store in a decrepit, abandoned mall. He felt a kinship with the building; they were both crumbling shells of their former selves, vestiges left over from a time when they were mildly successful, but never fulfilled.

As Franklin's mind drifted toward a blackness that he assumed was nothingness, he wondered if he'd see Joanna again. The previous time he'd almost died—shot by Phoenix on the deck of that ferry six months ago—he'd had a vision of his ex-wife. To be honest, he wasn't sure if it was a vision, a dream, a hallucination, or if it was somehow real. A glimpse into an afterlife.

Though Joanna had, Franklin wasn't sure he believed in an afterlife. He'd grown up in church—dragged most Sundays by his mother. He'd even called himself a Christian—if pushed—for years before he finally gave up the facade. But he never liked to talk about it. Or let whatever little faith he did have interfere with the rest of his life…his real life.

He'd seen too much death, too much destruction, too much misery to believe God truly cared, either about him or about humanity in general.

It wasn't that he didn't believe in God; it was a safe bet something supernatural, something beyond the material world existed. Maybe of the Intelligent Design variety. But he doubted any 'god' would debase himself to the level of humans, to stick around and get involved in the messy, cruel lives of people. Humanity was too corrupt, too cruel, too pathetic even to believe that God would intervene or somehow orchestrate this world for the better from the great beyond.

Maybe God was a spectator, watching humans ruin their own lives from afar, like a drunk, suburban housewife binging on a daytime television soap opera. But that was it.

Yet...that last time, as he neared death, he'd experienced something he hadn't been able to explain. And though he hadn't spoken to anyone about it, that vision and conversation with Joanna had shaken him. It'd uprooted his beliefs about what lay beyond this life, even if he'd never settled on what that meant. He'd meant to talk with his brother—a Christian, like Joanna—about faith, but everything had moved too quickly after the events of the Spring and it, as with too many things, had fallen by the wayside. And now, he worried it might be too late.

And as his mind faded, the blackness crept inward in increasingly smaller circles. But this time was different. Rather than a supernatural conversation with his ex-wife about his future, he began to witness flashes of his past.

That Christmas he and Jay had opened their first bikes.

A family vacation in middle school to the Maine coast, storm waves rolling into a bay from two directions, sending massive plumes of water into the air as they collided.

His senior prom.

His first sip of alcohol, which he hated.

An illegal street race that nearly killed him when a cat leapt into his path out of nowhere and he swerved to miss it, instead hitting two trees.

The moment he first met Joanna, Day 3 of an Introduction to Philosophy course.

His first time as a lookout for the Bratva, followed soon after by his first time running point as their Wheelman.

Meeting Silas. Meeting Hamlin. Getting shot and left for dead.

Publishing a book, Helios Rising, a loosely autobiographical and anonymous novel.

His mother's death. Her funeral, the first time he'd cried in years.

Joanna's death.

And then it was gone, replaced by a fuzzy blackness that engulfed his senses. It wasn't quite nothingness, though. It was faint, but he could just barely make out an ever-so-slight buzz that hung in the air like a fog. Almost, but not quite, white noise humming in the background of the blackness. Franklin couldn't identify its source; it appeared to be both all around him and nowhere at once.

It started getting louder, though. And it was definitely a buzz. Almost insect-like.

Locusts? Wasps? A swarm of bees?

He wasn't sure. But whatever it was kept getting closer.

He abruptly realized too, the blackness wasn't quite as pitch-black as it had been a moment ago. It was still dark as night, but a pulsating quality to it made it seem almost... conscious. It was a living, dynamic entity. A mass.

It was an amorphous blackness, but somehow... alive. And buzzing, louder and louder. The noise was almost deafening.

And worse, he couldn't explain it, but the buzzing seemed to have infected him, making the leap from the living darkness to his own body. The hum was inside him now, vibrating every cell and it began to hurt. Within seconds, the buzzing threatened to rip his cells apart from the inside and he began to scream in agony.

But his own scream was drowned out in the buzz.

He was dying and he knew it.

His own body rebelled against the very notion of death as any last shred of hope he had of a positive afterlife was shattered in this twisted, pulsing, agonizing darkness.

He understood, in an instant, this was what it felt like to be damned. Terror ripped through him, competing with the buzz to be the first to shred him into pieces. His mind teetered, hinging on the fence between anger and madness.

Right as those last threads ripped apart, condemning him to this agony for eternity, something grabbed him.

With a sudden jolt, his eyes snapped open and he gasped. He sucked air into his burning lungs like a man who'd just escaped drowning.

Fluorescent light bulbs flickered above him, as severe and bright as the ones that lit up the school football field. They seemed to burn his retinas, but he forced his eyes to stay open as he was overcome with the urge to weep.

The room slowly came into view.

He was still in the mall, in that empty shoe store, but he was no longer alone. Kneeling next to him, cradling his torso in her lap, was Eve Chase.

Where did she come from? How did she find him?

He tried to speak, but his mouth was too dry for words to form.

"You're okay. It's going to be okay," she kept whispering, over and over, her voice echoing around the edges of his consciousness. "Help is coming."

"Well, he's clearly guilty," Shannon remarked, as soon as Hartwell marched away.

"It's not enough though," Sloan retorted. "And look at him. He's got the people eating out of the palm of his hand."

Shannon turned to watch the proceedings and Sloan was, indeed, right. The audience sat on the edge of their seats, eating up every word of Hartwell's speech as he spoke about his impoverished upbringing. In their eyes, in the eyes of almost everyone, he was a near victim of the bombing, a hero.

The worst part was, if she didn't know what she knew now, she'd understand their admiration. He embodied the American dream.

He grew up poor, in the slums of Camden, New Jersey, staring across the river at the thriving city of Philadelphia. Raised by grandparents until they passed when he was eight, then in the foster system. He was the first in his family to graduate high school, overcame a teenage drug addiction, and worked his way out of poverty. He tended bar to pay his way through college, won a local mayoral election in a small suburb near his childhood neighborhood and soon became a darling of the Democratic party.

He was somewhat controversial for a handful of his more radical economic beliefs, but no one could deny his rags-to-riches story was admirable.

"So what do we do now?" Shannon asked.

"I'm not sure, but this is the closest we've been in months to a break," Sloan answered. "We need to run down every avenue of this."

"If Hartwell really is Volya, there's no way he's here alone," she mused aloud.

"You mean at this event?"

"Exactly. There's no way they would have one of their leaders in such a high-profile position by himself, right?"

"That's a good point. But who?" he asked, his eyes scanning the audience. "Snap some photos of those in the seats. Maybe Eve can run facial recog and we'll get lucky. I'll circle around the back. Last time, we caught Phoenix lurking on the outskirts of the roped-off area."

"Speaking of Phoenix..." Shannon began, but Sloan had already turned away. *I can tell him about Phoenix and O'Brian later...*

Shannon did as requested, pulling out her cell phone and taking photos. No one looked suspicious to her, but then again, she didn't expect them to be wearing matching anarchist t-shirts. As she snapped the shots, she started to listen to Hartwell's speech. She tuned in halfway through a sentence...

"...the spirit of America," he concluded a thought to a round of applause.

He paused for the clapping to abate before continuing. "America was targeted by this group because we are a beacon. Our role as world leader makes us a target. And our foundations were rattled. But rest assured, none of us will ever forget that day. And we will remember it not as the anniversary of a vile terrorist attack, but rather, we will remember it as the day of new beginnings. It will be a day that America—nay, the entire world—looks back on as the moment we came together to push forward for a new future. And I promise, under my watch, the steel that was shattered in the bombings will be rebuilt into something new, something better."

Shannon grunted. His words about rebuilding took on a different meaning in the context of knowing he was partially behind the anarchist attacks.

"And so...in the spirit of rebuilding..." he continued, his voice growing louder and more powerful. "I have an announcement."

Shannon paused photo-taking and turned to listen.

"I have spent many years in Washington. Long enough to recognize what makes America great. But also long enough to know the ways of Washington must change as we enter this new world. The founding fathers of this country designed a system of government that allows for change and we've done it many times, facing down tyranny, secession, depression. Every generation faces its great challenge and every time, that generation rises up to do what needs to be done. But every idea...every movement...every great change...needs someone to lead the way. And so, as I stand in the shadow of the man who once promised that 'America will never be destroyed from the outside,' I am here to formally announce my candidacy for President of the United States of America."

Shannon felt her jaw drop as the crowd erupted.

Hartwell stepped out from behind the podium and raised his arms to the sky as he basked in the applause. Shannon was horrified as she watched the crowd go crazy, hooting and hollering as they cheered. She could barely hear herself think over the roars.

But as she watched, something changed. The cheers turned to screams and she spun back to the stage.

The Congressman's arms had fallen to his sides and he'd stumbled backward. One hand moved to his chest where a spot of red seeped through his white shirt, growing by the second.

He dropped to his knees and then fell on his side.

Was he shot?!

Shannon's mind whirled and she instinctively pulled her weapon. Chaos erupted as Secret Service agents had swarmed Hartwell and people were running in every direction.

After a few seconds, she spotted Sloan and moved toward him.

As she neared, however, she could tell something else was wrong. He stared down at something black on the ground, but as she neared, he looked up at her and mouthed one word.

"Run!"

She froze in place, unsure what to do, but he grabbed her by the arm and dragged her away. He pulled her in the direction of the road.

"What's going on?" She demanded.

"It was my gun," he muttered.

"What?" Her mind reeled. *His gun? What did that mean? How could it be his?"*

"My gun," he spat, louder this time. "Someone used my gun to shoot Hartwell."

"But...how? Are—are you sure?" she stammered. They power walked quickly, but didn't run to draw attention.

"Yes. It was a rifle from my apartment. Customized. They must've broken in and taken it when they realized I hadn't been killed in Budapest."

"But...why?"

"Isn't it obvious? Someone tried to kill a Congressman, a man who just announced he's running for President." Sloan paused and looked her directly in the eye. "And I'm being set up for it."

Epilogue

One month later...

Franklin loved the month of September. The stifling grip of summer humidity was finally weakening, making it bearable to go outside again. But the bleak, barren cold of winter had yet to set in either. The weather was perfect, the air crisp and fresh, and the vibrant colors of the leaves, aflame with reds and yellows, ripe and just beginning to fall, made every view a picturesque one. Especially in the mountains, where everywhere you turned, leaves swirled in the light breeze. Up above, the autumn clouds drifted like smoky cloaks over the treetops.

He took a deep breath, inhaling the fragrant, airy aromas of the forest, and closed his eyes. *This,* he thought, *this is perfect.*

That's what he kept telling himself, anyway.

It'd been over thirty days since Congressman Marcus Hartwell had announced his candidacy for President, since someone took a shot at him, putting a hole in his clavicle and a jolt of electricity to his campaign. Rumor was he had recovered and left the hospital as a self-proclaimed martyr, and the new frontrunner for the Democratic nomination. His approval rating shot through the roof in an instant for surviving an assassination attempt.

And no one outside their team knew who he really was, what he really was.

Jacob Sloan had been blamed for the shooting; Franklin, Shannon, and Eve were all soon publicly named as accomplices. They all stood at the top of the FBI's Most Wanted list, with their photos hanging in every post office in the country. The rifle used to fire the shot was registered to Sloan and his fingerprints were all over the weapon. To make matters worse, audio of his threat of the Congressman moments before ascending the steps to the stage had accidentally been captured in the background of a video on someone's phone. When it leaked to the press an hour later, all hell broke loose.

Sloan chose to run rather than face prison and a trial, believing the stakes too high to sit behind bars for months while a terrorist dug his claws into an unknowing American populace. He'd be tried in the court of public opinion versus a supposed victim and newly-minted media darling. And the evidence didn't look favorable.

Shannon—at the top of their list since she'd been spotted at the ceremony with Sloan—was captured a day later by tracking her through a fitness app on her watch that she forgot to deactivate. She'd been brought in for questioning, ultimately arrested as an accomplice, and now sat alone and helpless in a federal detention center.

Eve still hadn't revealed exactly how she knew he was in danger, or where to find him, but she'd procured black market medical services to bring Franklin back from the brink of death and arranged for usage of this cabin for their band of outlaws. Somehow she'd gotten the message to Sloan about their hideout, who showed up on their doorstep after evading capture on his own for a couple days. She'd never explained where or how she'd located the property, but it was remote enough to keep away prying eyes and—she swore—completely off the grid. Her old home had been raided less than 24 hours after she'd fled, but by then, her system was fried. She swore they'd never be found here; it became a place to regroup and plan. A place to stay off the radar. They hadn't had even a smidge of contact with the outside world after that first day or two. The only way they even knew about Hartwell's recovery was from a fortuitously overheard conversation while Eve was on a supply run.

Still, Franklin's desperate attempt to save his father by confronting Hook had succeeded. Kind of. It turned out his father wasn't even there; one of Hartwell's goons, a man named Typhos had been stopped and arrested while trying to kidnap Irving Holt. But Franklin had bested Hook and ultimately killed him, but not before taking a beating. His whole body had been covered in bruises, a maze of deep purple.

It had taken a full week before Franklin managed to sit up on his own and hold his own weight. Another two weeks before he felt comfortable enough to stand, if only for a minute at a time. And he was just now relearning to walk, albeit with a heavy limp.

But of all the places he could've chosen to recover, a picturesque cabin in the middle of nowhere wasn't a bad option. And, despite his body's best efforts, he was alive and grateful for it. His second near-death experience had shaken him deeply and he had spent the last month reading everything he could on theology and the afterlife.

He desperately wanted to talk to his brother, the closest person to him who was a Christian, to pick his brain and try to arrive at some logical understanding of what had happened to him. And perhaps, if it made sense, to find a way to make sure he never had to experience that hell again.

This evening, he'd limped out to the porch that overlooked an encroaching forest and leaned against the railing for balance. He watched a couple rabbits obliviously hop across the leaf-covered grass below.

This porch was his favorite spot at the cabin. He'd always appreciated the mountains for the serenity and quiet. And something about being out in the middle of nowhere as the sun dipped below the horizon was calming. It felt safe, protected in a way he hadn't felt in many years. He had found a peace with the deaths of Phoenix, Hook, and O'Brian. He knew the larger fight was still far from over, but his personal fury had abated. And any threat that the group had been to him or his family seemed to have died with them.

As he observed the rabbits, he sensed a presence join him at the railing and glanced out of the corner of his eye to see Jacob Sloan.

"I finally figured it out," Sloan claimed.

"Figured what out?" Franklin turned and recognized a familiar gleam in Sloan's eye, the one reserved for when he had an idea. He knew the Director—well, former Director—had been going crazy at the cabin with all of his theories about the Volya and plans for how to take them down.

"The man. From the ceremony, before Hartwell's speech. I figured out who he is."

338

"You mean the one you and Shannon noticed talking to Hartwell?"

"That's the one. I recognized him. It's been decades, but I never forget a face. It just took me time to place it...more time than I'd have liked, but I did it. Without his beard, dressed in a Western suit, he looks so different from how I remember him. But I'm sure of it. That was Sharif bin-Qadir al-Rashid."

"Al-Rashid? Who's that?"

"Before I became Director, I spent two decades doing missions around the globe. One of those missions was a two-year operation in Kuwait. Well, not Kuwait, exactly...but the precise location was—still is—classified. It was one of my first fieldwork missions; I manned a reconnaissance team. We listened to terrorist chatter every day for months on end. Took some photographs. And finally, took down a weapons cabal."

"And al-Rashid was part of that group?"

"I must've listened to al-Rashid every day. He wasn't just a part of the group. He ran the operation. But he was absent that day we raided the cell; he got away. He became one of the major players funding terror throughout the entire Middle East. But if he's here, in the US, in Washington DC, meeting with a Presidential candidate...well, that's a terrifying thought."

"You think he's the real brains behind the Volya? I thought this was a Russian anarchist group passed down through generations."

"It is. But Sharif al-Rashid...he wasn't an ideologue. He funded Islamist groups, but he wasn't a true believer. In anything, I think. Except maybe money. He may not be the force behind the ideology or the brains, but he might be the moneybags. Or the weapons supplier. Either way, he's too big of a name to ignore."

"So, what are you saying? Is this the break you've been looking for?"

"I'm not sure. But despite our losses—and our current situation—we now have an angle. And I can work with that."

Two months after that...

Franklin shivered outside an office building on the corner of a street in Reykjavik, Iceland. Catching a glimpse of himself in the mirrored windows, he was stunned to see the transformation. He was barely recognizable from even August. Bundled in a long, black trench coat and toboggan-style beanie to escape the cold, crisp November air, he'd let both his hair and beard grow out as well, leaving both uncombed and a touch unruly. A pair of sunglasses to obscure his eyes and no one outside maybe his own brother would recognize him. And even then, it would probably take a second glance.

Iceland in November is a cold, dark time. They'd get maybe six hours of sunlight and temperatures hovered just above the freezing point. It wasn't uncommon to get both rain and snow on the same day, topped off by a heavy layer of fog that made it difficult to see at a distance.

It wasn't an ideal time to be outside as it was late in the afternoon and the sun was already setting. It would dip below the horizon in minutes, but that was the time their contact had insisted on seeing them. The approaching dusk and the fog would hide their meeting from prying eyes, but it made it challenging for Franklin to see who was coming.

For the past couple months, Eve had set about creating ironclad identities for the three of them to move around without the watchful 'big brother' of law enforcement, either local or the feds. As soon as they were able, they'd fled the country. Sloan was still being sought in a nationwide manhunt for questioning in the attempted assassination of Congressman Hartwell and Franklin wasn't taking any chances either, given their association.

Even Europe itself was a risk given the extradition treaties the European Union had with the United States. And, while not all nations had signed on, a new treaty ultimately approved Rufus Hastings's idea of creating an international strike force to combat terrorism on the global stage, independently operated, but answering to their new alliance of powers. So it was more than just the United States looking for them. But Iceland had been known to refuse extradition requests on occasion, despite their treaties, so it felt like a risk worth taking to meet this guy.

One of the notable things they'd learned is that, despite their photos and story being plastered all over mainstream American media sources, their presumed guilt was not universal abroad. There were others who believed in their innocence and worked behind the scenes on the Nasha Volya problem as well. This man claimed to be a political affairs analyst for the EU out of Luxembourg City, though had been cagey about his name and revealing any identifying information in their communications for his own safety.

Tonight was their first time meeting in person. The whole thing sounded fishy, but he promised to have information to help them. Sloan had decided it was worth the risk, but Franklin insisted on being the one to take the meeting. He was less recognizable to the general public, especially in a foreign country.

After about ten minutes of waiting, a figure emerged out of the fog and approached Franklin. He also wore a dark trench coat, but had chosen to forgo a head covering. A cheap pair of glasses teetered precariously on the bridge of his nose.

"Nice weather we're having, isn't it?" The man said, as he approached. A faint quasi-German accent was evident. He removed his glasses and wiped them on the lapel of his jacket.

"I wish I'd brought an umbrella," Franklin responded with his designated response. "How far are we from the nearest bus stop?"

"I wouldn't know," he claimed. "I never take the bus."

Satisfied that his answers checked out and this was their guy, Franklin finally smiled.

"It's nice to finally meet you," he said, extending a hand.

The man took it and beamed. "You, as well. It's an honor."

"As much as I'd enjoy chatting, I don't think it's wise to linger. You said you had something for me? For us?"

Franklin's phone buzzed, interrupting their conversation. Was it Jay, calling for the fourth time this week? Or perhaps Sloan, telling him to abort and get out of there? He glanced at the caller ID. But it wasn't Jay. Or Sloan. The number on the caller ID was an unknown, local number. He didn't want to, but something in his gut told him he needed to answer.

"I'm sorry, I need to take this," he told the man. "It'll only be a second." He stepped several feet away, to speak softly without being overheard.

"Hello?"

"Something is about to happen and you're going to want to react and say something, but you cannot." A voice that sounded electronic and monotone whispered through the speaker.

"What?"

"Do. Not. React. Don't," the voice hissed.

"Who is this?"

"Lives are at stake, Franklin."

Click.

The line went dead. *He knows my name?!*

Franklin stared at the device for a second, confused, before shoving it into the breast pocket of his coat. He slowly turned back toward his contact.

"Is everything okay?" the man raised an eyebrow.

"I—I'm not..."

"Oh, bloody..." His contact swore. "I didn't want to have to do this so soon." He reached into his jacket pocket and pulled out a gun.

"What—what is that for?"

"What all guns are for, Mr. Holt," the man said. He lifted the gun to Franklin's head. "I'd hoped to get more out of you first, but that phone call...that was your warning, wasn't it? About me?"

At that moment, another man appeared out of the mist. He kept his head down and walked quickly, but as he lifted his face, Franklin froze.

This...that...it couldn't be...

The man walking up to him was a dead man. Literally.

Silas Sherman. They'd buried him months ago, after he'd died in a hospital bed. Killed. The police had verified his identity.

The phone call. That had to have been Silas, warning him not to react to his resurrection.

His EU contact noticed him staring and turned to look.

"You!" he gasped and whirled his gun around. But he was too late.

Silas raised his own weapon and fired once. The man in front of Franklin grunted, then fell to the cobblestone, lifeless. Franklin yelped and stared at the dead man laying before him, utterly confused by this sudden turn of events. He looked back up to ask Silas what was going on, but the man had vanished back into the mist.

Questions whirled through Franklin's mind.

How—how could it be? How had Silas survived?

Who exactly was he? Some immortal superhero? A zombie? The luckiest man in the world?

And was he here to help?

And finally…

What in the world just happened?

To Be Continued...

"Hope itself is like a star—not to be seen in the sunshine of prosperity, and only to be discovered in the night of adversity."
Charles Haddon Spurgeon

****

"Fear is a reaction; courage is a decision."
Winston Churchill

About the Author:
Justin (J. Robert) Kinney is an author, analyst, researcher, speaker,

 and teacher. He has a PhD from the University of Tennessee, where he studied International Relations and Terrorism Studies. He specializes in analyzing extremist radicalization and recruitment, conflict, and security studies. His dissertation examined social media usage by terrorist organizations. Kinney has also earned degrees in Psychology from Duke University and Forensic Science from George Washington University.

Kinney has worked in federal public policy, performed security research, published in a political science journal, and taught university classes in global politics. He has lectured at the Killer Nashville International Writers Conference and community events, discussing everything from modern terrorism threats to weapons of mass destruction to crime scene investigation.

Kinney's first novel, *Precipice*, debuted in 2016, followed by *Splintered State* in 2018, the first in The Volya Series. Storytelling has been an interest from an early age, and with the help of some great teachers, morphed into a love and skill of writing. Now, he writes mysteries with an element of political suspense. Justin hosts a global politics podcast called Nutshell Politics, is active in his local church, competes in weekly trivia nights with friends, plays basketball and tennis regularly, and loves to travel the world.

Connect with Kinney online:
www.justinrkinney.com
www.twitter.com/justinr_kinney
www.facebook.com/jrobertkinney
jrobertkinney@gmail.com

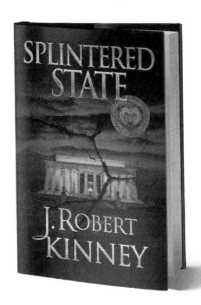

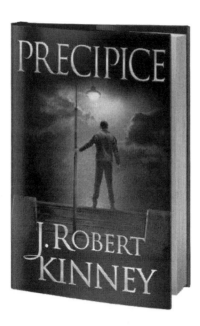

Made in the USA
Middletown, DE
07 November 2023